Red Hot Murder

A Charlie Kingsley Mystery

Books by Michele Pariza Wacek
MPWNovels.com/books

Secrets of Redemption series:
It Began With a Lie (Book 1)
This Happened to Jessica (Book 2)
The Evil That Was Done (Book 3)
The Summoning (Book 4)
The Reckoning (Book 5)
The Girl Who Wasn't There (Book 6)
The Room at the Top of the Stairs (Book 7)
The Search (Book 8)
The Secret Diary of Helen Blackstone (free novella)

Charlie Kingsley Mystery series:
A Grave Error (free prequel novella)
The Murder Before Christmas (Book 1)
Ice Cold Murder (Book 2)
Murder Next Door (Book 3)
Murder Among Friends (Book 4)
The Murder of Sleepy Hollow (Book 5)
Red Hot Murder (Book 6)
A Cornucopia of Murder (Book 7)
A Wedding to Murder For (novella)
Loch Ness Murder (novella)

Stand-a-lone books:
The Taking
The Third Nanny
Mirror Image
The Stolen Twin
Today I'll See Her (novella)

Red Hot Murder

A Charlie Kingsley Mystery

by Michele Pariza Wacek

For my family, for always believing in me.

Chapter 1

"Charlie, you are a lifesaver," Cherry gushed as I handed her a bag of tea. "I don't even want to think about what I would have done if I had run out."

"I'm glad I didn't let you down," I said, trying to keep my face composed. Cherry was a good customer and fun to talk to, but she had a tendency to exaggerate.

"So am I," she said, swiping at her strawberry-blonde curls and pushing them out of her green eyes. "With my wedding coming up, I can't afford any setbacks with my complexion. You should see my beauty routine." She rolled her eyes. "It takes *hours*. What we women subject ourselves to in the name of youth and beauty! It's nuts. At least I can relax when I drink a cup of your tea."

"It's tough," I agreed, with real sympathy. Even though Cherry was in her late twenties and still as cute and perky as she likely was when she was the captain of the Redemption High School cheerleading squad, she was already terrified at the prospect of getting old. She reminded me of the women I used to associate with when I was back in New York—all the rich wives who didn't work and spent their days worrying about being replaced by a younger model when they grew "too old." I wished there was something other than tea I could give her that would make her feel better about aging gracefully.

Alas, even though I was a firm believer that the right tea could pretty much cure anything, that was a little out of my league.

I ran a tea business out of my home, and I grew many of the herbs and flowers I used in my blends in my backyard. While I had a few popular recipes, like my lemon-lavender and Deep Sleep teas, some of my customers wanted specialized blends. Cherry was one of them. Hers was customized to help her skin maintain its youthful appearance.

"Oh," I continued. "I almost forgot. It sounds like congratulations are in order. You've finally set a date!"

Cherry's face faltered. "Well, it's not official. Yet. But that should all change tonight."

"Oh, that's exciting! What's happening tonight?"

She leaned closer to me as if we were in a crowded restaurant rather than my empty kitchen, and she didn't want anyone to overhear us. Well, empty other than Midnight, my black cat, who didn't appear to be listening to us anyway as he napped in the sun. "It's a surprise. All I know is I'm supposed to get dressed up and be ready at 7 p.m. sharp."

"Oooh, a romantic surprise. How fun," I said, feeling a little pang. I immediately pushed it away, though. It was better for everyone if I didn't date. Especially one specific member of the Redemption Police Department named Brandon Wyle.

"I know, I can't wait," Cherry said, tucking the bag of tea into her purse and rooting around for her wallet. Her cheeks had flushed pink, which made her look even more appealing. "Marcus has never done anything like this before, so what else could it be but to finally set the date? And it's perfect timing with Valentine's Day just a few weeks away."

"You did tell me how much he loves making grand gestures," I said.

Cherry nodded as she finally fished her wallet out. "He does," she sighed. "Like the time he threw that surprise birthday party for me. Or when he whisked me off to that romantic bed-and-breakfast for last year's Valentine's Day celebration."

"He's definitely a keeper," I said. Truth be told, I had no idea if he was or not, as I had never even met the man. All I knew was what Cherry shared with me, which on the surface, sounded amazing.

But dig a little deeper, and things weren't quite so rosy. The fact they had been engaged for a while now, at least a couple of years, with no actual wedding date in sight set off more than a few alarm bells. However, it wasn't enough to deter Cherry from closing the deal with him.

"He is," Cherry agreed as she opened her wallet. "You're definitely invited to the wedding. I can't wait for you to meet him. In fact, I'd love for you to be my Bride Whisperer. Anastasia has raved about you."

"Well, I appreciate that," I said, even though I wasn't sure how keen I was to step into that role again. Dealing with one Bridezilla was enough. Plus, I ended up having to solve a murder while carrying out my Bride Whisperer duties.

"You really are the best," Cherry continued as she handed me a few bills. "And I know I should have called you sooner, but it was only yesterday that I realized I had hardly any tea left. It's been so crazy busy; I can't keep anything straight anymore. Between the wedding and work, and now getting ready for this unexpected business trip, it's been madness. Absolute madness."

"I get it," I said, although a part of me wanted to ask her how she, of all people, was complaining about going on a business trip. She was a travel agent, after all. "Luckily, I had all the ingredients ready, so all I had to do was put it together."

"Well, thank you again," Cherry said as she slung her purse over her shoulder. "I hate to run like this, but I still have a million things to do today."

"Oh, well, hold on a second. I need to get you your change." I moved toward my own purse, hoping I had enough singles.

Cherry waved me off. "Don't worry about it. I appreciate you doing this rush job. Besides, I really do have to go. I've got a hot date to get ready for." She winked at me and hurried away, her heels clacking on the kitchen floor as she made her way toward the front door.

Midnight picked up his head and stared at me with his emerald-green eyes. "Don't give me that look," I said. "You and I both know the last thing I need is a romantic surprise date."

He yawned, showing off an impressive array of teeth.

"I'm not going to argue with you," I said, briskly moving into the kitchen. I had a sudden urge to bake a fresh batch of my famous chocolate chip cookies.

Chapter 2

The phone rang, jerking me out of a sound sleep. I fumbled for it, my heart instantly in my throat. At that hour of the night, I automatically assumed it was my sister, Annabelle, calling from New York with terrible news.

But then I reminded myself it was more likely someone like Dana, calling with a middle-of-the-night tea emergency. Again.

"Charlie?" The voice was so choked with tears, I could barely make it out.

"It's me," I said, swinging my legs out of bed as fear started to take hold again. "Who is this?" I almost asked if it was Annabelle, but I wasn't sure if I could get the words past the lump in my throat. Plus, it sounded nothing like my sister. Was it my best friend, Pat? No, it didn't sound like her, either.

"It … it … it's me," the voice said between sobs. "Cherry."

"Cherry?" I wasn't sure I'd heard her right.

Cherry burst into a fresh bawl. "You have to come," she said. "He's not moving. You have to help him."

"He? Do you mean Marcus?" My mind raced as I thought about her romantic surprise date. "Is something wrong with Marcus?"

Another hiccup. "Please come. He needs help. I need help."

"Cherry, if there's something wrong with Marcus, call 9-1-1."

"You don't understand," she cried. "I don't remember. He wasn't here. So, I don't even know how he was attacked."

Attacked? What was she talking about? Was she in the middle of a bad trip? Was THAT the romantic surprise? I tugged a hand through my wild, brownish- blondish hair, trying to decide if maybe *I* should hang up and call 9-1-1. "Cherry, what is going on? Talk to me."

"I ca … can't. Please just come. Hurry." There was a click, and the phone went dead.

I stared at the receiver. Really, the smart move would be to call 9-1-1 myself. I had no business heading over to her house in the middle of the night, especially if I was going to end up in the middle of some dangerous situation. Best to let the professionals take care of it.

Yet … her voice tugged at me. She sounded terrified … like something had gone very wrong.

What she really needed was someone in her corner she could trust.

Before I was even aware I had made the decision, I was striding over to my closet to pull on a pair of jeans and an oversized University of Wisconsin sweatshirt. I headed into my en suite bathroom to quickly brush my teeth, wash my face, and try to do something with my wild hair. I finally managed to gather it into a loose ponytail, although a few tendrils had snuck out and were framing my face. I stared at myself in the mirror. My hazel eyes were puffy from lack of sleep, and I looked far older than my early thirties.

Well, it's not like you're going to a party, I scolded myself. *If you're gonna do this, then hurry up and do it.*

I left the bedroom and hurried to find my keys.

* * *

Upon my knock, Cherry immediately opened the door and nearly fell into my arms. "Oh, thank goodness it's you."

She looked dreadful. Her eyes were red and swollen, and her hair, which looked like it had been carefully styled in a complicated up-do, had fallen halfway out. There were black streaks down her face where her makeup had smeared, and black flecks stained her red dress, which was now wrinkled. There was also a huge run in her pantyhose.

"Let's get inside," I said, gently pushing her into her front hallway as I quickly glanced around to see if anyone had seen us. Cherry was renting an apartment on top of a garage. Her landlords were a very sweet, retired couple. The wife was actually one of my tea customers, and the one who had referred Cherry to me. The property was in a quiet neighborhood filled with other retirees. While it was still dark and very much the middle of the night, if there was one thing I knew about older, retired people, it was that they were often up and wandering around at all hours of the night. In many cases, they also liked to take a peek out of their windows to make sure all was quiet in the neighborhood. Until I knew precisely what was going on, I would prefer not to be identified showing up at that particular time.

Cherry's body was limp and pliable as I maneuvered her back into her apartment. I couldn't figure out if it was shock or something else, but I didn't like how she looked. There was a glassiness to her eyes, and her skin was extremely pale.

"Charlie, you have to help him. You have to. I don't know what happened. Nothing makes any sense." The words were tumbling out of her so fast, they were practically on top of one another. Her breathing had sped up so much, she was practically gasping, and I was a little afraid she might hyperventilate.

I took hold of her shoulders and gave her a little shake. "Cherry, calm down. Breathe. I'm here. We'll figure it out, but first you have to breathe for me. Okay? Can you do that?" As much as I wanted to get a look at whoever it was who wasn't moving, I also knew I had to at least calm Cherry down enough to stabilize her before I ended up with two medical emergencies on my hands.

She gulped, her breath catching in her throat, but I could see her trying to mimic my breathing. I kept encouraging her until she finally seemed calm enough to disclose some information.

"Can you tell me what's going on?"

Almost immediately, her agitation accelerated again. "I told you … I don't remember. Someone must have broken in and attacked him, but I don't remember."

"Okay," I said quickly. "Why don't we go into the kitchen, and I'll make some tea? And you can …" I was going to say, "tell me where he is," but her eyes went wide, and she started gasping again.

"I can't go in the kitchen," she said, her voice high and panicked. "That's where he is!"

Well, that answered it. "Okay, why don't we go sit down in the living room? And then I can go check on him."

That appeared to be the right solution, as she immediately calmed down again and allowed me to lead her there.

The room was oddly lit, as both lamps were on the floor, but there was enough light to show that it was a disaster. One of the end tables had been knocked over, along with the coffee table. There was a pool of mail and magazines on the floor in front of the latter along with a mug lying on its side, lipstick smeared across its rim. Next to that were two wine glasses, one broken and one with lipstick marks, along with a bright-red phone. The television was also smashed. A gold-framed photo was lying in front of it, and I wondered if that was what had been used to break the screen. It was difficult seeing who exactly was in the photo, as the glass was cracked, but as far as I could tell, it appeared to be a picture of Cherry and a man with curly, black hair.

"I don't know what happened," Cherry said again. Her hands were pressed together at her palms, and she was shaking her head. "I don't understand what's going on."

"Okay, let's just sit down," I said, leading her to the loveseat, which was still intact. I suspected the reason why she had only one chair and a loveseat was because the room was too small for a full-sized couch. I quickly shed my jacket and slung it over the side, trying to keep it out of the way of the wreck. "I promise you, we'll sort this all out, but first I need to go into the kitchen and check on whoever's in there." Cherry's eyes filled with tears, and I hesitated, wondering if she was on the verge of another breakdown. But I also had to know the truth. "So it *is* Marcus?" I asked, my voice as gentle as I could make it.

Her breath caught in her throat, and she nodded.

"Did you call 9-1-1?"

Her eyes widened with horror. "No! No cops. Charlie, you can't call them. I can't talk to them. I don't remember anything."

"Okay, no cops," I cut in, trying to head off another hysterical outburst. "I'll go into the kitchen and see what's going on. I'm going to make you some tea, as well."

She nodded again. I led her to the loveseat and sat her down. I was about to pick up both the lamps and the end table, as then the living room would stop looking like some freaky horror show, but stopped myself at the last second. Surely, the cops wouldn't want anything moved.

Which means the only task left was to check out the kitchen. I took a deep breath and headed in.

I steeled myself before I walked in, more than a little apprehensive about what I would find. If the living room was in shambles, how much worse would the kitchen be, considering the array of weapons and knives within easy reach?

Luckily, my fears turned out to be unjustified. Other than a sink full of dirty dishes and both chairs overturned on the floor, it appeared more or less normal.

Well, other than the body on the floor.

I knelt down next to Marcus, intending to check for a pulse, but I wasn't holding out much hope. One look at him, and it was clear he was dead. When I touched his neck, it was already cold.

Oh no. I felt sick. What had Cherry done?

And what on Earth was I going to do?

For a moment, I could only sit there, staring intently at a man who was just a few years younger than me. Even in death, he was beautiful, with a head of black, silky curls, high cheekbones, and a perfect mouth. Although I couldn't tell for certain, I suspected he was the man in the shattered photo.

Thanks to hours at the gym, his chest was broad and muscular, and he wore dark jeans and a button-down blue flannel shirt. He looked relatively peaceful, and I wondered just what had killed him. Had Cherry poisoned him? I thought of the two wine glasses in the living room. But if he drank poisoned wine there, wouldn't his body be there, too? Why would he have come into the kitchen? Especially since it looked like he and Cherry had one heck of a fight in the other room.

It didn't make any sense.

Well, sitting frozen next to his body wasn't going to get my questions answered. I pulled myself to my feet, trying to decide how to best approach Cherry, when I noticed a pillow next to Marcus's head. Why would there be a pillow there? Was Cherry going to put it under his head? And if that was her intention, why didn't she?

So many questions, and the only person who could answer them was still teetering on the verge of hysteria. I glanced toward the stove, really wanting to make tea, but I also didn't know if I wanted to take the time for that. The sooner I could get through to Cherry, the sooner I could get the cops involved.

Taking another deep breath, I headed back into the living room.

Cherry was still in the same place I'd left her. She was slumped over, her arms dangling between her knees.

Gingerly, I sat down next to her and reached out to take one of her hands. It was frigid, and for a fleeting second, I was reminded of how cold Marcus was. She inhaled a deep, shuddering sigh when I touched her, and slowly turned her face toward me. "He's dead, isn't he?"

There was no use sugarcoating it. "I'm so sorry."

Her face scrunched up, and I could see fresh tears well up in her eyes. "We were going to get married," she whispered.

I gently squeezed her hand. "I know. I'm so, so sorry for your loss."

She turned her head to stare at the carpet as fat tears began to drip down her face. "We were to get married and have kids and grow old and die together."

I squeezed her limp hand again. There were no words. Unfortunately, that didn't mean there weren't things that needed to be done. And the sooner, the better.

"Cherry," I said very gently. "We need to call the cops."

She shook her head, but a bit less adamantly than before. "No cops." She was like a shell of her earlier self, almost as if my confirming what she knew had drained the hysteria from her body.

"We have no choice," I said. I kept my voice gentle, but I also made it firm. If she thought I was going to help her hide a body, she was going to be sorely disappointed.

She lifted her head to meet my eyes, her face a mask of grief and despair. "You don't understand," she said. "It's like I told you … I don't remember."

"What don't you remember?"

She threw her hands up in the air. "Anything! That's the problem, I don't remember anything." Her voice became agitated again.

"Okay," I said soothingly. Maybe I should have taken the time to make some tea after all. "Why don't you tell me what you DO remember, and we'll take it from there?"

She looked back down at her lap as she took a deep, shuddering breath. "I remember getting ready," she said, her voice soft. "I was so excited. I was sure tonight was going to be the night when we'd finally set a date, and I'd be that much closer to being Mrs. Marcus Whitlock. I had my hair done and spent extra time on my makeup. I was still getting ready when I heard a knock at the door. As you can imagine, I panicked. It was only 6 p.m., and the note had said I should be ready at 7. Had I gotten something wrong? I headed over to the front door, all set to tell Marcus I still needed more time, but there wasn't anyone there."

A shiver of unease reverberated through my body. "No one?"

Cherry shook her head. "No. But there was a package with a single rose on top of it." Her smile was soft at the memory. "It was a box of my favorite dessert … chocolate-dipped strawberries. There was a note, too. 'This is just the beginning of the treats I have in store for you tonight.'"

"Wow," I said. "He really does go all out, doesn't he?"

She nodded, another tear leaking out of her eye. "He was amazing. He had this way of treating me like an absolute princess. I felt like I was the only one in the world in his eyes." She swallowed hard.

I squeezed her hand again. "So, then what? You finished getting ready?"

"Yes. Well, after I put the rose in water and had a strawberry. Well, maybe two." She ducked her head, a faint bloom of pink appearing on her face. "I didn't want to spoil my appetite because I was sure whatever Marcus had planned, it would be spectacular. But they were sooo good. I had to force myself to stop. I put the box in the fridge, so I wouldn't be further tempted, and I went back to the bedroom to finish getting ready. The next thing I knew, I found myself on the floor of the living room, and Marcus … Marcus …" Her face scrunched up as more tears streamed down her cheeks.

"It's okay," I said as she started to sob, burying her face in her hands. I wrapped my arms around her shoulders, holding and rocking her as she cried. It took a little bit for the worst to move through her, but when it finally did, I realized she was in need of tissues.

"Wait here," I said, giving her another squeeze. "I'll go find some tissues and make that tea."

She kept her face in her hands as her head bobbed up and down. I stood up and headed back to the kitchen, figuring I would start by getting the water on the stove and then hunt down tissues. I knew I needed to convince Cherry we needed to call the cops, and soon, and I was hoping once she was calmer, she would finally see reason.

I clicked on the kitchen light and nearly gave myself a heart attack seeing Marcus still lying on the floor. It wasn't like I didn't know he was there, but somehow, I didn't expect to see him. Or the pillow lying next to his head. I was going to have to ask Cherry about it.

I moved to the stove where the teakettle sat on one of the back burners. I filled it up, avoiding the pile of dirty dishes in the sink, then figured out how to turn the burner on before hunting around for a couple of clean mugs.

Something was niggling at the back of my head, but I couldn't figure out what exactly was bothering me. I set out the mugs, found the tea, and stood for a moment just looking around the kitchen. Something was off, but … what?

Of course, it could have just been the dead body and pillow throwing me. I picked my way out of the kitchen and found my way to the bathroom, which was just as messy as the kitchen. The counter was strewn with various makeup brushes, sponges, and potions, along with pink and green streaks of color. A crumpled tissue stained with lipstick was in the sink.

I had no idea Cherry was such a slob.

I picked up the box of tissues sitting on the back of the toilet and went back into the living room to hand it to Cherry. I still couldn't shake the sense that something wasn't right with Cherry's account of the night.

It was only while digging around in the fridge looking for cream or milk to add to Cherry's sugar-loaded tea (to help her get past the shock of what she had been through) that it finally hit me: there WAS something missing.

The box of chocolate-dipped strawberries.

Nor was there a rose anywhere to be found.

I shut the fridge and went back into the living room thinking maybe I'd missed it on the floor, or it was mixed in with the half-broken wine glasses and coffee mug. But as far as I could tell, there was nothing more than the wine glasses and a coffee mug. No rose or vase.

I paused, my brain running through the story Cherry had told me. How was it that the two gifts she mentioned—the rose and the chocolate-dipped strawberries—were nowhere to be found, but two other items—the coffee mug and wine glasses—were never mentioned in Cherry's recounting of the night's events?

Cherry was mopping her face with tissues when I entered the room, but when she saw me standing there, she raised an eyebrow. "Do you need something? Are you having trouble finding things?"

"I was just wondering about the rose. Didn't you say you put it in a vase?"

She gave me a curious look. "Yeah. I left it right ..." she pointed to where the coffee table used to be. Her mouth formed a perfect O. "Oh, no. That vase was a graduation present from my grandma. It was Waterford crystal. Don't tell me it's broken."

"No, it's not broken. I just don't see it there."

She stared at me. "What do you mean, there's nothing there? Of course it was there. I remember putting it there last night."

"Well, it's not there now."

"What? That can't be." Cherry craned her neck as she searched the floor.

"But there *are* two wine glasses there," I said. "Do you remember having a glass of wine? Maybe before Marcus got here?"

"Why would I have opened up a bottle of wine if Marcus wasn't here?" she asked as her eyes continued sweeping the floor.

Good question. And now that she had asked it, I realized I hadn't seen an opened bottle of wine in the fridge, either. "What about the coffee mug?"

"Oh!" Her face brightened. "That, I remember. I had some of your tea yesterday. I try and have at least one cup every day. I had just finished it when I heard the doorbell."

Well, that at least cleared up one mystery from the night before. "So you must have brought the empty mug into the living room." Normally, I would have found that strange ... especially since Cherry would have walked right by the kitchen on her way to the front door, but after seeing the general lack of housekeeping in the apartment, it was probably not a big surprise a dirty mug might first take a detour into the living room before finding its way into a sink of hot soapy water.

She hesitated, a puzzled look on her face, before looking at me. "No. I'm sure I didn't do that. I would have left it in the bathroom where I was getting ready. I was sipping it while putting on my makeup."

"Is that the mug?" I pointed to where it lay on its side next to the wine glasses.

She frowned. "Ye-e-es." She drew out the word. "But why is it there? And … where did those wine glasses come from? And where IS my vase? What is going on?" She struggled to get to her feet as the shriek from the tea kettle startled her and caused her to fall back onto the loveseat. I hurried into the kitchen to take care of the tea, leaving Cherry muttering to herself. When I returned, tea mugs in hand, she was on her hands and knees searching through the debris by the coffee table.

"You may not want to touch any of that," I said.

She glanced up, but a hunk of her hair had fallen across one eye, so she gave her head a quick shake to move it out of the way. "Why not?"

"Because the cops will need to investigate."

"No!" She shook her head violently, causing more hair to fall out of her updo. "I told you, no cops!"

Inwardly, I sighed. I had hoped once some time had passed, she would see reason and come to the right conclusion on her own, without me pushing her. But it didn't look like that was going to be the case. I squatted down and wordlessly handed her a mug. She gave me a suspicious look, but took it.

"Cherry," I said after she had swallowed a couple of sips. "You must know we're going to have to get the cops involved. You have a body lying in your kitchen." Her face blanched at that, but I kept going. "It's not like you can leave him there. What would you do with him?"

"I can't have the cops here," she burst out. "I just told you, I don't remember what happened! How am I going to answer their questions if I can't remember anything?"

I tilted my head. "Cherry, do you honestly think if you don't call the cops now, you won't have to answer their questions? What do you think is going to happen when someone realizes Marcus is missing? They're going to call the cops, which means the cops are going to talk to all of Marcus's family and friends." I gave her a pointed look. "Including his fiancé. Who was supposed to have a surprise romantic date night with him the last day anyone saw him." As I talked, Cherry's lips pressed together tighter and tighter until they turned white.

"I know I wasn't the only one you told," I said as gently as I could.

She didn't respond. Instead, she sat back on her heels and took another long drink of tea. It seemed to be working its magic, as she was visibly calming down.

"So, can we call them?"

She lowered her mug until it was resting on her lap. I could see the smear of pink lipstick on the rim, though most of it seemed to have somehow ended up on her chin. "They're going to think I killed him," she said softly, staring into her mug.

I lowered myself to the floor, sitting cross-legged, so I could rest a hand on her knee without tipping over. "Don't you want to know the truth?"

Her face jerked up, her eyes wide. "I didn't kill him. I couldn't! Someone else killed him. Even if he wasn't the love of my life, I don't have it in me to kill *anyone*!" But, despite how sure her words were, I could hear the doubt trembling beneath.

"I know you don't. But something happened here, and we need to get to the bottom of it. We owe it to Marcus. Don't you agree?"

Her shoulders slumped, like she was deflating in front of my eyes, the last vestiges of resistance draining out of her. "You're right. We better call them."

Chapter 3

"So you don't remember when Marcus arrived?" Officer Brandon Wyle asked, his body a little too tall and broad to fit comfortably in the white, wooden chair. His too-long dark hair was already a mess, like he hadn't bothered to comb it that morning. His eyes weren't fully open, either, as if he hadn't been able to grab coffee on his way over, and he was still trying to wake up.

We were all crammed in Cherry's messy bedroom, which was no surprise to me after seeing the state of the bathroom and the kitchen. Piles of clothes were strewn about on the floor, and a large variety of necklaces, bracelets, and earrings lay scattered across the top of her dresser.

A pile of partially folded towels lay on the one and only chair in the room. Wyle had shifted those to the foot of the bed and dragged the chair over to sit across from Cherry and me as we perched on the side of the unmade bed. Another officer stood in the corner, taking notes, as there wasn't enough room to easily fit another chair in there, even if one had been available. The ones in the kitchen were now blocked off as part of the crime scene.

"No, I don't," Cherry said. She had cleaned herself up some before the cops arrived, having washed most of the makeup off her face and changed into an oversized blue sweatshirt and matching sweatpants. Her hair was still a train wreck, though. I suspected it was because of all the hairspray—whoever had styled her hair had taken no chances on it falling apart before the big date. Cherry would probably need to wash it before getting it back under control. But, even with her sticky, messy hair, she still looked better than earlier. Younger, more innocent even, making it even more difficult to imagine her killing her fiancé.

My more cynical side couldn't help but wonder if that was part of the reason she had made those changes.

"What about the living room? Do you remember how it got trashed?"

"No, I told you, it was like that when I woke up."

"And you were in the living room when you woke up?"

"Yes."

"But you don't remember how you got there?"

"No."

Wyle made a note. "Precisely where in the living room were you when you woke up?"

"On the floor." She reached to touch the back of her head. "I remember feeling woozy, and my head hurt. I thought maybe I had fallen and hit it."

Wyle's eyes narrowed. "Did you fall?"

She shook her head. "I don't think so. I don't remember falling."

"So, what did you do after you woke up?"

"Well, as you can imagine, I was in shock. I couldn't figure out what I was seeing. Then I thought maybe I was robbed, and someone had hit me on the head, and that's why I couldn't remember. So I dragged myself to my feet to check the rest of the apartment, and that's when I found Marcus."

Wyle gave her a sympathetic look. "That must have been a shock."

She swallowed hard. "It was. At first, I thought maybe he had been attacked, too, by whoever had robbed me, so I tried to wake him, but … he was so still and so … cold." She shivered, folding her arms across her chest.

"Why didn't you call 9-1-1?"

"I was going to. But he was so cold." Her voice dropped. "And I couldn't remember. Why was it such a blank? I couldn't even remember when he had arrived. I must have let him in … otherwise, how could he have gotten in? Or … had I accidentally left the door open? When I picked up the package? Was that how whoever did this got in? So I raced to the door to check. But …" She stopped talking to lick her lips. I noticed her hands were trembling, and I was suddenly worried she was going into shock again. Maybe I needed to ask Wyle if I could make her another cup of tea with lots of sugar and milk. That seemed to have worked before.

"And then?" Wyle asked, his voice gentle.

"The front door was locked." Her face was pale, her eyes huge. "How could that be? How did the person who attacked us get out? More importantly, how did Marcus get in? He had a key, just like I had a key to his place, but we never used them. They were for emergencies only."

"Maybe he heard something inside, and when you didn't answer the door, he thought it was an emergency and used his key," Wyle offered.

"He would have had to go back to his apartment to get it," Cherry said. "He doesn't carry it with him. It was just for emergencies. Not anything else. That was part of the agreement."

Agreement? Wyle's gaze flicked to mine, and I saw the same question reflected in his eyes. Even if they weren't living together, they were engaged, at least in theory. So why such restrictions on using each other's keys?

"What happened after you realized the front door was still locked?" Wyle asked.

Cherry's mouth worked, but no words came out. She swallowed hard again. "I … I called Charlie."

Wyle's lips twisted, like he had just bit into a lemon. "You called Charlie? Why didn't you call the police?"

Cherry squirmed. "I … I was confused. I needed a friend."

Wyle's eyes flickered over to mine again, but this time, they were filled with exasperation. I flashed him an innocent "It's not my fault" look in return.

Along with operating a tea business out of my home, I had also become something of an amateur sleuth. This wasn't completely by choice. Initially, when I moved to Redemption and started selling teas, my goal was to keep my head down (as much as you can when you have a business to promote) and live a quiet life gardening, baking, and making teas. Instead, as luck would have it—or maybe because I lived in Redemption, Wisconsin, and strange, unexplained things were always happening in Redemption—my tea customers regularly found themselves in some sort of hot water and in need of my help to get them out.

Wyle was not a fan of my playing amateur detective. He had made it clear numerous times how he would prefer I left the investigating to the professionals. But unfortunately for him, it turned out I had a knack for solving crimes, so he and I found ourselves in something of a reluctant partnership.

"You said you thought you were attacked, and you don't know how the attacker left," Wyle said. "Did it occur to you that that person might still be here?"

Cherry's face turned chalk-white. "What? No."

"You could have been in terrible danger," Wyle continued. "Not to mention how, by calling Charlie instead of the cops, you could also have been responsible for bringing Charlie into a dangerous situation."

Cherry was shaking her head. "No. No. That couldn't be."

"Of course it could be," Wyle said, his voice grim. "People walk in on home invasions all the time. He could have been in the bedroom or the bathroom, and you wouldn't have seen him."

"No, no … I was alone," Cherry said. "I … I walked around. I'm sure I did. I had to use the bathroom. I remember that. I knew I was alone. Whoever did this, he had already left."

To me, she sounded like someone trying to convince herself that she hadn't done anything wrong.

Wyle, however, was still stuck on someone being in the apartment. "But did you search? Did you look in the closet, under the bed, in the bathtub?"

Her eyes widened. "N-no … I didn't think …"

"That's why you need to call the cops," Wyle said. "There are things you don't know that we do. When you try to handle them yourself is when mistakes are made, and tragedies happen."

Cherry glanced at me, chagrin all over her face and shame in her eyes. "I didn't … I didn't think. I'm so sorry."

"It's okay," I said reassuringly.

Wyle pressed his lips together tightly. "It most certainly isn't okay. I could be investigating three bodies right now, instead of just one."

Cherry's face turned ashen, and her hands flew up to her mouth. "I'm so, so sorry. I didn't know. I was just confused. I couldn't think straight. My head was foggy."

I reached over to pat Cherry's knee. "Honestly, it's fine. Wyle here," I turned to give him a look. "Needs to be extra cautious, because that's his job. But I would have thought the same as you. This apartment is pretty small. It wouldn't be easy for an adult to hide."

"You would be surprised," Wyle muttered and dragged a hand through his hair. "Sorry, it's a little early for me without any coffee. So, you called Charlie …" his eyes shifted to mine, and I could see the lecture in them that he was saving for once we were alone. "And then what?"

"I waited for her."

"Did you do anything during that time? Maybe check on Marcus, or try to straighten up?"

Cherry shook her head violently, dislodging more hair from her updo. "Are you kidding? I couldn't bear to be anywhere near either room. I sat on the floor, right across from the front door." She folded her arms across her middle, hugging herself.

Wyle transferred his gaze to me. "Did you touch anything?"

"Marcus," I said. "I checked his neck to see if there was a pulse or not. Oh, and I made tea."

Wyle closed his eyes briefly. "Of course you made tea. In a crime scene."

"Well, there didn't appear to be a crime in the kitchen itself," I said. "Marcus was under the table, not in the kitchen proper. And, besides, Cherry needed the tea to calm her nerves."

"I did," Cherry agreed.

"I could make you some coffee if you'd like?" I offered. "As I already made tea, the damage is likely done. And I bet everyone here would like some coffee."

"I'd love a cup," the officer standing by the wall interjected. He was young—actually, he appeared way too young to be a cop. He was thin and gangly, like he hadn't grown into his body yet, and a spray of acne dotted his nose.

Wyle snapped his head around, and whatever look he shot the officer caused him to quickly duck his head and become instantly busy fiddling with his notes.

"I appreciate the offer, but we've got coffee covered," Wyle said, his voice dry. "So, to be clear, neither of you touched anything in either the living room or kitchen? They're exactly the way you found them?"

I gave Cherry the side-eye, but she had her head down and was plucking at her sweatpants.

Wyle didn't miss a beat. "What did you do?"

"I … I might have moved the coffee table," Cherry said, her voice so low, I had to lean in closer to hear her.

A muscle twitched in Wyle's jaw. "You might of?"

"It's not my fault," she said quickly. "I had to look for the vase."

Wyle kept his expression flat, his cop face, as I called it. But I could see the frustration swirling underneath. "Vase? What vase?"

"The vase I put the rose in," Cherry explained. "Remember how I told you about the package I got? There was a single red rose on it, so of course I had to put it in water."

"Let me guess—you put the vase on the coffee table," Wyle said.

Cherry leaned forward, her head bobbing up and down. "Yes, yes. I mean, that was part of the romantic surprise, so of course I wanted to display it where Marcus would see it as soon as he walked in."

Wyle nodded and made a few notes. "I take it the vase isn't in the living room?"

"No, it's not. And I don't know where it went. It was a graduation gift from my grandmother. It's Waterford crystal. I don't think they make that design anymore."

Wyle cleared his throat. "Is it possible it was broken?"

"That's why I picked up the coffee table. There would be pieces, if it were. But there's nothing."

"There's no rose, either," I added. "Not even any petals."

Wyle's eyes sharpened. "Are you positive you weren't robbed?"

Cherry raised her hands helplessly. "That's the only explanation that makes any sense. Someone broke in, trashed my living room, attacked me, and …" she seemed to stutter on the word. "Attacked Marcus and took the vase. But if they wanted to rob me, wouldn't they have taken more? It looks like all my jewelry is still there," she waved at the haphazard tangled mess on the top of her dresser. "There are some expensive pieces, too, passed down to me from my grandmother. A diamond tennis bracelet and matching earrings are probably the most valuable. Plus, there's some cash in the top drawer."

Wyle glanced at it. "Are you sure it's all there?"

"It should be. It doesn't look like anything has been touched." Cherry unfolded herself from the bed and walked over to the dresser as I wondered how on Earth she could possibly know if anything had been moved in the bedroom. She started poking around at the jumbled collection. "Yeah, here they are." She pointed to an open box where the necklace and earrings were nestled on a small, pink satin pillow. "The cash is here, too," she said, opening up the top drawer and peeking inside. She then looked back at us and must have seen the question on both mine and Wyle's faces. "My grandmother's family used to be quite wealthy. They lost most of it, but there are still a few things left."

Ah, that made more sense. I was wondering why Cherry would have chosen to live in this tiny garage apartment if her family was able to give her gifts like Waterford crystal vases and diamond earrings.

"And you checked the rest of the house for the vase? Maybe you put it somewhere else?"

Cherry gave him a look. "It's not like there's a lot of options to display the vase in here."

Wyle inclined his head as if to concede the point.

"Actually, it's not the only thing that's missing," I said.

Both Wyle and Cherry turned their heads to look at me. "What else is missing?" Wyle asked.

I looked at Cherry. "I didn't tell you this sooner, but your chocolate-dipped strawberries are gone, too."

Cherry's mouth dropped open. "Someone took my choco-late-dipped strawberries?" She looked almost more upset about that than the vase.

"They're not in the fridge, which is where you said you put them. Or did you put them somewhere else?"

"No, I definitely put them in the fridge." She started marching toward the door, clearly on a mission to find her favorite dessert, but Wyle held out a hand to stop her.

"You can't go in the kitchen yet," he said.

"But they must be in there. Why would someone take my chocolate-dipped strawberries and leave diamond earrings and cash?"

"I don't suppose you finished them and just don't remem-ber?" Wyle asked.

Cherry's expression was horrified. "Oh! I better not have. That would suck, if I ate them and don't even remember getting to enjoy them."

Wyle's lips quirked up a tiny bit, as if he were trying to hide a smile. "We'll check around. It may be that Charlie just missed them."

As there was very little food in Cherry's fridge—a gallon of milk, a container of half and half, some condiments, and a box of leftover Chinese food—I doubted that. But I also knew better than to say anything.

"And as for why no one took your cash and jewelry," Wyle continued, "it's possible whoever robbed you never made it to the bedroom. Maybe they were so freaked out over what happened in the living room and kitchen, they just grabbed the vase and fled."

"But then why was the front door still locked?" I asked.

"Is there another way out?" Wyle asked Cherry.

"There's a fire escape off the kitchen," she said. "The door is broken, so it's kind of a pain to open. I keep it locked."

Wyle made another face, like he wanted to lecture her on the safety aspects of having a working fire escape door, but decided to save it for another time. "We'll check and see if he could have left another way." He flipped his notebook closed. "I need to follow up on a few things with this investigation. Both of you stay here. I'm sure we'll have more questions, but just sit tight for the moment." He shot me a hard, unreadable look before standing up and striding to the door. The other officer quickly scurried after him.

Cherry remained where she was by the dresser, her arms wrapped around herself. "Charlie, I'm scared," she whispered.

The bedroom door was still open, and as I could see the second officer hovering nearby. I got up and moved closer to Cherry. "I don't blame you," I said, keeping my voice low. "You've gone through a horrible ordeal this morning. You probably should be checked out by a doctor once Wyle clears you. Just to be sure."

"It's not that," Cherry said quietly. "Well, not that exactly. What happened? Why can't I remember anything?" There was a note of desperation in her tone.

"That's why you need to see a doctor," I said. "Memory loss can be caused by all sorts of things. Like a head injury. You woke up on the floor in the living room, so maybe you did get hit in the head. Or …" I paused, wondering how much I should say. Cherry seemed relatively stable now, and she had handled Wyle's questioning well, especially considering the circumstances, but there was something swimming beneath the surface that seemed fairly close to hysteria. I had a feeling she was barely holding it all together as it was, and I didn't want to push her over the edge … especially with the cops only a few feet away.

On the other hand, all I had to do was look into her terrified blue eyes to know deep down she was already thinking the worst, and whatever I said wasn't going to be as bad at the scenarios her mind was likely coming up with.

"Stress and trauma can cause memory loss, too," I said. "It's usually temporary, but if you saw something happen to Marcus, that could cause amnesia."

Cherry squeezed her arms tighter around her waist. "But if that's the case, shouldn't I remember *more*? Like letting Marcus in? Or even finishing my makeup?"

"Memory is a funny thing," I said. "It's hard to predict what you will or won't remember."

She looked away from me, gnawing at her lip. "That's the other thing. Why am I still alive? Why is Marcus dead and not me? Or both of us?"

"I don't know. We'll have to find the person who did it and ask them."

She kept chewing at her lip. "It doesn't make any sense. None of this makes any sense." Her face was so pale, I was afraid she might faint. "There has to have been someone else here, right?" She was nearly whispering, and I had to move closer to hear her. "That's the only explanation. Someone had to have broken in and done this. Nothing else makes sense."

"It sure seems that way," I said.

"I mean, the vase is gone." She almost sounded like she was talking to herself. "And my chocolate-dipped strawberries. Why would they take those?"

"If it was a robbery, they would have had to go through the kitchen, so that's how they probably saw them," I said. "Maybe you didn't put the box in the fridge like you said, but left them on the counter. The attacker could have just grabbed the box as they walked by."

She shook her head. "No, I distinctly remember putting them in the fridge. I know I did. Because I didn't want to keep eating them." She pressed her fingers against her temple. "But maybe I took them out and ate a third after all, and that's part of what I don't remember. Maybe I did leave them on the counter. But why wouldn't I remember that?"

"Like I said, the mind is unpredictable."

"And why would whoever broke in go out through the fire escape? It's really hard to get that door open. Not to mention how loud the process of unfolding the metal stairs is. It would wake up half the neighborhood. It for sure would have disturbed the Joneses. It's a lot easier to go out through the front door. Especially if they were carrying a vase. Why wouldn't they have done that?"

"I don't know."

"But it had to have been someone else," she said again. "What else could have happened? There's probably a perfectly reasonable explanation as to why they left through the fire escape. That has to be it."

"Charlie." Wyle had stuck his head in the door, his face flat. "Can I see you for a moment?"

"Sure." I glanced at Cherry, who was still biting her lip. "Are you going to be okay?"

She didn't seem to be paying attention to me, so I reached out to touch her arm. She jolted, like I had shocked her with a cattle prod. "What?"

"Will you be okay?"

She whipped her head around, her eyes slightly wild. "Oh, yeah. Sure. Don't worry about me." She forced a smile.

I most certainly was worried about her, but I could sense Wyle's impatience, so I just patted her arm and left.

Wyle did not look happy as he led me through the apartment. As we passed through the living room, which was crowded with investigators taking pictures and dusting for prints, he pointed at my jacket that was still slung over the side of the love seat. "Is that yours?"

"Oh, yeah." I started to go fetch it, but he put a hand out to stop me. "I'm sure you've already done enough damage trampling through the crime scene," he muttered as he continued to lead me outside.

"But it's cold out," I protested. February in Wisconsin was always cold, gray, and bleak. And that was especially true before sunrise. "You just asked me if that was my coat … can't I get it?"

"Don't worry about it," he said, his dark eyes shuttered. He opened the front door and ushered me out and onto the small front porch.

I folded my arms across my chest. I at least had on a thick sweatshirt, but it could only do so much. To my surprise, Wyle removed his own coat and handed it to me.

"Aren't you going to be cold?"

"Don't worry about me," he said through gritted teeth. "My anger will keep me warm."

Oh. This doesn't sound good, I thought as I draped Wyle's coat across my shoulders. But at least I'd be warm. I could smell the combination of soap mixed with Wyle's unique scent on the fabric. It was a little distracting, but I firmly pushed it out of my mind. I had bigger things to worry about.

He folded his arms across his broad chest. The sky was starting to turn that silvery gray that meant dawn was right around the corner. It also meant I could make out how much he was glowering at me.

"Have you lost your mind?" he hissed. "What were you possibly thinking?"

Chapter 4

"You know exactly what I'm doing," I said. "I'm helping my client."

"The cops are who should be helping her," Wyle said. "Not you."

"She needed a friend," I said. "It's not every day that you wake up and find your fiancé dead in your kitchen with no memory of what happened. Having a bunch of cops swarming around wasn't the help she was initially looking for."

"It doesn't matter what she wanted," Wyle said. "She's obviously not thinking straight. It's up to you to keep a level head."

I stamped my feet, as the cold was starting to seep into my tennis shoes. "Look, she didn't want to call you at all. I was the one who convinced her. You should be thanking me."

"You shouldn't even be here," Wyle insisted, his frustration clear. "After she called you, why didn't you hang up and call me?"

"Because I had no idea what had happened," I said. "Do you think she told me on the phone that Marcus was dead in her kitchen, and she had lost her memory of the night before? She wasn't making any sense, so I came over to see what was going on."

Wyle's expression grew even more thunderous. "Did it ever occur to you that maybe that wasn't a good idea? You had no idea what you were walking into. If Cherry had been attacked, her attacker could still have been here and gone after you."

"It didn't sound like anyone else was still here," I said. "Well, except for whoever she said wasn't moving, who I assumed was Marcus." I didn't want to admit to Wyle that I hadn't considered the possibility that she wasn't alone. I was more focused on getting Marcus some help.

Wyle closed his eyes briefly. "That's why you should always call me when you get these types of calls. You haven't been trained, not like I have, and you're going to miss things."

"Wyle, I get what you're saying, but it was the middle of the night, and I didn't want to wake you if it was nothing."

His eyes widened. "Nothing? There's a man lying dead in the kitchen. How could that be nothing?"

"Well, I didn't know that then," I said. "For all I knew, Marcus was drunk and passed out somewhere. This could have all been the result of too much alcohol or pills or a bad combination of both. You certainly didn't need to be dragged out of bed for that. It would have been enough for me to have been."

"I would rather that than arriving later in the day and finding you in the kitchen lying next to Marcus."

"Well, I agree that would have been bad," I admitted.

He ran a hand roughly through his hair, messing it up even more. "Charlie, how many times do I have to tell you …"

"Sir." The front door opened, and one of the officers poked his head out. He glanced between us, his expression uncertain. "I … uh … you need to see this."

"I'll be right in," Wyle said, shooting me a hard look. "Don't think this is over."

"Wouldn't dream of it," I said.

He pursed his lips, like he had just bitten into something sour, but didn't answer. Instead, he flung open the front door and stormed back in. I was right behind him.

"What is it?" he asked the officer who was still awkwardly lingering by the door. I quietly removed Wyle's jacket and folded it in my arms.

The officer started to answer, but Cherry's disembodied voice interrupted him. "What? That's impossible."

Wyle glanced at me, the same question in his eyes that I had, and we both hurried forward.

Cherry was standing in the doorway to the kitchen, her back to us, but even if I hadn't heard her voice, I would have known her mood just by looking at her. Her entire body seemed to be vibrating with tension. "Why would someone do that?" she was asking. "To mess with me?"

"Do what?" Wyle asked.

Cherry whirled around to face us, and I caught a glimpse of a female cop wearing thick, black-rimmed glasses and holding what appeared to be a crystal vase.

"Put it back in the cupboard." She made a stabbing motion with her hand toward the cop. "Why wouldn't he have taken the vase?"

"Is that the vase you said was missing?" Wyle asked.

She flapped her arms. "Yes! Aren't you listening?"

Wyle put a hand out as if to try to calm Cherry down. "Where did you find it?" he asked, directing the question to the officer.

"It was in the cupboard." She pointed to the one next to the fridge, her hand covered with a blue glove.

"It doesn't make sense," Cherry said. "Why didn't he take it with him? It's quite valuable."

"Is that how you found it?" Wyle asked.

"Yes, just like this."

"What about a rose? Was there a rose in it?"

"No rose."

"Why would he take the rose and not the vase?" Cherry asked. "And what about my chocolate-dipped strawberries?"

"We didn't find any chocolate-dipped strawberries," the officer said.

"How about in the trash?" Wyle asked.

Cherry gasped. "You think he threw out my chocolate-dipped strawberries?"

"Nothing in the trash," the officer answered. "At least no rose or chocolate-dipped strawberries. Mostly just empty take-out containers and a bottle of wine. White."

"You found a bottle of wine in my trash?" Cherry asked.

The officer bent over and rummaged around for a moment before holding up an empty bottle.

Cherry stared at it. "I don't understand. I can't remember the last time I bought a bottle of wine. I only drink when I go out with friends, and usually only a couple of glasses."

Wyle frowned as he dug out his notebook. I was starting to get a bad feeling.

"I don't understand," Cherry repeated. "Could the attacker have left it? Did he bring it with him, or something? This makes no sense."

Wyle didn't seem to be paying any attention to Cherry's questions as he flipped back through the pages. "Did you find anything else? Like a note?"

"No note," the officer said. "At least not in the garbage or anywhere else in the kitchen. Not so far, anyway."

"What note are you talking about?" Cherry asked, but Wyle didn't answer. Instead, he turned to ask the officers working in the living room the same question. They confirmed they hadn't found anything yet, either.

"What are you talking about?" Cherry asked again. "What note?"

At that, Wyle turned back to her. "You said there was a note with your package, correct?"

"Well, yes, but I don't see what that has to do with …" her voice trailed off as her jaw dropped open, as if the implications of what Wyle was saying had finally sunk in.

"Do you remember where you put the note?"

Cherry swallowed hard. "I … I put it on the coffee table. Next to the rose."

Wyle's expression didn't change. "Was there anything else with that package? Maybe some wrapping paper or an envelope?"

"There was an envelope." Cherry's voice was so quiet, it was hard to hear. "I put the note back in the envelope."

Wyle glanced sideways at the investigators in the room who shook their heads again. He turned to look at the female officer, who had moved out of the kitchen and was still holding the vase, probably to hear what was going on better, who also shook her head.

Wyle glanced back at Cherry, who looked like she was watching her entire life crumble before her eyes. "Are you absolutely sure you got this package yesterday?"

"Yes. I'm sure." Her voice cracked, sounding anything but sure.

"Maybe it happened a different day," Wyle said. "Maybe last week? And with your memory loss, you're just remembering it wrong."

"No, it was yesterday," she said. Now, her voice sounded hollow, like a distant echo of herself. "I remember because I was getting ready for my surprise date when I heard the knock on the door. I distinctly remember panicking because he was an hour early, and I wasn't anywhere near ready."

"So tell me about this knock," Wyle said. "When you went to the door, did you see anything at all?"

"No. Other than the package, of course."

"You didn't see Marcus walking down the stairs or hiding?"

Cherry was shaking her head. "Nothing."

"What about his car? Did you see it in the street?"

"No."

"Weren't you surprised by that?"

Cherry's tongue darted out, and she licked her lips. "No. I mean, I thought it was all part of the surprise … that he didn't want us seeing each other until date time. I figured he parked down the street, or something like that."

Wyle shot her an unreadable look as he dug his pen out of his pocket.

"I got the package," Cherry muttered softly. Her voice wavered, and she swallowed hard before trying again. "I'm telling you, I got the package. Don't you see? He must have taken it."

"Who's 'he'?" Wyle's voice was neutral.

Cherry waved her arms. "Whoever broke in here and did this, that's who! He must have taken everything with him."

"Why would he want to do that?"

"I don't know. To make me look bad?" Her voice was rising. "We're going to have to ask him."

Wyle finished writing and flipped his notebook closed. "We'll be looking into all possibilities." His voice was neutral.

Cherry stared at him. "All possibilities?"

He tucked his notebook back in his pocket. "It might make sense for you to wait in your room while we finish our investiga- ..."

"What are you saying?" Cherry's voice was rising. "It had to be someone else. Don't you get it?"

"Like I said, we're going to look into that," Wyle said, gesturing for her to make her way to the bedroom. But she didn't budge.

"You said you were going to be looking into all possibilities. I want to know what you meant by that."

"Just what I said. All possibilities."

"What other possibility could it possibly be?"

"I don't know." Wyle's voice remained steady and calm even as Cherry's agitation increased. "At this point, no one knows what happened. Including you. Or are you saying you remember now?"

Cherry folded her arms. "No, I don't remember, but ..."

"Well, then, you should probably let us do our job and find whoever was behind this. Okay?"

Cherry's only response was to glare at him.

Wyle sighed. "The longer you stand here, the longer it's going to take."

I walked over behind Cherry and gently put a hand on her shoulder. "C'mon. Let's get out of their way, so they can catch the bastard who did this."

Her shoulder stiffened beneath my hand, and for a moment, I thought she was going to ignore me, too. But finally, she tossed her head, flinging her collapsed updo in my face. "Fine. I'll go." She squared her shoulders and marched forward. Wyle took a step back to allow us to pass.

We had almost cleared the kitchen when, without warning, Cherry slammed to a halt. It was so sudden, I bumped into her.

"What are you doing?" she asked.

I took a step back, swiping at her strands of hair-sprayed hair that had landed in my mouth.

Cherry didn't seem to notice. She was too intent as to what was going on in the kitchen. "I said," she repeated, taking a step forward. "What are you doing?"

I peered over Cherry's shoulder, trying to figure out what had gotten her so upset, but all I saw was the female officer standing in the kitchen next to an open cupboard, still holding the vase.

Wyle took a step closer to me, his expression pained. "Cherry, what's going on?"

Cherry pointed. "That."

Wyle looked as confused as I was. "What?"

"What is she doing? What are you doing?" The second time, she directed her question squarely at the female officer.

"I'm … I'm putting the vase back," she stammered. She glanced at Wyle. "Shouldn't I? Or did you want me to enter it into evidence?"

"But that's not where it goes," Cherry said before Wyle could answer.

The female officer looked confused. "I'm sorry?"

"Is that where you found the vase? In that cupboard? The one that's open?" Cherry asked.

The officer glanced behind her and back at Cherry. "Uh, yeah …"

"Well, that proves it," Cherry's voice was triumphant. "Someone WAS here."

"How do you figure?" Wyle asked.

"Because that's not where I keep that vase," she said. "I keep it in the bottom cupboard under the sink. It's more out of the way there. Plus, it's easy for me to pull out and fill with water when I need it."

"Makes sense," Wyle said, his voice agreeable. "Is it possible you put it in the wrong cupboard?"

"Absolutely not." Cherry's voice was firm. She pointed toward the open cupboard. "That one is for glasses. See? Why would I put it in there? It would block me from easily getting my glasses out."

"Do you remember the last time you used the vase?" Wyle asked.

Cherry screwed up her face. "It was at least a couple of months ago. No, longer than that. Maybe six months? I think the last time Marcus brought me flowers was my birthday." She winced, her expression full of pain.

"Again, I'm sorry for your loss," Wyle said, acknowledging her emotion. "And I'm sorry if these questions make it worse for you, but unfortunately, I have to ask them."

Cherry straightened her shoulders. "I'm okay. I want you to find who did this to Marcus."

Wyle nodded. "I know you do. So, I just need to ask. Do you remember the last time you saw the vase under the sink?"

Cherry looked at him blankly. "Yesterday. I told you. I got it out to put the rose in it."

"Before yesterday," he said. "Maybe one of your friends moved it?"

"But there's no reason for them to," Cherry said. "And I would have noticed if they had put it there next to the glasses."

Wyle started to ask another question when the doorbell interrupted him.

"Are you expecting anyone?" Wyle asked.

Cherry shook her head. She pressed her hand to her chest, almost as if the sound of the doorbell had startled her.

Wyle gestured to one of the officers to take care of it.

"Good morning! I hope it's not too … wait, what's going on?" The voice was female, and it floated through the small apartment. Next to me, Cherry sagged with relief.

"It's just Lola. My friend."

Wyle glanced at the kitchen clock. "Does your friend often stop by this early?"

"Not really, but …" Cherry's eyes shifted toward the front door where Lola was peppering the officers with questions. "Maybe we can just let her in and see what she wants?"

Wyle looked conflicted. On one hand, I was sure he wanted to know as much as I did about why Lola had decided to show up bright and early the day after something terrible happened, but he likely also didn't want to contaminate the crime scene any more than it already was … especially since Lola was going to have to walk through the living room to get to the bedroom. "Give me a second," he said. Then, he disappeared.

After a few moments of quiet conversation, Lola appeared, one hand holding a cardboard tray with three drinks on it, and the other, a white bag. Her eyes were wide as she tried to take everything in. "Good heavens. What happened?"

"It's been a nightmare," Cherry said, her eyes filling with tears. She stepped toward her as if to give Lola a hug, but then she hesitated, noticing Lola's full arms. She dropped her arms awkwardly. At the same time, Wyle had repositioned himself in the kitchen doorway, so it would be more difficult for Lola to see Marcus, who was still lying on the floor.

"Let's go in the bedroom, and we can talk about it," I said. "I'm Charlie, by the way."

Lola turned to me, and I could almost feel her sizing me up. She had long, thick, chestnut-colored hair that hung halfway down her back in waves. It seemed to almost overpower her delicate, heart-shaped face. Her eyes were a lighter brown than her hair, and I could see flecks of gold in them. She wore a long, black, wool coat with a white silk blouse and a tight, black skirt with very high heels. Even with them, she still only came up to my shoulder. "Charlie? Wait, are you the tea lady?"

"I am," I said.

"You really need to call her for some tea," Cherry said.

"Trust me, I've been meaning to, but …" Lola looked around again. "I still don't understand what's going on. And where is Marcus?"

I glanced sideways at Wyle, who shot me a look I had no trouble interpreting. He still wasn't happy I was there, but since I was, I might as well make myself useful and find out why Lola had showed up out of the blue.

"Let's go talk about it," I repeated.

Chapter 5

"What is going on?" Lola asked again as I ushered both her and Cherry into the bedroom. She bee-lined for the bed, plopping the bag and drink carrier on top of the wrinkled comforter.

Cherry sat down next to her while I took the uncomfortable-looking wooden chair Wyle had used. It wasn't that bad, but I was smaller than Wyle, so that probably helped.

Lola handed Cherry one of the cups. "It's a mocha. Your favorite. I figured we could celebrate."

Cherry took the mocha but didn't drink it. She rested it on her lap and stared at it, blinking back tears.

"Is that why you're here?" I asked Lola, wanting to give Cherry a moment to collect herself. "Because you wanted to hear about the surprise date?"

Lola turned to me as she sipped her coffee. "Isn't that why you are?"

I almost said no, I was there because Cherry called me, but something about the way she was sitting, the way her body seemed to almost vibrate with tension, made me change my answer. "I definitely wanted to know what happened last night, yes."

"Did you set a date?" Lola asked. Clearly perplexed, she turned back to Cherry, who was still staring at her cup. "I was hoping we could start some initial planning. Just as long as I wasn't interrupting anything."

Cherry winced. Lola leaned forward to put a hand on Cherry's leg. "Cherry, what on Earth happened? Why are the cops here? Where is Marcus?"

"Marcus was … we were … attacked," Cherry said.

"*Attacked*?" Lola's eyes went wide, and her hand paused midway on its way toward her mouth. "By who? Is Marcus alright? Is he in the hospital?"

A couple of tears started to leak from Cherry's eyes, so I decided to jump in again. "Unfortunately, no. Marcus is dead."

I knew I was being blunt, but I also couldn't think of any other way to say it. Marcus was most likely murdered, and saying he had passed away or something equally gentle wasn't accurate either.

As Lola was obviously a good friend, I figured she would take it hard, but I wasn't prepared for how hard. She froze, her face draining of all color. The hand holding the coffee went limp, causing her to drop the cup into her lap, where it sloshed out all over her black skirt. Unfortunately for the skirt, it appeared Lola had either gotten some sort of latte or dumped a ton of cream into a coffee, because the liquid was nearly white.

I muttered an "oh no" as I leaned forward to help mop up her skirt. But she didn't seem to even notice. Her face had grown even more pale, and her eyes were glassy and unfocused.

"Hey," I said, jumping out of my chair and putting a hand on her shoulder. "Lola, breathe. You gotta breathe."

She didn't react, so I shook her, first a little, then a little more, and she suddenly started gasping.

"Are you okay?" I asked. Even Cherry was staring at her.

"I … I … he can't be dead. There must be some sort of mistake." Her voice was too high, bordering on hysteria, and her eyes still didn't look right. Was she going into shock? I really wished I could get into the kitchen and make more tea.

"I'm so sorry," I said. "I wish it was a mistake. But it's not."

Her mouth opened and closed, but nothing came out. She started shaking her head violently and making a sort of strange, keening noise.

What in the world was going on? A part of me wanted to slap her in an attempt to jar her out of the fit she seemed to be having. Instead, I grabbed her shoulders with both hands and shook her again. Hard. Her head jerked back, and I could hear her teeth click together.

"Lola, you have to get it together," I said. "I know it's a shock, but think of Cherry. She just lost her fiancé." I almost mentioned how, if I didn't know better, I would assume Lola was the fiancé, but at the last moment, I thought better of it.

Especially when I glanced at Cherry and saw the confusion and surprise all over her face. Cherry apparently hadn't expected such a reaction either.

Lola blinked a couple of times and finally focused on me. "I'm … I'm so sorry," she said, her voice raspy. "You're right. It was just … just such a shock." She swallowed hard. "You don't … you don't expect someone our age to die. Especially someone like Marcus. I've known him for years … since freshman year in college."

"It's a terrible shock," I said, letting go of her and moving back to my chair. I nodded at the mess in her lap. "If there's sugar in your coffee, you might want to drink it. Sugar helps with shock."

She gave me a confused look before glancing at her lap. Her eyes widened, and she picked up her cup. "No sugar, but Equal," she said, taking a sip. "And skim milk."

"Sugar is best," I said. "But it's probably better than nothing."

"Sugar is bad for my diet," she said.

Looking at how thin she was, I didn't think a little sugar would kill her, but I also didn't think it was necessarily my place to say anything.

Cherry was still staring at Lola like she had just sprouted a second head. She obviously wasn't sure how to respond. Lola took another sip of coffee and seemed to finally get herself together. "So, what happened?"

"I don't know," Cherry said, finding her voice.

Lola was clutching her cup with both hands as she guzzled her coffee, but she paused to give Cherry a quizzical look. "You don't know?"

"I don't remember. I woke up and discovered the living room was trashed, and Marcus …" her voice trailed off.

Lola dropped her hands into her lap again. "You found Marcus dead? Right here?" Her voice cracked.

"In the kitchen," Cherry said.

"He's in the kitchen? Right now?" Her voice rose an octave, and her fingers squeezed the coffee cup.

"I think so," Cherry said.

"Lola, are you okay?" I asked, leaning forward again.

Lola gulped hard. "I'm so sorry, it's just … a body? Marcus's body? Right here? I can't … I have to go." She stood up suddenly. Her coffee cup had started to crumple in her hands, spilling what was left of her coffee. "Oh," she looked down at herself. "I'm a mess. I have to change before work. I'm so sorry. I'll call you later."

"Okay," Cherry said as Lola, still holding the crumpled cup in her hand, hurried from the room.

We could hear her asking the officers to get out of her way as she approached the front door.

"Is she … is she always like that?"

Cherry was still staring at the door, her eyes far away, but she jerked at the sound of my voice. "Oh, Lola? Yeah, she's always been a bit of a drama queen. Also, she and Marcus had gone out a few times. It was years ago. Before he and I started dating," she added hastily.

"Of course," I said. That explained Lola's reaction … especially if Marcus was the one to end it. It was also possible Lola never completely got over Marcus.

"She's with Flynn now, so it's all cool," Cherry continued. "She's my … she was going to be my maid of honor. I guess 'matron' of honor would be more correct."

"She and Flynn are married?" I asked.

Cherry nodded. "Yeah. They got married right before Flynn started law school. That way, they could qualify for the student housing for married couples on campus, which was not only cheaper, but a lot nicer. They were the first of our group to get married, and I think that's why she was so excited for us to set a date … so they wouldn't be the only ones married anymore."

"Makes sense," I said, even though I was thinking the exact opposite. I was having a tough time imagining how Lola could be both excited about Marcus getting married and that distraught over his death.

Cherry didn't seem to be listening, though. Instead, she stared at the remains of the breakfast Lola had brought, which was still on the bed. She lifted a hand helplessly, gesturing limply toward the bag and drink tray, which still had a single, lonely cup on it. "What should I do with all of this?"

I got up to gather it. "The cops would probably love a treat."

"Oh, that's a good idea," Cherry said. She was still sitting in the same place, her untouched mocha in her lap. I was halfway to the door with the bag and the drink tray when she called my name.

She held up her mocha. "Maybe one of them might like this, too?"

I shifted the bag and the tray to one hand so I could take the cup from her. "You don't want it?"

She shook her head. "I'm not in the mood to celebrate."

Her fingers were cold when I touched them, despite the fact that the outside of the cup was still warm. I watched her hand fall back into her lap, like she didn't have the strength to hold it up. She looked so sad, so broken, I desperately wished I could say something that would help ... like even though I knew what was happening was horrible, she would find a way to get through it, eventually.

But I also knew it wouldn't do anything to ease her pain at that moment.

Instead, I quietly left the room and went to find Wyle, who was frowning in the kitchen as he watched a small, dapper-looking man examine Marcus.

"Do you like mochas?" I asked.

Wyle raised an eyebrow. "Mochas? Why?"

I thrust the cup at him. "Lola brought it for Cherry, but she's not up to drinking it."

"Yeah, I'm not surprised," Wyle said as he took it. "Thanks. Someone is bringing coffee, but I suspect this is going to be a multiple-coffee day. Is that one Lola's?" He nodded to the one on the tray.

"No, Lola took hers. I think that one was supposed to be for Marcus, but I didn't ask."

"Oh … that makes sense." Wyle took a sip from his cup.

"I have no idea what kind it is, but if someone wants to drink it …" My voice trailed off as Wyle made a horrible face.

"I thought you said it was a mocha?"

"That's what Lola said it was."

He made a smacking noise. "It's got a weird aftertaste."

"Oh, it's probably sugar-free," I said, remembering Lola's Equal clarification. "Also, it might be skim milk."

Wyle rolled his eyes. "Of course it is." He took another drink and cringed again.

"Do you want to try this one?" I held up the tray.

Wyle shook his head, grimacing slightly. "I've had worse. Someone else can drink it. What's in the bag?"

I shook it open and peered inside. "Looks like muffins."

"That would probably help this go down."

"Unless they're sugar-free, too," I joked.

Wyle groaned.

"Yep," the well-groomed man kneeling on the ground said. He stood up and peeled his gloves off. He had black hair, cut very neat and short, and a perfectly trimmed black mustache. A pair of gold-rimmed glasses sat perched on his nose, and he wore a coat with the words "Medical Examiner" embroidered above the pocket. "I'm positive it was suffocation."

"Suffocation? But that makes no sense," Wyle said.

"Marcus was suffocated?" I asked.

"He was indeed," the medical examiner answered. He nodded at the pillow still lying next to Marcus. "I would assume with that, but obviously, I'll need to examine it before I can be sure."

I looked down at Marcus's broad chest and muscular arms. While Cherry wasn't as petite as Lola, she would have been no match for Marcus. How could she have held a pillow over his face long enough to smother him?

Wyle apparently had the same thought. "Make sure you run a tox screen, as well."

The medical examiner looked slightly offended. "Of course. I know how to do my job." He sniffed loudly.

Wyle rubbed the back of his neck. "Yeah, I know. This case has me on edge."

"Well, the sooner we get him back to my lab, the sooner you'll have your answers," the M.E. said, bending down to start packing up his black bag.

"I think we're about done here," Wyle said, turning to me. "I'm going to need your statement, but it's going to be a bit. Not to mention there isn't much room here. Why don't you meet me at the station later this morning? Shall we say ten?" It wasn't exactly a question.

"I'll be there."

Chapter 6

"I got here as quickly as I could," Pat breathed, sliding into the booth across from me at Aunt May's diner. She peeled her jacket off as Sue appeared, coffeepot in hand, to fill her cup and top off mine. I didn't normally drink a lot of coffee, as I preferred tea. But should a tea customer wake me up in the middle of the night, especially when a dead body was involved, I was definitely drinking coffee that day.

Pat was one of my best friends. I met her shortly after arriving in Redemption, when she became a tea client. Now, she was my unofficial sleuthing partner. Pat was a good decade or so older than I, and the best way to describe her was "round." She was plump, with a round face, round, black-rimmed glasses, and short, no-nonsense brown hair that was turning gray.

"Do you two know what you want, or should I come back?" Sue asked.

"I do," Pat quickly answered. "Blueberry pancakes. And a side of bacon."

"I'll have the same," I said. I was going to get the vegetable omelet, but I decided after the morning I had, I could use some pancakes.

"Good choice," Pat said, reaching for the cream to doctor her coffee. "So, what's up?"

I gave her the rundown of what happened at Cherry's apartment. Pat's eyes grew rounder, and she said, "That's crazy. What do you think is going on?"

"I have no idea," I answered honestly as Sue bustled over with our plates full of pancakes and bacon. "It's hard to believe that Cherry had anything to do with Marcus's murder."

"But ..." Pat said, as she drenched her pancakes with syrup.

"But at least right now, there's no evidence anyone else was there." I ticked off each point with one of my fingers. "There's no evidence of the package she claimed she got. There IS evidence she and Marcus shared a bottle of wine. But then what happened? Did they have a huge fight? Is that why the living room was trashed?"

"You said there was a broken photo of them too, right?" Pat asked.

"Yeah, it was next to the television set, like someone had thrown the picture and hit the TV."

Pat forked up a huge bite of pancakes dripping with syrup. "Maybe instead of setting a date for the wedding, Marcus told her it was over, and she flipped out," she theorized, her mouth full.

I played with my own pancakes. "Honestly, that's how it seems. They drank a bottle of wine and had a huge fight. At some point, Marcus became incapacitated, although I don't see how Cherry could have possibly suffocated him with a pillow unless he was unconscious. Maybe she hit him in the head with something."

"Maybe with the wine bottle," Pat offered.

"It's possible. It would have been heavy enough to knock him out." I picked up my coffee cup but didn't drink. "Although you'd think if she hit him hard enough on the head to knock him out, the wine bottle would have broken."

"What if he ducked, causing her to hit him on the shoulder, and he fell and hit his head?"

"That seems more likely," I said, although it still didn't feel right to me. "What doesn't make sense is how the bottle ended up in the trash. Nothing else was cleaned up, so why the wine bottle?"

"Shock?" Pat suggested.

"Shock would explain her lack of memory, as well," I agreed. "She was so furious at him, she wanted to kill him, and then when she actually did, her brain short-circuited."

"Just as long as she wasn't faking it."

I thought about Cherry's reaction—how she couldn't stop crying and seemed to be genuinely grieving Marcus's death. "I would be very surprised if she was," I said. "I would think you would have to be a sociopath or a psychopath to pull that off, and Cherry doesn't strike me as either."

"Probably not," Pat said, reaching for her coffee. "Would shock explain why she remembered things happening that didn't happen? Eating the chocolate-dipped strawberries, for instance?"

"I would imagine," I said. "I'm not a brain specialist or anything, but I would think the brain could just as easily create a false memory as it could block a real one. It's like the McMartin preschool case, where those kids had fake memories of being part of a satanic cult implanted in their minds. If therapists can do it to patients, why couldn't the brain do it to itself?"

"I'm no expert either, but it sounds plausible to me," Pat said, putting down her cup and glancing around for Sue and her ever-present pot of coffee. "It's still kind of a weird memory, though. Especially to use as a cover for potentially killing your fiancé. Putting a rose in water and eating a chocolate-dipped strawberry? Even stranger, to claim they were both gifts from him. Why not remember someone breaking in? That would at least provide a likely suspect."

"I agree; they're both weirdly specific memories," I said, reaching for my coffee. If Sue was going to come refill our cups anyway, it made sense to drink some more. "I wonder if those memories actually happened at some point before."

Pat tilted her head. "What do you mean?"

"Like maybe there was a time where Marcus *did* come to her apartment an hour before their date and leave her a surprise package of chocolate-dipped strawberries and a rose. Just not yesterday. Maybe it was even years ago, and her mind just resurrected that memory, making her think it happened yesterday."

"Hmm, that's an interesting idea. It actually makes a lot of sense," Pat said as Sue appeared at our table, coffeepot in hand. "I would definitely rather remember eating a chocolate-dipped strawberry than killing my fiancé."

"Oh, you must be talking about Cherry," Sue said, shaking her head. "Poor girl. Not that I blame her, though."

I did a double take. "Wait? What? You've already heard?"

"And what do you mean, you don't blame her?" Pat asked.

Sue put a hand on her hip. "Of course I've heard. Where do you think the cops order their coffee from?"

Ah, yes. Wyle had mentioned that someone was bringing coffee to the crime scene. "So what have you heard?"

"That Cherry killed Marcus." Sue glanced between us. "Isn't that right?"

"It might be," I said. "What did you mean when you said you don't blame Cherry?"

"Did you ever meet him?"

Pat and I both shook our heads.

"Oh, well, that explains it." Sue looked disgusted. "He was a womanizer. Oozed charm out of every pore. It's amazing how many women fell for his act." She shivered.

Pat and I exchanged glances. "Are you saying he wasn't faithful?"

"I doubt he even knew what the word meant," she said, her voice matching her expression.

"If that was the case, why would they even get engaged?" I asked.

"If I had to guess, I would say because of Cherry's family."

"Her family?" I was even more mystified.

Sue looked at me in surprise. "Don't you know who her family is?"

"No, we never talked about it. Except … wait a minute. She did say there was money at some point, but it's gone now."

Sue gave a bark of laughter. "Oh, yeah, I would say there was money at one point. She's related to the Duckworths."

"She's a Duckworth?" Pat asked incredulously. The Duckworths were a very wealthy family who lived in Riverview, Wisconsin, which was about 45 minutes away from Redemption. They owned a chunk of Riverview, as well. Check that—they owned a chunk of the rest of the state, as well.

"Basically. You do know there were two main families, right?"

"Yeah, two brothers who were basically building separate empires with their businesses," Pat said. "But eventually, one bought out the other."

Sue nodded. "Right. And while some of the family members who were bought out are part of the current Duckworth empire, not all of them were as lucky."

"I'm guessing Cherry falls into the latter," I said.

"Unfortunately, yes," Sue said, shaking her head and clucking her tongue. "I feel bad for her. She worked here for a while when she was a student, and she was just a joy. Always had a smile on her face and a positive attitude. I'm sure her family's financial situation must weigh on her, but she's never shown it … just rolled up her sleeves and got to work. And then, when she got together with that Marcus fellow …" She twisted her lips like she had eaten something bitter. "It was hard to watch."

"So you knew Marcus, too?" Pat asked.

"The whole gang worked here," Sue said. "They all got jobs here one summer. Worked during the day and partied at night. Ah, to be young again."

"Gang?" I asked.

Sue waved a hand. "A whole group of them. Thick as thieves. Let me see, there was Cherry and Marcus, of course. And Caleb. That was Marcus's best friend. And what's-her-name … the one with all the hair."

"Lola?" I offered.

Sue snapped her fingers. "Yes. Lola. And Flynn, who was dating Lola. And then that other girl … Sage. That was her name."

"Wow, that must have been something, to have them all here at one time," I said.

"You better believe it. Talk about drama. And angst." Sue rolled her eyes before noticing a customer across the room gesturing at her. "Oh, I better get back to work."

"Hmm," Pat said as Sue bustled away. "Lola is still in the picture. I wonder about the rest of them."

"I do, too," I said, thinking about Lola's near breakdown when she heard the news about Marcus's death. Based on what Sue had said, was it more than just her dating Marcus a long time ago? Was something maybe going on more recently?

"I wonder if that's true about Marcus not being faithful," Pat mused, going back to her pancakes.

"If it is, that's going to make things even more difficult for Cherry," I said. "That would give her two motives for killing him."

"Assuming he did break up with her," Pat said.

"Or at the very least, refused to set a date," I said. "But if he was also cheating on her …"

"Assuming she knew about it," Pat said. "The way you described her, it doesn't seem like she knew."

I thought back to Cherry and how upset she was. It sure seemed like she was genuinely grieving Marcus, but it was also possible some of that was from a guilty conscience, if she indeed was the one who killed him.

"I would assume she would break up with him if she knew, not push for a wedding date," I said. "But people are strange. She might have thought once they were married, he would change. Or maybe she thought she could change him. It's also odd that Lola showed up bright and early to start planning the wedding. If Sue knew Marcus was cheating, you'd think Lola would know, too."

"And, if she truly was Cherry's friend, why would she be happy about her marrying a cheater?" Pat asked.

I pointed my fork at her. "Exactly."

Pat picked up her bacon. "Well, it sure seems like there are way more questions than answers."

I went back to playing with my pancakes. "I agree. I also wouldn't be surprised if more people assume Cherry did it, with this new information."

Pat grinned. "Good thing she has you in her corner."

Chapter 7

"I appreciate you coming in," Wyle said. We were sitting at his desk, which was a towering paper disaster just waiting to happen. I was always amazed that the stacks of files and paperwork never seemed to tip over. He held up his mug. "I assume you don't want anything."

"I've had plenty of coffee," I said. "I just left Aunt May's."

He took a sip and winced. "Much better choice." He set the mug down and poked around his desk, eventually finding a yellow legal pad and pen. "Along with getting a written statement from you, I also have a few more questions."

"I would expect nothing less."

He eyed me. "Charlie, to be clear, I'm still not happy about any of this. You really should have called me. You had no idea what you were walking into."

"Duly noted. The next time a tea customer calls me in the middle of the night, I'll keep that in mind."

Wyle shot me a look. "That isn't terribly reassuring, as it seems you get a lot of those kinds of calls from your customers."

I held up my hands. "I can't help that they seem to regularly find themselves in trouble with the law." What I didn't add was I also couldn't help that I seemed to be better at solving cases than the cops were. Wyle was the only one I could work with, as he had been more interested in getting the right person behind bars than worrying about who got the credit. And while I appreciated his viewpoint that amateurs might be more likely to mess up the case—nor did I necessarily even think he was wrong—I would be more inclined to listen to him if I thought the cops didn't have a tendency to zero in on the wrong person. Which was precisely what I was worried about with Cherry.

"Yes, but you CAN help how you respond. As in, calling me or the cops instead of running over there in the middle of the night and into who knows what."

"Got it. Do you want to hear what else I've found out, or do you want to keep lecturing me?"

Wyle stared at me. I had the distinct impression he wanted to reach over his towering piles of paper and throttle me. Maybe the only thing that was saving me was if he did that, he would absolutely knock at least one of them over. Or that he knew whatever I was there to tell him, he really wanted to hear. He chewed on his bottom lip, his eyes narrowing, before finally clicking his pen. "I'll bite. What did you find out?"

"Before I tell you, hear me out," I said.

He frowned at me. "When have I ever not heard you out?"

"Well, never. It's just …" I rubbed my hands on my jeans, my palms suddenly sweaty. I wasn't sure why I was nervous. Was I afraid I was going to make things even worse for Cherry?

At the same time, Marcus's infidelities were going to come out sooner or later. If Sue knew, a lot of people knew. And those other people might assume Cherry was guilty. If I brought it up, then I would at least have the opportunity to present another perspective.

"So, it seems that Marcus wasn't exactly faithful," I said.

Wyle looked a little perplexed. "What does that mean? He either was or wasn't."

I sighed. "He wasn't. At least according to Sue."

Wyle was taking notes. "Sue?"

"The waitress at Aunt May's." I paused as Wyle kept writing. "However, despite how it looks, I don't think we should assume Cherry is guilty of killing him."

Wyle looked at me over his notebook. "Why would I assume that?"

"Well, because … I know it already looks bad for her."

Wyle sighed and put his notebook down. "Oh, for Pete's sake. Is this why you don't always call me? How long has this … 'arrangement' between us been going on?"

"A while," I said.

"Exactly. And have I ever assumed someone was guilty without looking hard at what the evidence was saying?"

"No, you haven't."

"Okay, then. So let's stop that nonsense." Wyle picked up his notebook again. "Quite honestly, if he was cheating on Cherry, which we will need to confirm, that opens up a lot more potential suspects. All the boyfriends and husbands and significant others who maybe wanted to kill Marcus for sleeping with their partner."

"Good point. And if that *is* the case, you might want to start with Flynn."

Wyle was busy writing again. "Flynn? Flynn who?"

"I don't know his last name. But he's apparently married to Lola."

Wyle glanced up at me. "Lola? As in Cherry's friend who showed up at her apartment this morning?"

"The one and same."

Wyle put his notebook down again. "You think Lola is having an affair with Marcus?"

"If she's not, something else is up with her." I told him about her overreaction to hearing about Marcus's death. "Later, Cherry said they had dated at one point, years ago, before she and Marcus got together, and maybe that's all it is. Lola just never got over Marcus. But …" I paused.

Wyle raised an eyebrow. "But?"

"It doesn't feel right. Even if she was still carrying a torch for Marcus, it still seemed over the top."

"People experience grief differently."

"Yeah, I know. And maybe she is just a drama queen, which is also what Cherry said. But if she was still sleeping with Marcus, her reaction would make a lot more sense."

Wyle had gone back to his notes. "It might also explain why she showed up there bright and early. It's possible she was aware there could be trouble."

I looked at him in surprise. "You think Lola was involved?" Thinking back to how upset she was, it was hard to imagine her being that good of an actress. Unless there was something else going on. Like guilt.

"Right now, everything is on the table," Wyle said. "But she doesn't necessarily need to be directly involved to have suspected something was going to happen. They could have fought about Marcus the night before, or Flynn could have disappeared in the middle of the night and reappeared with a questionable explanation. So, she shows up, bright and early, with coffee and muffins as a cover, so she could see for herself what, if anything, happened."

I mulled Wyle's explanation. The more I thought about it, the more sense it made. If Lola had a gut feeling something was very wrong and had been trying to convince herself she was overreacting, I could see how discovering that her worst instincts were right could have led to her meltdown.

"Anything else to report?" Wyle asked.

"You mean that's not enough?" I countered.

Wyle's lips twitched up in an almost-smile. "I would have preferred a confession, but I'll take what I can get." He paused for a moment, straightening up and busying himself with his notes. It almost felt like he was preparing himself for something, although I couldn't imagine what.

"Cherry is one of your tea customers, right?" He wasn't looking at me. Instead, he was focused on a spot on his desk.

"Yes," I said, wondering why he was asking. "We covered this already. It's why she called me."

He nodded. "We found a nearly full package of what looks like one of your teas."

"Because it probably was," I said.

"When was the last time she bought from you?"

"Yesterday." I was wondering where he was going.

"What type of tea does she normally buy?"

"A custom blend." I shifted in my seat, starting to get an uneasy feeling in my gut. For the life of me, I couldn't figure out why Wyle would be the slightest bit interested in what sort of tea I made for Cherry. "Why does this matter?"

"Everything matters in a murder investigation," Wyle said flatly, which of course was no answer at all. "We found an empty mug in the living room, and it appears as though Cherry had been drinking a cup of your tea when everything went down."

The uneasy feeling grew stronger, morphing into something that felt more like a serpent coiling its way around my stomach. "That would make sense. She said she'd had a cup."

"Did she tell you when she drank it?"

"You mean like a time?" I stared at Wyle. "No, she didn't tell me a time, nor did I ask. How on Earth is this relevant to what happened to Marcus?"

"Again, during a murder investigation, you never know which details will end up being relevant or not," Wyle said. He still wasn't looking me in the eyes, and appeared to be inordinately busy with his notes.

I leaned forward. "What aren't you telling me?"

"Nothing, because there's nothing to tell," Wyle said. "We found an empty mug in the living room. You confirmed that Cherry had indeed drank a cup of your tea the night before. So we of course have to send it to the lab to analyze it."

The lab? The serpent tightened its grip around my stomach, although a part of me tried to tell myself to relax. So what if they analyzed my tea blend? It wasn't like it was a big trade secret. "Seems like a waste of taxpayer's money when all you're going to find is tea."

"A lot of leads during an investigation end up going nowhere. That's the nature of the beast," he said.

"I take it you're also testing the wine glasses, as well?"

"And the bottle," he confirmed.

Well, at least my tea wasn't being singled out. Still, there was something off about the whole line of questioning. Even if my gut wasn't screaming at me, Wyle's whole demeanor seemed like a giant red flag.

The only question was, what was he hiding from me?

Chapter 8

I took a deep breath as I got out of my car, debating again whether or not my idea was a good one.

Pat had other plans, so I had spent most of the day puttering around my house pretending to work as I tried to not to think about what had happened at the police station with Wyle earlier in the day. Of course, trying not to think about something never works, and this case was no exception. So, every time one of his questions or the uncomfortable way he had held himself popped into my head, all the uneasiness rushed back in.

Something was brewing in the background. And whatever it was, I had a feeling it was bad.

Finally, I decided sitting in my house trying not to think about it wasn't doing me any good. What I needed to do was get ahead of whatever was happening, and the only way I could think of doing that was to spend some time with Cherry.

I wasn't sure how Wyle would react if he knew what I was planning. The last thing he'd said to me was that I should sit tight and let the professionals do their job.

The problem was, I didn't trust the professionals. Wyle, sure—I knew he would always be fair. But the rest of the station? Especially after what happened a few months before, when some members of the police department tried to pin a murder on me.

No, I didn't trust them at all.

I squared my shoulders and headed up the driveway. The day was gray and cold, a typical February in Wisconsin. Banks of dirty snow lined the driveway. Ugh. February was the worst month. The only good thing about it was that it was short. Okay, Valentine's Day wasn't so bad, either. Which reminded me that I needed to start my Valentine's Day baking, since it was the following week. Cookies made everything better. Actually, the more I thought about it, maybe that was my problem with Wyle.

I hadn't baked him any cookies for a while. I felt a little flutter in my stomach when I thought about giving him a Valentine's gift.

No. I firmly squashed that thought. It wouldn't actually be a Valentine's gift. It was a bribe, to get him to tell me what was going on.

Up ahead, I could see the yellow police tape fluttering in the cold wind, blocking the door. Well, mostly blocking. There were a couple of pieces that weren't attached dangling down.

I could feel my stomach sinking. Great. Now what would I do? I had no idea how to find Cherry. Was she staying at a hotel, or a friend's house? Maybe Lola's? Not that I knew where Lola lived, either. Nor did I know her last name, so checking the phone book wouldn't do me any good.

I chewed on my bottom lip, motionless at the bottom of the driveway near the steps to her apartment. Should I leave a note? No, because chances were high that the cops would see whatever I wrote, as well. Maybe I should try to ask her landlords. It was possible Cherry told them where she was staying, but even if she hadn't, they might at least know Lola's last name.

Although, if she was staying at Lola's place, did I really want to show up uninvited? Maybe calling would be a better idea.

Regardless of what I did with the information, the first step was to see if I could track Cherry down. I was just about to walk over to the main house when the door to Cherry's apartment flew open. All I saw was a black shadow framed in the doorway, and I involuntarily took a step back. Great. Running into the cops right now, especially Wyle, was not part of the plan. I was trying to formulate a plausible excuse for why I was standing there when the figure stepped forward, and I heard a distinctly female voice say, "Oh drat. I forgot about this stupid tape."

"Cherry?"

The figure paused, and I saw a head pop up over the tape. "Charlie? What are you doing here?"

"Looking for you," I said, breathing a sigh of relief that it was her. "I wanted to make sure you were okay."

She scowled. "I will be, once I'm able to get out of here."

"Do you need help?" I asked as I started climbing the stairs. "How did you get in?"

"I was able to duck in under the tape, but I don't think I can do that now."

"Why not?" I reached the top of the driveway and paused to catch my breath. Now that I was on her stoop, I was able to get a better look at her. It seemed she had finally gotten a chance to clean herself up. Her strawberry-blonde hair was slightly damp, like she had just showered, and hung loosely around her shoulders. Under her red, wool jacket, she wore a red sweater, jeans, and a pair of red boots. The only thing that wasn't back to normal was the lack of makeup on her face. Her eyes were red-rimmed and puffy, and her nose was also bright red. I wondered if she had simply decided not to bother.

Along with taking a shower and changing her clothes, she had also appeared to have spent some time packing. She had loaded herself down with several large bags, their black straps crisscrossing her chest, in addition to a suitcase that sat at her feet.

"Because of this." She gestured to the bags. "They're too heavy. I don't think I can bend down, and I don't know how else to get them out."

"Here." I stuck my hand under the tape. "Pass them to me."

It took a few minutes, as she had to unwind the luggage from her body first, but eventually, between the two of us, we got her three bags, her suitcase, and her out of the apartment.

"I take it you're staying somewhere else," I said.

She made a face. "The cops can't tell me how long they need my apartment, and Lola said I could stay with her. But before I did, I thought I'd come pack a few things."

Surveying the amount of luggage around us, it seemed like more than just "a few things," but I suspected Cherry wouldn't appreciate me saying so. "Where are the cops? Didn't they offer to come with you when you packed?"

Cherry snorted, tossing her head so her damp hair flew around her face. "The cops. Like I would tell them what I was doing. I let them know I would find somewhere else to stay until they cleared my apartment, and that's exactly what I did. It's none of their business if I want to take a shower in my own bathroom first or pack a few things." Her voice was uncharacteristically bitter, and I wondered if her questioning had been as rough as mine.

"Do you want help carrying it all to the car?" I asked, changing the subject.

Her face, which had been tight with her mouth pressed together and her eyes narrowed, relaxed, and she almost smiled. "Oh, that would be wonderful. Thank you."

I picked up one of the bags and nearly dropped it. I couldn't believe how heavy it was. What had she packed in it? If I hadn't seen the cops take Marcus away, I would have thought she had stuck his body in the bag.

It took a bit, but between the two of us, we managed to drag everything to her car and load up her trunk. "You have been such a lifesaver," she said. "I don't know what I would have done without your help."

"I'm happy to do it," I said, dusting off my hands while trying to figure out a natural way to get myself invited to Lola's. I needed more information, and standing out in the cold, gray Wisconsin winter wasn't going to cut it.

Luckily, I didn't have to sweet-talk my way into an invitation. "Want to come with me to Lola's?"

"Oh, I wouldn't want to be a bother," I said.

She waved a hand. "No bother. She's having a few people over to talk about ... what happened, anyway." Cherry swallowed and swiveled her head to look at the apartment. After a moment, she shook herself and turned back to me. "And as you were there this morning, I think you should be there."

"If you're sure she won't mind," I said. I thought about how upset Lola was that morning and was amazed she had been able to pull herself together enough to have a group of people over. "I don't want to intrude. Especially if there're going to be other people."

"It's not just anyone. It's the gang. And I know they won't mind." She glanced around and spotted my car. "Do you want to just follow me?"

"Sure," I said, digging my keys out of my purse and trying to contain the frisson of excitement that shot through me. If "the gang" meant what I thought it did, I was going to be meeting Cherry and Marcus's closest friends—the ones Sue had talked about.

And if any of them were responsible for Marcus's death, this would be my chance to figure out what was going on.

Chapter 9

"I still can't believe he's gone." Cherry reached for a tissue from the box in the middle of the glass coffee table and blew her nose. Along with the tissue boxes, there was a cheese and meat platter, a basket of crackers, and a couple of open bottles of wine.

We were all in Lola's tastefully decorated living room. Unlike Cherry, Lola and her husband lived in a duplex rather than an apartment. And it was a pretty nice one. The furniture was cream-colored leather, and the floors were hardwood. Dark-blue area rugs accented them. Throw pillows and afghans in various colors of blue were draped around the couches and chairs. A huge entertainment cabinet covered one wall, and a fireplace accented the other. The fire was lit, along with several long, tapered, blue candles on the hearth. On a side table, a brown candle in a glass jar flickered. It smelled of smoke, wood, and cinnamon.

"I can't either," Lola said. She was sitting next to Cherry on the loveseat. She had changed out of her smart-looking work attire into an equally smart-looking casual outfit consisting of dark jeans, cream-colored knee-high boots, and a matching cream-colored cable-knit sweater. She had also redone her makeup, so her face was back to flawless. Other than her blood-shot eyes, there was no trace of the woman who had very nearly lost it early that morning.

"I agree that what happened to Marcus was terrible. But what about you?" The third woman, whose name was Sage, slid forward in her chair, resting her elbows against her knees. She wasn't exactly beautiful; her face was too sharp, and her lips were a little too thin, but there was something compelling about her. She too was carefully made up with Farrah Fawcett hair and a purple sweater paired with white jeans. One mani-cured hand casually held a glass of red wine over her spotless white jeans.

"How do you think I'm doing?" Cherry asked, a hint of acidity in her tone. "My fiancé was just killed in my kitchen."

"That's not what I meant," Sage said, her expression chastened. "I meant you could have been killed, too. I'm amazed at how well you're handling it. I would be a complete basket case right now."

"I don't think I'm handing it very well at all," Cherry said, reaching for her wineglass. "It's all I could do all day to not just constantly cry."

"Well, as far as I'm concerned, it would have been perfectly fine if you had, after what you've been through," Sage said.

"Have you been checked out by a doctor?" the man next to Sage asked. His name was Caleb, and he was Marcus's roommate and best friend. He was good-looking in a clean-cut way, with short brown hair, a square jaw, and high cheekbones. But picturing Marcus's curly black hair and striking looks, I had a feeling Caleb generally faded into the background whenever they were together.

Cherry sniffed loudly. "Yes, the cops took me to the hospital to get checked out. I'm fine. A little dehydrated, so I was instructed to drink lots of water." She held up her wine glass. "Not quite water, but close enough."

"It's still liquid, so it counts," Flynn said, leaning over to reach for the bottle on the coffee table. He was sitting in the chair opposite me, so he was the furthest away from it. Like Lola, his "casual" outfit was pretty dressy, consisting of a blue turtleneck sweater and creased dark jeans. The sweater brought out the blue in his eyes, and his longish, dark-blond hair was carefully styled. "Besides, you know Marcus would approve."

"Flynn," Lola said, a warning in her tone.

"What?" Flynn asked. His voice was only slightly slurred, like he might have started drinking before the rest had arrived. "I'm not saying anything we all don't already know. Well, except for Charlie, of course." He tipped his drink to me. "Marcus wouldn't have wanted us sitting around crying into our drinks.

He would have wanted us toasting him as we swapped stories and got rip-roaring drunk. Isn't that right, Caleb?"

"Sure, if he had died as an old man in his sleep of natural causes," Sage said. "Not as a 29-year-old murder victim."

The only response was a gasp, although I wasn't sure who was responsible for it. A shocked silence fell over the room, broken only by the crackling and snapping of the fire.

Sage looked around. "What? Is this how we're going to act? By putting our heads in the sand and pretending that Cherry and Marcus weren't brutally attacked in Cherry's home?"

"I wasn't ... I don't think I was brutally attacked," Cherry said, her eyes fixed on her wineglass.

Sage stared at her, disbelief all over her face. "You woke up in your completely trashed living room with no memory of what happened last night. How would you describe what happened?"

"I don't know," Cherry snapped, jerking her head up. Her red wine sloshed in her glass, dangerously close to spilling on the cream-colored couch. "That's the whole point. I don't know what happened."

Sage seemed unperturbed about her outburst. "Well, someone obviously did something to you. That's what we should be focusing on."

"That's not what the cops think," Cherry said before slamming her mouth shut, so hard I could hear her teeth click together.

The rest of the group stared at her. "What are you talking about?" Caleb asked.

"It's nothing," Cherry quickly answered.

"It's not nothing," Sage said. "If you weren't attacked, what do the cops think happened?"

"I shouldn't have said anything," Cherry said.

"Of course you should have," Sage continued. "We're your friends. We're here to support you."

Cherry glanced at Sage, her lips twisted in a grimace. "Thanks, but I don't think you can support me."

"What are you talking about? Of course we will," Sage started to say, but Lola interrupted her.

"Oh, for heaven's sake. Sage, you can't be that dense." Lola took a long swig of her wine, draining her glass as Sage sputtered, her words slurring together in a way that I hadn't picked up on earlier. It suddenly occurred to me that it wasn't just Flynn who seemed a bit intoxicated, but all of them. "Who do you think the cops are focusing on, if they don't think Cherry and Marcus were attacked by another person? Or do you think Marcus died of natural causes?"

Sage blinked as if she was trying to process Lola's words. "You can't be serious."

"Where do you think I was all day?" Cherry asked, her voice bitter.

Sage's eyes widened. "You were with the cops all day? But didn't you say you went to the hospital?"

"I was there, too, but yeah, I spent most of the day surrounded by cops," Cherry said. "First at my apartment, then being questioned. It's been a long day."

"What about a lawyer?" Caleb said. "Flynn, are you representing her?"

Flynn shook his head. "I'm not a defense attorney."

"Did you give her any names of good defense attorneys?" Caleb asked, his voice rising.

"Yes, I did." He looked at Cherry. "You hired one, right?"

"I'm going to," Cherry said. "I have an appointment scheduled with one of them tomorrow."

"Which one?" Flynn asked.

"Bonnie something."

"Oh, Bonnie," Flynn nodded. "She's excellent. I was hoping she would have an opening for you."

Sage was staring at both of them. "Wait a second." She held up a hand. "Let's back up here. If you're under suspicion for killing Marcus, why don't you have a lawyer right now?"

Cherry made a face as she finished her wine. Lola leaned forward to pick up the bottle and started to refill her glass. "Because I didn't realize until later today that I was going to need one. I thought … I thought …" her voice caught. "I didn't really think they suspected me. I couldn't believe that was what was happening. When it finally started to sink in, it was already this afternoon, so Bonnie moved some things around to meet with me in the morning."

"Unbelievable," Sage said, shaking her head as Lola emptied the bottle into Cherry's glass. Flynn got up and headed into the kitchen, most likely to fetch another one. "I still don't understand how they can think you had anything to do with it."

"They claim there's no evidence of anyone else being in our apartment last night," Cherry said.

"What do you mean, no evidence?" Sage asked, her voice indignant. "There's all sorts of evidence. Look at the mess in your living room!"

Cherry winced. "They said that Marcus and I could have done that."

"What?" Sage's voice went up an octave as she jerked her hand, spilling wine over the edge. "Why would you trash your living room like that?"

"They think we might have fought," Cherry said as Lola flung a couple of paper napkins toward Sage, who finally got the hint and started mopping up the drips that were heading down her glass, dangerously close to the leather furniture.

"Honestly," Sage grumbled. "People fight all the time, and they rarely throw things around."

"Is there any other reason why the cops think you did it?" Caleb asked as Flynn returned, fresh bottle in hand. He started by topping off his own glass.

"They didn't really say," Cherry said. "Honestly, they didn't say much. But as the day went on, some of the ways they were phrasing their questions made me realize the direction they were heading in."

"Well, even if they're headed in that direction, they still need evidence," Sage said. "Even if you and Marcus did fight and ended up tearing apart your living room, they still have to find evidence that you actually killed him."

"But if you two did fight that violently, it's going to look bad for you," Caleb pointed out matter-of-factly.

Sage's head snapped around. "Whose side are you on?"

Caleb held up his hands, one palm facing forward, the other still holding his almost empty glass. "Hey, don't attack the messenger. I'm just stating the obvious."

"What, that you think Cherry killed Marcus?" Sage asked as Flynn refilled Caleb's glass. "You think Cherry has it in her to actually *kill* Marcus?"

"Of course I don't," Caleb said as Flynn held the bottle toward me and waggled his eyebrows. I shook my head and put my hand over my still-full glass. I glanced over at the largely untouched snacks on the coffee table, and wondered if my taking some might spur the others to help themselves, as well. The energy was starting to feel dangerous, and the more wine that was consumed with no food, the more likely it was going to explode into something bad. "But if we're going to help Cherry, we have to know what the prosecutor's case will be."

"*Prosecutor's case?*" Sage nearly dropped her glass in shock as all the blood drained from Cherry's face. "Have you lost your mind? Cherry hasn't even been arrested yet, and you've already got her going to trial?"

"We have to stay two steps ahead," Caleb said stubbornly. "Otherwise, we lose."

"We're getting ahead of ourselves," Flynn added as he took a seat. "Cherry is innocent. We all know she's innocent. Maybe we should just wait and see what the cops do before we get too excited."

"Finally. Someone with some common sense," Sage said.

Caleb looked around the room, his expression bewildered. "I don't understand you all. This isn't how you help Cherry. We need to know what the cops know, so we can start planning a defense …"

"Caleb, you're not her attorney," Flynn said.

"What does that matter?" Caleb asked. "We can all still help her. Don't you want to know what's going on? And who killed Marcus? Don't you want to figure out the truth?"

"What are you talking about?" Sage asked. "What do you think we've been doing here? Of course we want to know the truth. You're the one putting Cherry on trial."

"Excuse me," Cherry stood up abruptly. Her face was pale, other than her lips, which were stained red from the wine. "I think I need to go lie down. I'm not feeling very well."

"Do you want someone to come with you?" Lola asked as Cherry struggled to stand, trying to get her feet balanced under her without spilling her wine. I was already on my feet and ready to move toward Cherry if she started to fall, which I was a little concerned about. She was swaying on her feet, as if she were about to faint.

"No, I'm fine," she said as she took a few halting steps forward. She held her hand up as I started to move toward her. "Really, I'm okay. I probably just need a little alone time. Everything is happening so fast … I just need a moment."

"You probably need more wine, too," Flynn said, holding out the wine bottle. Cherry hesitated for a moment before offering her wine glass for him to top off. I wanted to say the last thing she needed was more wine, but I bit my tongue. There was no question she had a terrible day, and if getting rip-roaring drunk helped her deal with it, then who was I to tell her otherwise?

"Just make yourself at home," Lola said. "Help yourself to whatever you need. I think you know where everything is, right? And if you need anything else, just let us know."

"Thanks," Cherry said. She forced a smile on her lips as she looked at everyone. "I appreciate what all of you are trying to do."

"Of course," I said along with everyone else as Cherry shuffled out of the room, stumbling only once.

Sage waited until she disappeared before slamming both feet on the ground and resting her hands against her thighs. Her movement was so sudden, wine came sloshing out of her glass, spilling on her white jeans, but she didn't notice. "This is all your fault," she hissed to Caleb.

"My fault?" Caleb looked startled. "I'm the one trying to help her here. All of you," he pointed toward all of us, "are the ones who are hurting her. Encouraging her not to face reality …"

"Face reality?" Sage interrupted. "Caleb, her fiancé, died *today.* She woke up this morning and found him dead. In her kitchen. For Pete's sake, can you give her a moment to grieve before she has to worry about defending herself in a court of law?"

"The law doesn't care if you're grieving. The wheels of justice are still going to move forward. And if you're in the way, you're going to get run over," Caleb insisted, but he no longer sounded as sure as he had before. He had dropped his gaze, but not before a flicker of shame crossed his face.

"While there's some truth to that, I will add that the wheels of justice move awfully slowly," Flynn said. "It's probably not time to panic. At least not yet."

"Fine," Caleb snapped as he jumped up, stumbling slightly. "Obviously, none of you are taking the threat to Cherry seriously enough. I might as well be talking to the walls of my apartment. I'm out of here."

"Too bad you didn't think of that before you chased Cherry away," Sage said. "Don't let the door hit you on the way out."

Caleb shot her a dangerous look before snatching up his coat and striding toward the front door. A moment later, it slammed shut.

There was a moment of silence, broken by the sound of a particularly loud crack from the fire. Then, Flynn raised his glass.

"To Marcus. May he always be remembered for all the joy and laughter he brought with him wherever he went."

Lola glared at him before storming out of the living room. Flynn shrugged and drained half his glass.

"Flynn, you can be a real jerk sometimes, you know that?" Sage said, but unlike with Caleb, her voice lacked any real edge. She simply sounded tired and drained.

Flynn reached for the bottle. "Just trying to send our friend off with a proper farewell."

Chapter 10

I had just finished putting the finishing touches on my raspberry jam Valentine's cookies when the phone rang.

It had been a couple of days since the disastrous get-together at Lola and Flynn's house. I had left shortly after Lola disappeared, leaving me with a morose Sage and increasingly drunk Flynn. Even though I had questions—a lot of them—it didn't feel like the right time to ask. Instead, I thanked Flynn for his hospitality, and he nodded absently. When I told Sage it was nice to meet her, she said she was sorry I had to experience all the drama that had gone on.

Since then, things had been quiet. I hadn't heard anything from Wyle or Cherry, which I kept telling myself was a good thing—no news is good news, and all of that—but rather than reassuring me, it only seemed to make me more and more anxious. I couldn't stop thinking about the case and struggling to fit all the pieces together. And seeing how nothing *was* coming together, I couldn't shake the feeling I was missing something important … maybe a few important pieces, even.

But every time I thought about calling Cherry or Wyle, I stopped myself. Sage was right; Cherry needed a little time to grieve. I didn't need to keep pushing her, especially since she was probably overwhelmed with the logistics of finding a lawyer and defending herself during such a painful time. As for Wyle, he was surely busy with the case and also didn't need me distracting him.

However, two days of repeating to myself how much I needed to give everyone some space was over. It was time to think about getting some answers, which was why I was up at the crack of dawn to start my Valentine's Day baking.

After all, it was never a bad idea to have baked goods on hand. Especially when there was a murder investigation lurking in the background and a lot of strange questions I still wasn't sure why I had been asked in the first place. Having some beautiful and delicious cookies around to dispense as needed certainly couldn't hurt. Wyle loving raspberries had nothing to do with anything.

The ringing of the phone startled me, making me jump and squirt some of the frosting out of the pastry bag I was still holding. Luckily, it wasn't anywhere near a cookie, so my hard work remained perfectly intact. Licking the frosting off my wrist, I headed for the phone.

"Have you seen the paper yet?" Pat asked.

"Good morning to you, too," I said.

"I'm serious. I'm coming over right now." There was a click.

I replaced the receiver, trying to push down the uneasiness that was starting to stir in my gut. Normally, when Pat said she was coming over early in the morning because of something she saw in the newspaper, it wasn't good news.

In my mind's eye, I again pictured Wyle asking me about my tea. Why would he ask me about it unless it was part of the investigation? Yet for the life of me, I couldn't imagine how or why it could be involved.

I reminded myself that when it came to murder investigations, cops tended to ask all sorts of questions that seemed to have little to do with the case, but it still wasn't sitting right. I also reminded myself that Wyle hadn't called or stopped by, and if something had changed and my tea *had* somehow become relevant, he surely would have reached out.

None of that reassured me as much as it should have.

Part of me wanted to race outside and grab the newspaper, but I also knew Pat would arrive in just a few minutes, and it made more sense to use that time to get ready for her. I started another pot of coffee, as I had almost finished the first. Considering I hadn't been able to get a decent night of sleep since the middle-of-the-night call from Cherry, I needed all the caffeine I could get. I also arranged some zucchini muffins on one plate and homemade dog biscuits on a second, as I assumed Tiki, Pat's miniature poodle, would be with her.

I had just finished setting the table and topping off my coffee when I heard the front door open. "I can't believe you still haven't looked at today's paper." Pat's disembodied voice floated into the kitchen. A minute later, I heard the sounds of Tiki's nails as she ran across the tile floor to greet me. I saw Midnight lift his head from where he was napping in the early morning sun to keep a close eye on the little dog. The start of Midnight and Tiki's relationship had been rocky, but they'd more or less warmed up to each other since.

"How do you know that?" I asked as I straightened up, Tiki in my arms. She was dressed in a little red sweater with pink hearts all over it and matching pink ribbons in her fur. I glanced over at Pat, who was in the doorway, and I immediately realized the answer to my own question. Pat was brandishing my rolled-up newspaper in one hand, like it was a sword. "Oh."

She shook her head and plopped it on the table. "I see you have a full cup, which is good. You're going to need it. I'll help myself."

I eyed her. "Why? What am I going to find?"

"Just read it," she said, filling the empty mug I had left for her next to the pot.

"Is it Tad?" I asked as I moved toward the paper. Even as I said the name, I found myself cringing inside. Tad Clark was the reporter for the *Redemption Times* who had been a thorn in my side since the day I'd first moved to Redemption. If there was a story that made me look bad, rest assured Tad would cover it.

"Who else? But that's the least of your concerns." Pat's voice was dark.

I eyed her again as I put Tiki on the floor and picked up the paper, the uneasy feeling becoming more intense. I slid off the rubber band and started to unroll it. I caught a whiff of the unmistakable scent of warm ink and fresh paper I always loved when first opening a newspaper, but it didn't do much to calm my anxiety.

"Oh. You've been busy," Pat said, gesturing toward the frosted Valentine's cookies. "These are gorgeous. Are they for something special, or can anyone have one?"

"If you want a cookie for breakfast, go for it, but I do have muffins on the table," I said absentmindedly as I smoothed the paper.

And I felt my heart stop.

"I told you, you should have looked at it," Pat said, her mouth full of cookie. "These are amazing, by the way. Should I bring you one? As you always say, sugar is good for shock."

I wasn't listening to Pat. My knees had buckled, and my hands were shaking so much, I was struggling to pull a chair out before I ended up on the floor.

"Hey," Pat said. Suddenly, she was right beside me, helping me into a chair. "Breathe. It's going to be okay." A moment later, I felt a warm bundle of fur land in my lap, along with a few worried licks to my face. Tiki was watching me closely, her little black eyes fixed on mine. I automatically petted her, trying to reassure her, even though the last thing I felt was reassured. I couldn't think, couldn't focus. I tried to read the words, but they were all jumbled together.

"I can't … why didn't Wyle call me and warn me this was going to happen?" My one hand that held the paper was still shaking, so Pat gently re-positioned my arm, so it was resting on the table.

"It's possible he didn't know," she said as she went back into the kitchen, no doubt adding sugar and more cream to my coffee. I felt a moment of deep appreciation for my friend. She knew exactly what I would do in this situation for someone else and was doing it for me.

"How could he not know?" I kept thinking about how Wyle had questioned me about my tea. Did he know something and didn't tell me? Was there something wrong with my tea after all?

She didn't immediately answer, just busied herself with my coffee. I could do nothing but stare at the headline, the letters larger than life.

"The Tea Made Her Do It" — Woman Claims She Killed Her Fiancé Because She Was Under a Spell

"I don't understand. What spell? Everyone knows I don't cast spells," I said as Pat gently pushed the mug into my hand. "And how could a tea make anyone do anything, much less kill someone?"

"Slow down," Pat said, pulling up a chair to sit next to me. She pushed a plate toward me. "Have a cookie. It's definitely a cookie type of morning."

I picked up the cookie, even though my stomach was so twisted up in knots, I wasn't sure I would be able to keep anything down. But Pat was right; I needed sugar. I took a bite. It was warm and chewy, nearly melting in my mouth while the raspberry jam I had made from scratch added just the right pop of sweetness and acidity.

"You're right … it is good," I said, reaching for my coffee to take a drink. It was a little too sweet, especially after the cookie, but I forced myself to drink it anyway. Between the sugar and warm little dog body in my lap, I started to feel more grounded. After a few moments, my brain started to clear, and my hands stopped shaking. "Thanks."

"What are friends for?" Pat asked, reaching for a muffin. "As good as your muffins are, I suspect the cookie is better, but I'll restrain myself."

I half-smiled at her as I took another sip of coffee before setting the mug down. I stared at the paper lying flat on the table. "I'm not even sure where to start."

"Yeah, there's a lot to unpack. But let's start with Wyle." She tapped the paper. Her fingers were short and thick, and her hands were red and chapped from her constant cleaning to keep her house spotless. Still, she kept her nails neat and well-cared for. "If you read the article, it sounds like Cherry went to Tad and gave him an interview as to what she thinks happened to her. The only quote from the cops was basically 'No comment'—the typical 'We don't comment on existing investigations,' etc."

"But that would mean Wyle knew this article was going to be in the paper, right? He could have warned me. And what was Cherry thinking? How could she do this to me? I thought we were friends." I pressed my hand against my chest as if I could somehow take away the pain that was lodging itself there. As if the anxiety and uneasy feelings weren't enough, there was now the sharpness of a betrayal intertwined, as well.

"Cherry is a whole other story, but back to Wyle, again, he might not have known. He was not mentioned in the article, so it's possible no one said anything to him about this being published."

I slumped down in my seat. "I find it hard to believe that, in our small-town police station, he wouldn't know."

Pat gave me a sympathetic look and reached out to put a hand on my arm. "We both know he's not always in the loop anymore. By design. It's possible it's getting worse for him, not better."

I closed my eyes, trying not to grimace. When we had worked on a recent case together, it became apparent that there were people in the Redemption Police Department who were, well, let's just say not my biggest fans. Wyle did what he could, but as our relationship wasn't a secret, everyone against me knew to keep him in the dark. I knew he was still poking around, trying to get to the bottom of it, but it was slow going, and not just because it was tough to get people to talk to him. He also had to do it between real, actual cases.

"I get what you're saying. But that doesn't explain why he was asking me about my tea the other day."

"He what?" She stared at me, her forehead wrinkled.

"He kept questioning me about the tea I sold to Cherry. When was the last time I sold her a batch, and what kind was it … that sort of thing."

"Why would he do that?"

I held my hand up, palms facing upward. "I haven't a clue."

"Did you ask him?"

"Of course I did. He just kept saying that's what happens in a murder investigation … that you have to ask a lot of questions, even when they didn't seem relevant."

Pat's brow was still furrowed. "But I still don't understand. Why would your tea matter at all? Was he investigating the grocery store, too? About the food she had in her apartment?"

"Well, maybe, but probably not. I'm guessing it's because Cherry had a cup of my tea the night everything happened. That's one of the few things she remembers, apparently."

"How do you know that?"

"To begin with, I saw the empty mug was on the living room floor."

Pat's eyes grew wider. "Do you think they might have found something in the tea?"

"I don't know what they could have. There was nothing in that tea that wasn't in all the other blends I've sold to her and everyone else."

"But …" Pat frowned. "Charlie, is it possible you made a mistake? Maybe put something in that batch accidentally?"

I thought back to when I was making her blend. It was true that I was a little rushed. Cherry had called me in a panic earlier that day and wanted to pick it up a few hours later. But it wasn't like I was using some complicated recipe; I was just combining herbs and flowers. "I guess anything is possible, but even if I did, there wouldn't have been anything in there that would have caused her to do anything, much less kill her fiancé."

Pat took a bite of muffin as she thought about what I said. "Okay. So, I don't think this changes anything with Wyle."

"What are you talking about?" I flapped my hands around in frustration, causing Tiki to duck. "It changes everything. He was asking about tea, and now my tea is being publicly blamed."

She shook her head. "No, it really doesn't. Just hear me out. If you really were under suspicion, you wouldn't be sitting here right now. You would be at the station, likely in a jail cell. So, again, Wyle may very well have just been asking because Cherry had some of your tea earlier in the night, and he has to cover all his bases. I mean, *something* caused Cherry to lose her memory, right?"

"It might not have been anything she ate or drank," I said. "It could have been trauma."

"True, but they're not going to know that unless they elimi-nate everything else," Pat said. "Just like if they had been drink-ing wine, they would test the wine glasses too, right?"

I chewed on my bottom lip. Pat's words jogged my memory. Wyle did say they were testing the wine glasses and bottle, as well. "Well, now that you mention it, there were wine glasses, along with an empty bottle of wine. And yes, Wyle was testing those, as well."

"Well, then. You see. It's just what I said. Covering all the bases." Pat popped another bite of muffin into her mouth.

I considered her words. While it was true she wasn't saying anything to me that I hadn't told myself over the last few days, that still didn't explain Wyle's body language as he questioned me. He was acting like someone who knew more than he was letting on. And now, with this newspaper article out …

Although maybe Pat was right, and I was just reading more into it than what was actually there. Maybe Wyle truly was just uncomfortable questioning me about my teas even though he knew it was standard procedure. And Pat did have a point; if the cops had found something wrong with my tea, I would defi-nitely be sitting at the station answering questions rather than in my nice warm kitchen with Pat and Tiki, consuming way too much sugar.

"You're right. I'll give Wyle the benefit of the doubt. For now, at least. But what about Cherry? Why would she throw me under the bus like that?"

Pat picked up her mug, looking at me over the top of it. "I would imagine to save herself."

"To save herself?" I pulled the paper closer to me to make it easier to skim the story. "Are you saying she was arrested?"

"No one was arrested. At least not yet," Pat said. "But that doesn't mean she doesn't see the writing on the wall. Especially if the cops don't appear to be investigating anyone else. Do you know if she hired an attorney yet?"

"I know she was interviewing at least one," I said. "According to Flynn, the best one."

"Well, if that's the case, it might have been her attorney's idea. Plant the seed for another explanation of what happened, not to mention another suspect."

"But how could I be a suspect?" I asked. "First off, what on Earth would I have put in her tea that would have 'made' her kill Marcus? Nothing like that even exists. And even if there *was* something in the tea that contributed to her killing Marcus, she was still the one who did it, not me."

"I'm no lawyer, but I'm guessing she could claim diminished capacity or something like that," Pat said. "If they're able to prove that whatever you put in her tea rendered her out of her right mind, then it wouldn't be her fault. Technically."

I threw up my hands. "But nothing like that even exists!"

"What about some sort of drug?" Pat asked. "Like LSD, or some other hallucinogenic?"

"I suppose it would be possible, if she was on some sort of acid trip," I said. "If she was on a bad trip and thought Marcus was a giant spider attacking her, for example, then sure. But if that were the case, I don't think she would have smothered Marcus with a pillow. She probably would have hacked him to death or something."

"Maybe she thought he was a small spider," Pat joked.

"Maybe," I said with a slight smile. "Anything is possible. But regardless, I don't see how Cherry's defense attorney could pin anything on me."

"I don't think that's what Cherry's attorney is trying to do," Pat said. "If they were trying to get the police to charge you for the crime, then they would be talking to the police. And if the police were buying their argument, again, you wouldn't be here right now. Cherry simply gave an exclusive interview to the *Redemption Times,* which tells me they're trying this case in the court of public opinion."

"Wait," I said, holding up a hand. "You're saying Cherry trashed my reputation even though she hasn't even been charged with a crime just in case they end up going to trial?"

"Pretty much," Pat said.

I was having trouble getting my mind around Pat's theory. "But what if she never IS charged with Marcus's murder? She would have hurt me for no reason."

"It's possible her attorney is worried there might be some sort of gag order if Cherry is charged," Pat said. "In that case, she couldn't talk to the press. But if she hasn't been charged, there's no gag order."

I stared at the paper. The headline blared at me. *The Tea Made Her Do It.* "Unbelievable. Doesn't she care that this could hurt my business? Maybe permanently?"

"If she's found guilty of Marcus's murder, she's going to end up in jail for a long time," Pat said. "I suspect if you asked her, she would say, 'What's worse? Spending your life in jail, or making a few less bucks?'"

I slumped in my seat, feeling both bad for Cherry and angry about what she was doing. "I know you're right," I said. "And she's probably terrified right now and not thinking straight. But still."

"I get it," Pat said. "It's a seriously crappy thing to do, especially to friend. But as you said, she's not in her right mind. Along with the fear over what's going to happen to her, she's still grieving Marcus. We can't forget that."

"No, I haven't," I sighed, rubbing my forehead before reaching for the rest of my cookie. Maybe I'd even have a second. What a morning.

Before I could take a bite, though, Tiki's cold, wet nose nudged my hand holding the cookie. I dropped it back onto the plate, picked up one of my homemade dog biscuits, and gave it to her. "You don't need a cookie," I told her as she gobbled down the biscuit. "Of course, I don't necessarily need one either. And I definitely don't need a second, especially if I want to give some to …" my voice trailed off as it occurred to me that I was saying things out loud I probably shouldn't be.

Pat glanced at me. "You want to give some to who? As if I can't guess." Her smile was mischievous.

I shook my head. "It's not like that. I was going to use the cookies as a bribe."

Her smile widened. "Oh, of course. A bribe."

"I need to find out what's going on with my tea," I said. "Especially now, with this newspaper article. Is there a connection or not? I can't just sit here and assume there isn't just because the cops aren't talking to me. There might be something going on under the surface that hasn't revealed itself yet."

Pat finished the last of her muffin and picked up a napkin to wipe her hands. "Good point. And there's no time like the present to bring one of our hardworking men in blue an early Valentine's Day present. Shall we?"

Chapter 11

Unfortunately, just because we were ready to talk to Wyle didn't mean he was able to talk to us.

"He's not here." The desk sergeant scowled at us. He was older, with graying hair, bushy eyebrows, and a substantial paunch. "He's busy."

"Is he busy, or is he not here?" Pat asked. At the sound of Pat's voice, Tiki's head popped out of the purse she carried him in.

His scowl deepened, but whether it was because of what Pat said or the dog, or both, was difficult to tell. "What does it matter? He can't see you. Do you want to leave a message for him?"

"Do you know when he'll be in?" I asked as I shifted the box of cookies to my other arm.

"It's hard to say. He's got a lot going on. You can leave a message or make an appointment."

"We'll try back later," I said with a friendly smile.

"Suit yourself," he said, going back to his paperwork.

"So now what?" Pat asked as we left the building and headed for my car. "Do we just go home and wait a few hours?"

I didn't immediately answer. I was still bothered by Cherry's interview. "We could. But I was thinking we could make another stop first?"

"Where?" Pat asked as I unlocked my door.

"Lola's apartment."

Pat looked at me in confusion as she opened her door. "Lola? Who's that?"

"Cherry's friend. Cherry is staying with her," I said, getting into the car.

Pat got in as well. "Do you think that's a good idea?"

"I have no idea, but I'd like to hear her side of the story," I said, buckling my seatbelt.

Pat did the same. "She's probably not going to be home. It's a weekday. Wouldn't she be at work?"

"She might be, but there's a chance she's home, as well. Remember, she just lost her fiancé, and she's been talking to the police. It's possible her employer told her to take some time off. But regardless, it's worth a shot."

"Might as well," Pat agreed, sitting back as I started the car. "We've got a few hours to kill anyway. So why not?"

***

As it turned out, it appeared Cherry was there, as her car was parked on the street. I parked in front of her, and Pat and I headed to the front door.

Pat positioned herself front and center as I stood off to the side. After reading that article, I wasn't sure how Cherry would react to me showing up uninvited to Lola's doorstep, and I thought maybe she would be more likely to answer the door if she didn't see me standing there.

Pat glanced at me, eyebrows raised. "Ready?"

"Let's do it."

She reached over to ring the doorbell. As we listened to the sound echo in the house, Tiki poked her head out of Pat's purse.

Perfect timing. How could anyone feel threatened by someone with such a cute dog?

After a few moments, we heard footsteps, and the door opened.

In some ways, Cherry looked even worse than when I'd last seen her. Seeing how that was only a few days before, I could hardly believe the difference. Her face was puffy, and she had black circles under her eyes, like she hadn't slept for days. Her strawberry-blonde hair was scraped back into a tight ponytail, and her face was scrubbed clean of makeup, which didn't help.

She was dressed in a pale-blue tracksuit and white tee shirt that were clean, but didn't seem to fit. They hung off of her body, at least one full size too big. I wondered if she was sleeping or eating at all.

"Can I help you?" she started to say, but then her eyes darted over to me and went very wide. Her mouth formed a round O, and she started to slam the door shut, but I was too fast for her. I jumped forward and blocked the door with my body.

"What are you doing here? I'm not supposed to talk to you," she said.

"Why not? You called me in the middle of the night to come help you."

She turned her face away. "That was different."

"Why was it different?"

She chewed on her bottom lip. "I didn't know then what I know now."

"And what do you know now?"

She still wouldn't look at me. "You know. What you did to me."

"What? What did I do to you?"

"I don't know, exactly. But you definitely did *something*. Otherwise, I would remember what happened."

"Cherry, I didn't do anything to you. I tried to help you."

She was shaking her head violently as her ponytail flew around. "No! You did something to me! That's the only explanation."

"How can that be the only explanation ..." I started to say, but just then, I was interrupted by another voice.

"Cherry, what's going on? Wait, what are YOU doing here?" Lola appeared next to Cherry. Like Cherry, she was dressed casually in a faded pair of blue jeans and a black turtleneck sweater. Unlike Cherry, her hair was carefully styled, and her face made up.

"I'm here to talk to Cherry. Why are you here? Shouldn't you be at work?" I asked.

Lola sniffed. "I took a week off. Cherry needs me." Her eyes narrowed. "Not that it's any of your business. You need to leave."

"I'll leave once I get some answers. Starting with, why did you throw me under the bus to the media? I read the article in the *Redemption Times*."

Cherry started to answer, but Lola took a step forward and put a hand on her arm. "She doesn't have to talk to you."

I ignored her. "Cherry, why did you do that to me? I thought we were friends."

She lifted her head, but she still wasn't looking at me. "I thought we were friends, too. But you made me kill Marcus."

"That's absurd. I didn't do anything of the sort."

"But that's the only thing that makes sense," Cherry said.

"You keep saying that. Why would you think that?"

"She doesn't have to answer you," Lola repeated before turning to Cherry. "You don't have to answer her."

Cherry ignored her. "Because the only thing I remember drinking was your tea," she said. "So there must have been something in it that made me do it."

My mouth dropped open. "That's not true. What about the chocolate-dipped strawberries?"

"Don't you get it?" Lola interrupted. "There were no chocolate-dipped strawberries. Only tea."

"What about the wine?" I asked. "There were wine glasses. And an empty bottle."

Lola took a step forward, her eyes glittering. "Cherry doesn't remember drinking the wine, only your tea. And everyone knows you're a witch."

"A witch?" I almost laughed, but there was a grimness in Lola's expression that caused the laughter to die in my throat. "You can't be serious."

"I'm very serious," Lola said. "You put a spell on poor Cherry, and look what you made her do."

"That's crazy. There's no such thing as witchcraft," I said.

Lola grabbed Cherry's arm and started to pull her backward, her eyes never leaving mine. "If you don't leave, I'm calling the cops. You're trespassing."

"You do know we're not living in Salem, and this isn't hundreds of years ago," I said. "No judge or jury in the country is going to take any of this seriously."

Lola straightened up. "Cherry, go call the cops. I'll handle this."

"Come on, Charlie," Pat was tugging me from behind. "Let's go."

Cherry still wasn't meeting my eyes. She was staring at her feet while Lola's gaze didn't waver.

"Fine," I said as I started backing up. "I'm leaving."

"Good," Lola responded, taking a step forward, her hand on the door. "And don't come back." She slammed it shut.

"Come on," Pat said again, still pulling at me. I took a final look at the door before turning around to head back to my car.

"How is this happening?" I asked. "Cherry and I were friends."

Pat's mouth was set in a thin line. "I don't know."

"It doesn't even make sense," I said. "Claiming I'm some sort of witch who put a spell on her is not any sort of defense. So why is she doing it? It's almost like she's trying to hurt me."

"You never know how people are going to react when their backs are against the wall," Pat said as we reached the car. "Sometimes, they act completely irrationally. It's like an abused dog that lashes out for no reason. You don't know what happened in her past."

"Or … someone talked her into it," I said, thinking about Lola and her self-righteous glare.

"Yeah, it sure seems like Lola has it in for you. Did you do something to her?"

We had reached the car, and I walked around to unlock the driver's side door. "I can't imagine what. I just met her for the first time that morning after it all happened."

"Hmmm," Pat said, opening her door and getting in. "It's weird that she decided to go after you the way she has. It does seem like more of a character attack than anything else."

I was about to put the key in the ignition, but I froze. A character attack. Of course.

"What if Lola isn't the one putting ideas into Cherry's head? What if there's someone else doing it?"

"Who would do …" Pat's voice trailed off and her eyes went wide. "Oh no. You think it was …"

"Louise," I spat, putting the key into the ignition and turning on the car. "This is completely up her alley."

Chapter 12

"Why shouldn't this surprise me?" I muttered, staring at the closed front door of Louise's home. I had already rung the doorbell twice, but the door remained stubbornly shut.

"She's hiding from us," Pat said. We both knew she was home, as her car was in the garage. Pat had walked over to peek into the garage after I first rang the bell.

"She has good reason to," I said, reaching for the doorbell again. "How does she even know Cherry? That's what I can't figure out."

"Louise is like me. We know everyone in town," Pat said.

I eyed her. "You know Cherry?"

Pat shrugged. "Of course. I mean, not well. My understanding is she's a pretty good travel agent. We have friends who booked several trips through her."

"Of course you do," I said, turning back to the front door. I was going to ring the doorbell again, but my frustration got the better of me, and I started pounding on the door instead. "Louise, we know you're in there. Just open up. We want to talk."

"What on Earth are you two doing?" a voice from behind me said.

Both Pat and I jumped before whirling around. "Oh, there you are."

Louise was on the sidewalk pushing a stroller. Both her and Jessica, her toddler, were well bundled up. "Yes. Here I am. What did you think? That I would be *hiding* from you two?"

"Well, the thought did cross our minds," Pat admitted.

Louise started pushing the stroller up the driveway. "Don't flatter yourself."

Jessica's eyes brightened as she got a look at Tiki, and she stretched her hands out. "Doggie. Doggie!"

Louise muttered something unintelligible. "Now look what you've done."

Pat knelt down as Jessica and Louise got closer. "Oh, stop it. Tiki loves kids. Don't you, Tiki?" In response, Tiki strained to get closer to Jessica, her tail wagging a mile a minute.

"You're not the one who has to listen to her spend the next four hours begging for a dog," Louise snapped.

Pat glanced up at her. "There's a solution to that."

"What?"

"You could get her a dog."

Louise's face, already red from the cold wind, turned even redder. Strands of her long blonde hair that weren't pulled back in her messy ponytail or under her dark-blue stocking hat flew around her face. While Louise would never be as gorgeous as Jessica, who was happily petting Tiki and looking even cuter than normal, if that was even possible, there was a time she would have been considered very pretty, if not beautiful. Unfortunately, the stress and disappointment of her life had taken a toll on her looks. She never wanted a second child, and she was still mourning the disappearance of her brother, Jesse, who had vanished several months before Jessica was born.

But her looks weren't the only casualty. Her personality had changed as well, and for the worse. Although admittedly, I might be biased. Even though we had started out as friends, she had since become my sworn enemy. Convinced I had something to do with Jesse's disappearance, she was doing everything in her power to drive me out of town.

And with this latest stunt, I was a little afraid she might succeed.

Louise finally tore her eyes away from her daughter who was playing with the little dog and focused on me. "Charlie, what are you doing here?"

I folded my arms across my chest. "Are you behind today's newspaper article?"

For a moment, she looked at me blankly. "Newspaper article?" Then, her expression shifted to a knowing look. "You mean the one accusing you of witchcraft?"

I glared at her. "You know darn well I'm not a witch."

"I know no such thing," she sniffed. "For all I know, you put a spell on Jesse, and that's why he's never returned."

"Oh, for Pete's sake. That never happened, and you know it."

"Well, something happened to Jesse," Louise said. "He never would have left without saying goodbye if he had been in his right mind. Just like Cherry wouldn't have done the things she did if she had been in hers."

"Are you kidding me?" I asked. "Jesse's not saying goodbye and Cherry killing her fiancé are two very different things. One does not equate to the other. And besides, I wasn't even making tea when Jesse disappeared, so there is no connection there."

"You still could have put a spell on him some other way," Louise insisted.

"No, I couldn't have, because I'm not a witch. Nor do witches or witchcraft exist. Which I know you know, so this is a ridiculous attack."

A small, dark smile touched her lips. "It can't be that ridiculous if you're here. Otherwise, you would have ignored it."

"Oh, come on," Pat said. "Cherry practically accused Charlie of murdering Marcus. It's beyond the pale, what you did."

Louise paused, tilting her head. "How do you know I did anything?"

"What are you talking about? You're the one who just said I put a spell on Jesse. Who else talks like that?"

"What, you think I'm the only one in this town who doesn't like you?"

"You're certainly the only one actively driving the dislike," Pat countered.

Louise rolled her eyes. "Oh, please. Charlie is excellent at getting people to not like her all on her own."

There was something in her voice that made alarm bells go off in my head. "Who are you talking about?"

Louise threw me that small, secret smile again. "Why do you think I know?"

"Because you know everyone in town," I said. "Especially people who don't like me."

Louise chuckled. "That's true. Although in this case, I suspect you know exactly who I'm talking about."

"*Who*?" I demanded.

Louise's response was to jerk the stroller backward, forcing Pat to snatch up Tiki, so she wouldn't fall. "Jessica, it's time to say bye-bye to the dog."

Jessica's face squished up. "No! I want to play with the doggie."

Louise's expression darkened. "No more doggie. It's time to go inside." She shoved the stroller forward, ignoring Jessica's cries. "Now see what you've done?" she hissed at Pat.

"Always nice to spend some quality time with you, too," Pat answered.

Louise scowled as she continued forward, pushing her way past me and onto the porch. She yanked her keys out of her purse, ignoring Jessica's cries as she wrenched open the front door and stalked into the house.

Pat popped Tiki back into her purse, shaking her head. "That poor child. I know how unhappy Louise is, but I would feel sorrier for her if she could put some of her issues aside when it comes to Jessica."

I came down off the porch to join her. "Yeah, I know. I feel bad for Jessica, too. I would probably feel worse for Louise if her sole purpose wasn't to get me."

Pat rolled her eyes as we started down the driveway toward my car. "How much do you want to bet she's lying?"

"Actually, I'm not so sure she is," I said.

Pat looked at me in surprise. "Who do you think she could be talking about?"

I shot Pat a look. "Who do *you* think?

***

I hadn't been to Psychic Readings by Madame Rowena Tanveer since the previous spring, when she first set up shop. It was located in downtown Redemption in what used to be the Redemption Hardware store, until they moved to a bigger location further outside of town.

Suffice it to say, Madame Rowena and I hadn't gotten off on the right foot. I blamed myself. I was unable to suffer fake psychics. Although, to be fair, not everyone believed in my assessment of Madame Rowena's psychic skills, or lack thereof.

"Are you sure about this?" Pat asked, her voice hesitant. I had to park about a block away, which wasn't all that surprising, considering how parking downtown was usually a challenge. Pat, Tiki, and I were hoofing it the rest of the way.

"If she's behind the rumor that my tea somehow caused Cherry to kill her fiancé, yeah, I'm sure," I said grimly.

"Yes, but … you do remember what she said the last time you saw her, right?" Pat asked, still sounding uneasy. Tiki poked her head out of her purse and nuzzled Pat's chest, as though to comfort her.

I did indeed remember the last thing Madame Rowena had said to me—to stay out of her psychic shop. "Desperate times," I answered. "What other choice do I have?"

Pat didn't look happy.

We had reached the front door, which was all glass. Madame Rowena's name was painted on the door, along with a crystal ball, a moon, and a few stars. In the shop window was a huge red, white, and pink display of crystals, hearts, and candles, presumably in honor of Valentine's Day.

I pulled the door open, listening to the tinkling of the bell as I stepped into the shop. A blast of heat mixed with the scents of sage and incense slapped me in the face. A skinny, awkward girl with stick-straight brown hair and braces was comparing various tarot decks while two other women, their backs to me, stood by a display of various essential oils.

There was a flutter of the curtain in the back, and Madame Rowena made her appearance with a flourish. She wore a flowing gold and silver robe over a long gold and silver dress covered in big, sparkling, red and blue stones. Her hair was tucked into a matching turban. Her face, which was heavily made up, fell when she saw it was me.

"Why Charlie," she said. Her voice was low and reminded me of buttery caramel. "I'm … surprised to see you here."

"I'm surprised to be here," I said. "But I was hoping, if it isn't too much of an inconvenience, of course, that I might have a word."

She paused as she deliberated for a moment before moving to stand behind the counter. "I have a couple of minutes."

"Maybe in private?" I asked, gesturing with my head to the brightly colored freestanding divider behind which she did her psychic readings.

She stared at me, an unreadable expression in her eyes. Maybe she was remembering the last time I had been back there. "I'm afraid that is a sacred spot to be used only for customers needing guidance." Her voice had grown just a shade colder as she stepped away from the counter and moved toward the back corner of the shop. "But I'm happy to talk with you over here." She sounded the exact opposite of happy, but I didn't question her, simply following her to the corner instead.

She waited for Pat and me, her hand on her hip and her eyes shooting daggers at us. "What are you doing here?" she hissed as soon as we were out of sight of her customers. Keeping her voice low, she added, "I thought we had an understanding."

"I thought we did, too," I said just as quietly. I tugged at my coat, wanting to at least unzip it as the shop was so warm, but I also knew I wasn't going to stay long and certainly didn't want to give Rowena the opposite impression. "So, why did you lie about me?"

She looked at me blankly. "What are you talking about? I didn't lie about you."

"Well, what would you call telling Cherry that my tea was what caused her to kill her fiancé?"

An expression I couldn't completely decipher—something like smug satisfaction—flitted across her face before disappearing almost immediately. "Ah, yes. That is a sad story. It would be heartbreaking to wake up with no memory of killing your fiancé."

"You know as well as I do that there's nothing I can put in a tea that would make someone kill someone," I said.

Rowena shrugged. "I don't know any such thing. How would I know what ingredients you use?"

I gritted my teeth. "You do know, because nothing like that exists."

A slight smile touched her lips. "Not in the normal world, of course. But you and I both know there is a shadowy world where the rules are quite different."

"If by 'shadowy world' you mean wherever your 'guides' hang out, I know nothing of it," I said.

Rowena cocked her head. "I'm talking about Redemption. You and I both know that not everything is what it seems here, and a dark side most definitely exists … even if most people want to pretend it doesn't."

Despite how uncomfortable the store was, I felt a sudden chill. Next to me, Pat sucked in her breath.

It was true that Redemption, Wisconsin, was not a normal town. It had a dark and haunted past. Back in 1888, all the adults disappeared, leaving only the children. To this day, no one knew what happened to the adults. The children all swore they had no idea—when they went to bed, the adults were there, and when they awoke, they were gone.

Since then, Redemption had been plagued by unexplained and strange occurrences, including hauntings, disappearances, murders, and more. For the locals, knowing that things were never quite as they seemed became a way of life.

Rowena wasn't wrong about Redemption having a dark side, but I couldn't see how that could possibly have anything to do with what happened to Cherry. I had seen Marcus and was fairly certain he had been killed by a person, not by some ghost. I highly doubted a ghost would need a pillow to smother him.

Although … there *were* peculiarities to the case. Why had Cherry been so convinced that she had eaten chocolate-dipped strawberries and had put a rose in a vase, when neither of those things were real? And why couldn't she remember what happened that night?

But even more troubling was the "who"—Marcus was a muscular, fit guy. Who would have been able to successfully smother him with a pillow, especially if he was fighting back? Other than the chairs that had been tipped over, the kitchen seemed relatively undisturbed, unlike the living room. So, clearly, someone was able to overpower Marcus, get him on the floor, and then smother him. The odds of that being Cherry were slim to none.

"What does that even mean?" Pat asked, her voice hoarse, as if she hadn't used it in days.

Rowena turned to Pat, her expression indicating she had forgotten Pat was even there. "What does what mean?"

"Your insinuation about Redemption. Are you implying that the town itself could somehow be involved with Marcus's murder?"

Rowena's lips, painted a dark red, stretched into an evil clown grin. "That's not what I said."

"You just said … "

"What I *said*," Rowena continued as if Pat hadn't interrupted her, "is that in the 'normal' world, the only one most people believe exists, it's true that there is nothing Charlie could put in a tea that would cause Cherry to kill Marcus. But we don't always live in a normal world, do we? At least not here in Redemption."

"What are you saying?" I asked, trying to tamp down the agitation that was getting stronger the longer the conversation continued. "That I'm somehow harnessing Redemption's dark side to make tea that causes people to kill each other?"

Rowena shrugged again. "You said it, not me. I have no idea what you're doing."

"This is absurd," I said, fully exasperated. "What you're suggesting is impossible."

"Well, something happened in Cherry's apartment," Rowena said. "And whatever it was, it happened after Cherry drank your tea. So if the shoe fits …." Her voice trailed off, and she smiled that creepy, predatory smile again.

"Seeing as Cherry doesn't remember, we don't know if she consumed any other food or drink," I said. "Or maybe whatever happened had nothing to do with anything she ate or drank at all."

Rowena's smile remained fixed on her face. "Keep telling yourself that. But if you want to know the truth…" she leaned closer, so close I could feel the warmth from her breath on my cheek. There was a sour smell to it, as well, like she had either eaten something unfortunate earlier or had forgotten to brush her teeth. "I'm kind of impressed with what you pulled off. You've surprised me, and that's not easy to do. So, good job."

My mind went blank. I had no idea what to say in response. Was she serious? Did she honestly think I was some sort of witch? Or was she yanking my chain?

"C'mon," Pat said, pulling on my arm. "We should go."

"Yes," Rowena said. "You should definitely go. I'm sure you have plenty of … preparations you should be doing. I know I certainly do."

Was that a threat? Was she *threatening* me? Even though Pat was tugging at me, I didn't move. Instead, I stared into Rowena's heavily made-up eyes rimmed with black eyeliner, trying to peer into their depths and figure out what she was doing. She couldn't possibly believe what she was saying. It was utter nonsense.

Could she?

"Charlie, let's go," Pat said, jerking my arm again. This time, it was hard enough to cause me to stumble, breaking eye contact.

"Bye Charlie, Pat," Rowena said, her voice back to a normal volume. "Always nice to see you." Even though her voice sounded friendly on the surface, underneath was a hard edge that revealed the exact opposite feeling.

"Thanks for your time," I said, matching her tone. "I'm sure I'll be seeing you."

Rowena's eyes bored into mine. "Oh, you can count on it."

Chapter 13

"What on Earth just happened?" I asked the moment we left Rowena's shop. A cold, damp wind slapped me in the face, which I normally wouldn't enjoy, but in that moment, it felt like a welcome relief after the too-warm, overly incensed shop. "She can't be serious. What game is she playing?"

"Charlie, I don't think you understand," Pat said. Her lips were pale, as if she had been pressing them together so tightly, the blood had run out. "It's one thing to claim you put something in Cherry's tea to make her do it. No one is going to believe that because, as you pointed out, that doesn't exist. The closest thing to it would be some sort of hallucinogenic, but even that's questionable, as most people don't turn into killers on those drugs. And why would you do anything like that? But if you're somehow tapped into the dark side of Redemption, everything changes."

"But that makes no sense. How could I tap into the dark side of a town?"

"That's beside the point," Pat continued. "Everyone who lives here knows there's a shadow side, even if they claim they don't believe in such things or never talk about it. For a small town, we have disproportionately high disappearance and murder rates, not to mention the dreams and other unexplained happenings."

"Dreams?" Something disturbing shifted inside me … something I was trying very hard to forget. It had been years since I'd had troubling dreams, since the first year I lived in Redemption. I thought I had moved past them, though perhaps "hoped" was a better word. But now, listening to Pat, I suddenly had the unwelcome thought that maybe those dreams hadn't gone away after all. Maybe they had simply gone temporarily dormant. Hibernating, waiting for the right time to emerge.

Pat waved her hand. "The point isn't the dreams," she said as I firmly told myself I was letting my imagination run away with me. The stress of the past few days was likely catching up with me. "The point is that it's now believable you could have tainted the tea like that."

"Wait." I stopped walking and held up my hand, as if I could stop the terrible feeling that had started to form in my gut. "Are you saying this could be an actual reasonable cause? That I somehow am connected to whatever darkness exists in Redemption, and I used it to infect the tea, so Cherry would kill Marcus?" Bile rose in my throat as the pieces continued to slide into place in my head. If Cherry could successfully use that as a defense, did that mean I could somehow be charged for Marcus's murder?

"Who said anything about reasonable cause?" Pat asked. "I have no idea what could be used in a court of law. That's not what worries me."

"Then what does?"

She took a step closer to me, her face as gray as the clouds scuttling across the sky. "Charlie, don't you realize what would happen to you if the majority of the town thought you were in cahoots with the shadowy side of Redemption?"

"Well, my tea business would probably tank," I surmised.

Pat shook her head. "Your tea business is the least of your worries. You would be a pariah. No one would want anything to do with you. More than that, there would be a lot more people than Louise actively trying to get you to leave."

"Great. More Louises ... that's exactly what I need." I dragged a hand through my hair.

Pat's mouth flattened. "You think Louise is a problem? Louise is nothing. She has no power to do anything other than complain and spread gossip, and most people ignore her anyway. I'm talking about your being unable to shop in certain stores, or getting your heat shut off during a particularly bad cold snap, for example."

I stared at Pat in horror. "You think I'm going to get my heat turned off? They can't do that ... that's regulated."

"Mistakes happen," Pat said grimly. "I'm sure it wouldn't be permanently shut off, but some 'glitch,'" Pat made air quotes, "could turn it off temporarily."

"But if things like that kept happening, I could sue. And win. And probably cause a lot of headaches for Redemption Gas and Electric as well. I can't imagine they would risk such a thing."

Pat gave me a look. "Is that what you really want your life to become? Constantly in the middle of some lawsuit or fight to get basic services? And what about if someone vandalizes your home, and the cops slow-walk their investigations? How would you sue over that?"

"Wyle wouldn't allow that."

"Wyle may not have much of a choice," Pat said. "He either gets with the program, or he's out."

"You think they would fire Wyle?"

Pat spread her hands out. "I don't know. I'm just saying, if enough people want you out of Redemption, there's no end to the things they could do to make your life very unpleasant."

"While I'm sure that's true, some of these hypotheticals seem rather unlikely, like my gas getting turned off."

"It depends on who decides they really want to see you go, and what job they have," Pat said darkly. "But anyone can drive by your house and toss a rock through your front window. Or something worse. Do you really want that to become your reality?"

I didn't. Nor did I have any intention of leaving Redemption. It was my home. Period. There was absolutely no question I was going to live in the very house that the town deemed "the most haunted house in Redemption" for the rest of my life. They would have to carry me out in a body bag to remove me.

But Pat was right; that didn't mean things couldn't get dicey for me. While it was true that I had a trust fund that was taking care of the mortgage and taxes, I still needed money to live on, so losing my business would be a huge problem. Especially if it turned out I couldn't get a job locally and would have to drive to Riverview or some other town. If that happened, it would mean long periods of my house standing vacant, and who knows what could happen then.

I was going to have to do something, and fast. And that probably meant solving Cherry's case and figuring out who was really behind the murder, preferably before the horrible rumor about me gained any more traction.

"Alright. I guess we have our work cut out for us," I said as I resumed walking toward the car.

"What are you going to do?" Pat asked as she hurried to catch up.

"Solve the case. What else?" I said. "I think it's time to pay Wyle another visit."

***

"I was just about to come see you," Wyle said as he met Pat, Tiki, and me in the lobby of the police station. His face was drawn and exhausted, and he wasn't meeting my eyes.

I was holding the white box with four frosted Valentine's cookies in it, but something in his expression told me to hold off handing it to him. Instead, that terrible feeling that had been slowly gaining steam as the day went on found its way to my chest, and I was having a lot of trouble breathing. "Well, glad I could save you a trip." I smiled as I said it, trying to lighten the mood, but both my smile and voice fell flat.

He didn't return the smile. Instead, he turned and began to lead us to the back of the station. I had assumed we were going to his desk, but he led us to an interrogation room instead.

I turned and saw the same question in my mind in Pat's eyes. Why an interrogation room? My throat seemed to close up, and I balanced the box in one hand so I could yank at the zipper of my jacket with the other, allowing me to tug at the white turtle-neck shirt I wore under my pink sweater.

"Have a seat," he said, gesturing toward the two metal fold-ing chairs next to a white plastic table. "I'm assuming you want Pat to stay."

"Of course I'm staying," Pat said. As if to second the motion, Tiki's head popped out of the purse, and she fixed her little black eyes on Wyle.

Wyle shook his head when he saw the little dog, but he didn't say anything. Instead, he disappeared to fetch another chair.

"What do you think is going on?" Pat asked, her voice barely above a whisper.

I shook my head, not sure I completely trusted my voice. My mind was racing. All I could think was that they had found something wrong with the tea after all. But what? I knew I hadn't done anything different than I normally did when I was making it.

Wyle returned with another chair and a notebook. "Do you want anything? Coffee? Water?"

"I'm fine," I murmured, removing my coat as I was already uncomfortably hot. I took a seat in the metal chair, the white box resting on my lap. My stomach was roiling so much, I was afraid if I tried to drink anything, I would throw it up.

Pat refused, as well. I expected Wyle to go fetch a cup for himself, as that's what he normally did. Instead, he took a seat in front of us and flipped open his notebook. "So, I have to ask you a few more questions about your tea."

I closed my eyes. Exactly what I was afraid of. "Why?"

Wyle cleared his throat and busied himself with his notebook and pen. "We got the lab results back, and it looks like there are traces of Rohypnol in it."

My jaw dropped open. "Are you talking about roofies? The date-rape drug?"

Wyle nodded. "Yes. Do you have any idea how Rohypnol ended up in that batch of tea?"

My mind was racing. "Is that why Cherry passed out and doesn't remember that night?"

"That's what we think happened," Wyle said. "So, do you have any idea how it got into your tea? Maybe it was an accident?"

I stared at him. "An accident? You think I have roofies just sitting around in my house?"

"It doesn't matter what I think. I have to ask the question," Wyle said. "Do you have any Rohypnol in your home?"

"I do not," I said sternly. "Nor did I add anything to Cherry's—or anyone else's—tea."

Wyle made a few notes and raked his hand through his hair. "It was a new bag of tea, correct?"

"Yes, but I don't see what that has to do with anything." Although that wasn't exactly true. I had a feeling I knew exactly where he was going, and it wasn't good.

"And you gave her that bag of tea the day of her date, correct?"

I rubbed my temples. "Yes."

"Do you remember what time?"

"She came by over her lunch hour, but she was taking a late lunch that day in order to give me time to make it for her."

Wyle was back to scribbling. "What time was her late lunch?"

"Sometime after two. I wasn't paying that close attention."

"And you made her tea that day?"

I closed my eyes again as I continued rubbing my temples. "Yes. She had called me over her morning break and asked if she could pick up a batch that day. She apologized for the urgency … said she thought she had more, but she had used the last of it the night before and thought it was too late to call me then."

Wyle looked up. "But she called you in the middle of the night on the night of the murder?"

"I guess finding your fiancé's body in your kitchen is a more acceptable reason for waking someone up than running out of tea."

"Is it possible you made a mistake when you were making her batch? Things happen, and you were in a hurry … it would be understandable."

"It might be more understandable if I had roofies in my kitchen," I said.

Wyle was still focusing intently on his notes rather than looking at me. "So, it sounds like what you're saying is you have no idea how that drug got into her tea."

"That's exactly what I'm saying," I said. "If you found roofies in her tea, they came from somewhere else. Not from me."

"Any idea where?"

"Maybe the person who broke in and took the rose and chocolate-dipped strawberries had something to do with it."

Wyle sighed, dropping his pen and rubbing his eyes. "The problem with that theory is that she drank your tea before getting that alleged package, not after."

"Maybe the person broke in earlier and doctored the tea."

Wyle sat back in his chair, looking more and more exhausted. "But according to both you and Cherry, she got the tea from you that day. So, even if someone had broken in earlier, for instance, while she was at work, the tea wouldn't have been there."

"Well, maybe he broke in later, like while she was getting ready," I said.

That got Wyle to glance up at me. "Seriously? Were we in the same apartment? You think someone could have been moving around in the kitchen while Cherry was in the bedroom without her noticing?"

"She's not the most observant person," I said, although even as I said it, I could hear how lame it sounded.

Wyle's expression was even more skeptical. "And then what? Are you thinking he hid somewhere while she waltzed into the kitchen and made tea?"

"Maybe that's when he snuck out the front door and left the package for her," I offered.

Wyle shook his head. "I suppose anything is possible, but that sounds very … farfetched."

"Well, maybe he broke into her car then." I was starting to feel more and more irritated, but I had a feeling it was less about the questions and more about the idea that my life was about to be torn away. How on Earth could my tea have gotten drugged, when Cherry had picked it up the same day I made it? The only explanation was someone else must have drugged it. But who? And how?

None of it was making any sense.

Pat reached over and squeezed my knee. I could feel her encouraging me to breathe, and I paused to inhale deeply.

"Is it possible that someone knew what herbs you would use for Cherry's tea and slipped into your kitchen and drugged them?" Wyle asked.

"I … ah …" I hadn't thought about that possibility. "I don't think so. I don't list the ingredients on the bag or anything like that."

"Do you have them written down somewhere?"

"Of course. I have files …" My voice trailed off, and I stared at him. "Are you saying you think someone knew Cherry bought tea from me, so they broke in, found my recipe, and mixed the drugs into the herbs I used?"

"It's possible," Wyle said. "Especially if it turns out Cherry, or Marcus, wasn't the true target."

It took me a moment to process what he was saying. "Wait. You think *I* was the target?"

"I think we need to look at all the angles," Wyle said. "But if someone wanted you to leave Redemption, destroying your reputation would be one of the most efficient ways to get that to happen. And what better way to do that than to slip something into your tea ingredients?"

I glanced at Pat and saw the same shocked expression in her eyes that I was sure was in mine. Could Louise be so determined to force me to leave that she would do something so drastic? Would she know enough about herbs and flowers to pull something like that off?

Rowena, though … I thought about the sage, incense, and essential oils in her shop. She would definitely know her way around a plant. And no, she didn't like me, but was it possible she hated me that much? To do something so elaborate?

"I can't imagine anyone wanting Charlie to leave so badly they would be willing to kill someone," Pat said. "That seems rather extreme." Even though she didn't say Louise's name, I knew she was referring to her.

"If Charlie was the target, I doubt whoever did this thought Marcus would be killed," Wyle said. "That was obviously an extreme reaction to the drug that no one would have anticipated."

"So you still think Cherry killed Marcus," I said.

"We're still investigating, but that does seem to be the most probable scenario."

"How could that be a probable scenario?" I asked. "Marcus was smothered with a pillow, right?"

"That's correct," Wyle confirmed.

"How could Cherry possibly overpower him? Look at the size difference between them. Not to mention he obviously worked out."

"The tox screen hasn't come back yet, but we're checking to see if she drugged him," Wyle said.

I held my hand up. "Hold on. Is your theory that Cherry drank a cup of my tea that had been laced with roofies at some point, and once it kicked in, she somehow had the mental and physical capacity to drug Marcus and smother him with a pillow?"

"It's not a perfect theory …" Wyle began, but I interrupted him.

"It's not even an imperfect theory," I said. "I don't think it's physically possible. Do you understand how someone would act if they were under the influence of roofies? They have trouble standing and walking. They slur their words, like you would if you were really drunk. Someone who is that impaired wouldn't be able to execute a plan like you're describing."

Wyle rubbed his eyes again. "I hear what you're saying, but the problem is, there's no evidence that anyone else was in the apartment."

"What about the fight in the living room? How does that tie into your 'not-so-perfect' theory?" I asked, making air quotes around "not-so-perfect."

"Another theory is they fought. They were both under the influence of some drug, along with the roofies in the tea. There was also an empty bottle of wine and two glasses, remember? It's possible Marcus hit his head, and that's how he was incapacitated."

"And Cherry was still so angry at him, she smothered him with a pillow," I finished.

"Something like that," Wyle said.

I glanced at Pat again. Tiki also turned her head to look at me, tilting her head as she gazed at me with her bright-black eyes. Neither looked terribly convinced.

"You said you were getting the wine tested, as well. Was there any trace of drugs in the wine?"

Wyle became very busy writing something down. "The tox results for the wine haven't come in yet."

"Oh, but they have for Charlie's tea," Pat said.

Wyle didn't look at either of us. "We put a rush on both, but we don't control what happens at the lab."

"Of course you don't," I muttered under my breath. I glanced at Pat and could see the same thought in her eyes. I was being set up.

"Well, what you said about Cherry and Marcus fighting makes more sense than Cherry planning the murder in cold blood," I said. "Or even planning a murder while under the effects of roofies. But it still seems … what was the word you used? Farfetched."

Wyle dropped his face into his hands, rubbing his forehead before dragging his fingers through his hair. "It's all farfetched. None of it makes sense."

"And what about the missing rose and chocolate-dipped strawberries? How do they fit in?"

Wyle straightened up. "Again, there's no evidence of either of those items ever existing. So right now, the working theory is that she hallucinated because of the roofies."

I shot him a look. "Yes, because eating chocolate-dipped strawberries is such a common hallucination."

He held up a hand, palm up. "Look, there's a lot we don't know. It's still early in the investigation ..."

"Yes, it is. Yet there's a newspaper article out telling the whole town that I did something to that tea," I burst out. "How did that even happen?"

"There was a quote from the police department in the article," Pat added. "It was just a standard, "We don't make statements on active cases," but they still could have shut this down if they wanted to."

"It depends on who the interviewer asked," Wyle said. "It's possible it went to someone who didn't know better and just gave the standard statement. But that's another reason why I would like to test your ingredients and see if you were the intended target." Wyle met my eyes again, giving me a very pointed look.

I opened my mouth to respond, then closed it. "Fine," I said. "Do you want me to bring them in now, or would you rather come get them?"

Wyle stood up. "I'll follow you to your home, if that's okay. I'd like to do this all officially, and maybe take another look around while I'm there."

"Sure," I said, standing up and fumbling with my jacket and the white box. Without a word, Pat took the box from me so I could get my coat on. I shot her a grateful look.

"Let's be off then," Wyle said.

Chapter 14

"As much as I love your tea and cookies, I think after this day, a glass of wine might be more appropriate," Pat said.

I was standing in the kitchen staring at the teakettle, still trying to get my head around what had happened that day. At Pat's voice, I roused myself.

"Actually, I think you're right," I said, turning the stove off and moving to the cupboard to grab a bottle of red and two glasses. "Today is definitely a wine day." I wasn't a big drinker, but occasionally—especially on days when I was being accused of drugging people and inciting murder—it felt pretty acceptable.

Neither Pat nor I talked much as I drove home from the station with Wyle trailing close behind us. Pat must have either sensed my brain working overtime, or hers was whirling just as fast as mine.

While Wyle watched, I went to my office to locate Cherry's file, which was right where I always kept it. It didn't look like anyone had moved it or touched it, but I wasn't the most organized businessperson, either, so there was no way to rule out the possibility that it could have been moved at some point. Wyle also took samples of all the ingredients I used to make Cherry's tea, then prowled around the house presumably checking to see if there was any sign of a break-in. He asked me a few questions about that as well, like whether I had noticed anything strange. I hadn't.

Before he left, I gave him the box of cookies I'd put together for him. He opened it, and with one eyebrow raised asked, "What did I do to deserve cookies like these?"

"They were intended as a bribe," I admitted. My voice felt wooden. "I wanted to know why you would ask me all those questions about my tea, and I thought you might be more likely to tell me what was going on if I brought treats."

He half-smiled as he closed the box. "I hope you know I'll always tell you as much as I can, regardless of whether you come bearing gifts. Not that I'm averse to eating a few of your cookies."

"I know," I said. "But as you know, I like to bake. Especially during times of stress. And making a few extra for bribery purposes isn't a big deal."

His smile disappeared. "We'll get to the bottom of this, okay? We're going to figure it out."

I nodded before biting my bottom lip. "Do you really think someone is trying to frame me? And that the police, or at least some of them, might be behind it?"

Wyle's face darkened. "I have no evidence that you're being framed or that anyone in the police department is involved. However, as a general rule, I think it's wise to keep an open mind during the early stage of any investigation."

That wasn't exactly an answer, but the expression on Wyle's face said enough.

Pat discreetly stayed in the kitchen while Wyle had searched the house, which is where I joined her once he left.

My intention had been to make tea, but Pat's suggestion was a better one, so once I opened the bottle of wine and poured two glasses, I took a long swig.

"Oh my," Pat said gently as I wiped my lips with my sleeve. "I wasn't expecting that response."

"Wine was a good idea," I replied, moving toward the fridge to put out an assortment of cheese, nuts, olives, grapes, and crackers. While I normally loved to cook, I really just wanted to drink wine and lick my wounds at that point. Maybe eat some cookies, as well.

"Hey," Pat said, her voice serious. I glanced over as I stood up from the fridge, my arms loaded with food. "We'll get through this."

"I'd like to think so," I quietly replied while arranging the ingredients on the counter and collecting my cutting board and knife to slice the cheese. "But I don't know, Pat. It looks pretty bleak right now."

"That's because you haven't started investigating yet," Pat said. "If anyone can crack this case, it's you."

I half-smiled. "I appreciate the vote of confidence, but unfortunately, I'm not feeling very clever right now."

Pat waved her hand. "That's only because today has been so stressful. You just need a break and a good night's sleep. Tomorrow will be a better day. You'll see."

"I hope so, but ..." I paused my chopping, staring at the slices of dark yellow cheddar cheese on the cutting board. "I honestly don't understand it. How could my tea have roofies in it?"

"Obviously, someone tainted it."

"Yes, but who? And when?" I put the knife down and picked up my wine. "When it was sitting in Cherry's car? I assume that's where it was while she was at work. Or did she bring it inside with her, and someone managed to drug it at some point that afternoon?"

"Both of those scenarios are possible," Pat said, but her face was troubled. "Or it happened at her apartment while she was getting ready. Someone broke in, like you said."

I reached for a platter and started arranging the cheese and crackers. "The first two options don't seem very likely," I admitted. "Someone would have had to know she had the tea in her car or at her desk. How likely is that?"

"About as likely as knowing she drinks a special blend made by you," Pat said. "My guess is that it's either someone she knows, or someone who has been watching her long enough to know her habits."

I shivered. I couldn't figure out which was creepier—that a stalker was behind the whole thing, just waiting for the right moment, or that it was someone Cherry knew.

"So, you think whoever wanted to do this to Cherry carried around roofies just waiting for the right product to add it to?"

Pat frowned. "Well, when you say it like that ..." her voice trailed off as she reached for a piece of cheese.

I added a selection of olives to the tray. "The problem is, the more I think about it, the more it seems like Wyle was right, and I was the main target."

Pat crinkled her nose. "I know Louise has been irrational toward you, but even for her, that seems over the top."

"It might not be her," I said, grabbing a couple of small plates and moving everything to the table along with the cookies and wine bottle.

"Well, who else would it be?" Pat asked, our wine glasses in hand as she joined me. She then of course, had to bring the platter of homemade dog biscuits for Tiki, too.

"Maybe Rowena."

Pat shook her head as she pulled a chair out to sit down. "No way. Rowena is even less likely to do something as crazy as break into your home and taint your tea ingredients than Louise is."

I flopped down in a chair in front of her. "Then who?" I stared at the food laid out in the center of the table. It was a nice spread, and I knew I needed to eat, considering how little I had that day. I picked up my wineglass instead. The depression that had been hovering around me since Wyle told me he thought I was the intended victim finally crashed over me. All I really wanted to do was curl up in a corner and have a good cry, but instead, I took a sip of wine. "Do the townspeople really hate me so much?" I could hear the waver in my voice and took another drink.

Pat looked stricken. "Oh, honey. No. Of course not. Louise is a little nuts, but we already knew that. And Rowena probably views you as competition, so that's not a huge surprise. Sure, there might be a few others who don't necessarily care for you, but that's normal. You're never going to be everyone's cup of tea … no one is. But to actively try to get you to leave by destroying your reputation? No one would do that."

"Yes, but according to you, what Rowena was saying about me tapping into the dark side of Redemption would be enough to destroy my reputation," I said. "Is it that much of a stretch to think she might take the additional step of drugging the tea to make sure I leave?"

Pat pressed her lips into a thin line as she reached down to plop an excited Tiki on her lap. "Breaking into someone's house to drug tea is a pretty huge leap from spreading false rumors. And besides, Rowena might not have known just how terrible spreading that piece of gossip would be for you."

"Maybe you're right," I sighed, reaching for some cheese and crackers. "Neither Rowena nor Louise feel right for this, really. Neither of them seemed particularly upset that Marcus died. Even if they hate me enough to drug my tea, I can't see either of them being okay with accidentally killing someone just to frame me."

Pat selected an olive and bit into it. "Exactly. I think if there truly is someone who would do something so drastic to get rid of you, they'd have to be a pretty horrible person to not feel terrible about causing someone's death."

I nibbled on the cheese and cracker, mulling over what Pat had said. "So, I guess we're back to Cherry being the victim."

"Or Marcus," Pat said.

"Marcus," I mused, popping the rest of the cheese and cracker into my mouth. "That's what I'm not sure about. Who was the intended victim? Was it Cherry? For some reason, someone wanted her roofied, and it all went horribly wrong? Or was Marcus the intended victim, and they wanted to take Cherry out of the picture?"

"But if Marcus was the victim," Pat continued the thought, "why would someone take the extra step of killing him at Cherry's apartment? Doesn't that seem like a lot more work?"

"It sure does," I answered. "If someone was going to break into an apartment anyway, why not break into Marcus's and kill him there? It could just as easily have been a robbery gone wrong at his place, which was what it seemed like at first glance with the trashed living room. But instead, they had to make the whole thing more elaborate by drugging Cherry's tea … not to mention the whole chocolate-dipped strawberries-that-don't-exist thing."

"Yeah, talk about a puzzle piece that doesn't make any sense," Pat agreed, reaching for the wine bottle to top off both of our glasses. "Who hallucinates eating chocolate-dipped strawberries? Or putting a rose in a vase?"

"I know. It's such an oddly specific yet mundane detail," I said. "Unless she didn't hallucinate it, and it actually happened."

"Except there's no chocolate-dipped strawberries or rose to be found," Pat reminded me.

"I know," I said as I picked up my wineglass, lost in thought as I gently tapped the rim. "Why would someone go through all the trouble of leaving a package and then taking such pains to make it look like it never existed? Even washing and putting the vase away. Although the vase WAS in the wrong cupboard."

"Maybe there was something in the package that implicated them," Pat said.

"Yes, but what would that be?" I asked. "Normally, I would have assumed there was something in the chocolate-dipped strawberries that would have knocked Cherry out. In this case, the roofies. But Wyle said they found it in my tea. So, what else would it be?"

"Maybe something that would have proved that Marcus didn't send that package," Pat guessed.

"Maybe, but whatever it was, it was enough to convince Cherry he had sent it," I said. "So it couldn't have been that obvious."

Pat opened her mouth to answer, but before she could get a word out, the doorbell rang. "Are you expecting someone?"

"No," I said, surprised. "Maybe Wyle forgot something." I stood up.

"Possibly," Pat said, standing up to join me. Midnight opened one green eye to watch her.

"You know I'm perfectly capable of answering the door on my own," I said.

"Doesn't hurt to be extra safe," Pat said. "It's been a strange day. A lot of strange things have happened."

I couldn't argue with that. And as we walked together toward the door, I also couldn't deny that I was glad she was with me.

I peered out the peephole, expecting to see Wyle, but dreading that I might find Louise or Rowena standing on my front porch instead.

It wasn't any of them, though. It was an older woman I had never seen before.

"Who is it?" Pat asked, her voice near a whisper.

I shook my head. "I've never seen her before. But if I had to guess, I would say it's a potential tea client." I unlocked the door and opened it. "Can I help you?"

"Actually," the woman said. "I'm here to help you."

Chapter 15

I blinked. "Excuse me?"

The woman stuck her hand out. "Allow me to introduce myself. I'm Tilde Tillerson, owner of the Redemption Detective Agency." She was much older than I had first thought, at least in her sixties or seventies. Her hair was dyed an orange-red, and she wore huge, orange-rimmed glasses.

"The Redemption Detective Agency?" I repeated as Pat nudged me out of the way.

"Tilde! What are you doing here?"

The woman's face brightened. "Pat! I should have known you would be here."

"You two know each other?" I asked, even though I knew as soon as the words left my mouth how redundant that question was.

"Pat and I have known each other for years and years," Tilde said.

"We go to the same church," Pat explained.

"I was one of Barbara's Sunday School teachers," Tilde added. Barbara was Pat's daughter. "And let me tell you, that apple doesn't fall far from the tree." She winked and elbowed Pat.

"What?" Pat asked, acting surprised. "Barbara was a much more obedient student than I ever was!"

"Okay," I said quickly, hoping to keep the conversation from derailing any further. The day had already been surreal enough. I didn't need to get sucked into a conversation about Barbara's Sunday School behavior. "Why have you never told me that there's a Redemption Detective Agency?" I turned to Pat.

"Because there isn't one," Pat scoffed. "Tilde is a retired nurse."

"There is so a Redemption Detective Agency," Tilde insisted, straightening her shoulders.

Pat put her hands on her hips. "And who owns it?"

"Well, me, of course," Tilde said.

Pat rolled her eyes. "Exactly. As I said. There is no Redemption Detective Agency."

Tilde started to say something, but at that moment, Tiki finally worked her way around the two sets of legs standing in her way and was able to greet the newcomer by jumping up on her calf.

"Why look at you," Tilde beamed, bending down to get a closer look. "Aren't you the cutest thing?"

"That's Tiki," Pat said as Tilde scooped her up. Tiki immediately covered her nose in kisses.

"Oh, what a little sweetie," Tilde gushed. "I didn't know you got a dog."

"It's a long story," Pat said. "Just like the Redemption Detective Agency story, so you might as well come in, so we can all get caught up."

Tilde glanced at me, and I nodded. "Of course. Come in. I'd love to hear all about it."

I led the way to the kitchen, asking Tilde if she wanted wine, tea, or something else.

"We're having wine," Pat added.

"Well, in that case, one glass probably won't hurt me," Tilde said. She had removed her jacket, revealing a fire-engine red-and-white polka-dot shirt that clashed with her orangey-red hair and glasses and a bright-green sweater that also didn't go with anything. "Oh, you have a menagerie here."

"That's Midnight," I said. Midnight opened one green eye at the sound of his name, but seeing that there wasn't any food involved, shut it again. "He's mine. Tiki is Pat's. So, a small menagerie."

"I have a cat as well," Tilde said. "Well, unless you count the other cats."

I glanced at Pat, who looked as puzzled as I was. "Other cats?"

"The ones I feed," she said, as if it should be obvious. She had turned her attention to the spread on the table. "Are you sure I'm not interrupting?"

"No, it's fine," Pat waved toward a chair, inviting her to sit. "We do this all the time."

"Yes, and help yourself," I said, handing Tilde a plate and a wineglass. "I'm dying to hear more about your agency."

"So am I," Pat said.

"Well, to be honest, you were my inspiration for starting it," Tilde replied as she carefully examined the food.

I glanced at Pat. "Are you talking to me or Pat?"

"You, of course." She began filling her plate with olives, cheese, grapes, and a cookie. "All everyone talks about is how great a sleuth you are and how lucky we all are to have you around to get to the bottom of all the crimes that occur in Redemption."

"That's very flattering," I said, although my mind immediately reverted to the grim look on Wyle's face when I mentioned the police department. I knew he didn't care who got the credit for solving cases; he just wanted to get criminals off the street and charged. But I also knew not everyone in the police department felt that way—some very much wanted the credit. Could that be why I was targeted? Because I was making the police department look bad, even though that was never my intention?

I refocused on Tilde. "I was kind of hoping they would be talking about my teas," I said, keeping my tone light.

Tilde waved her hand as she bit into a cookie. "Oh, that too. But mostly, it's about your ability to solve crime. You have no idea how many unsolved cases there are in Redemption. It's truly an epidemic. And as I was watching you work on them, it was like a lightbulb went on. It never occurred to me to take matters into my own hands to get to the bottom of them before you. But then I figured, how hard could it be? You're doing it."

"Indeed," I murmured, hiding a smile. Across from me, Pat rolled her eyes.

Tilde kept right on going, oblivious to our reactions. "So, I thought why not open up a detective agency of my own and get to work?"

"What do you know about doing that?" Pat asked.

"Well, again, I know it can't be that difficult," Tilde said. "Besides, you have no idea how bored I am. There's only so much bridge one can play."

"You could go on a cruise," Pat suggested.

"I get seasick. This is much better," Tilde said firmly as she finished off the cookie. "These are fantastic, by the way." She gestured toward the cookies.

"Thank you," I said. "So, is that why you're here? To tell me about the Redemption Detective Agency?"

Tilde shook her head, her hair flying around her head as she finished swallowing. "No, I'm here to offer my services."

"Your services?" I eyed Pat, who shot me an exasperated look. "You mean, you want me to hire you for … investigating …"

"Oh, heaven's no," Tilde said, selecting a piece of cheese. "I wouldn't dream of charging you."

"But you would charge other people?" Pat asked.

Tilde looked slightly embarrassed. "That hasn't been deter-mined yet."

"What do you mean?" Pat asked. "Have you solved any cas-es?"

Tilde busied herself with choosing another cookie. "It takes time to build a new business, Pat."

"And you somehow think you're going to be able to help Charlie?" Pat's voice was incredulous.

"Well, someone has to," Tilde said matter-of-factly. "I read all about it in the paper. It looks bad."

I closed my eyes and rubbed my temples. "Yeah, it sure does."

"You don't think Charlie had anything to do with it, do you?" Pat asked.

Tilde's eyes widened. "Of course not. Charlie solves crimes. She doesn't commit them."

I lifted my head, feeling a spark of hope. Maybe it wasn't as bad as Pat had said.

"Although," Tilde continued. "It's hard to deny that the facts are troubling. Cherry grew up in Redemption. She's one of those girls everyone knows. Always so bubbly and cheery. A smile for all. Everyone loves her. It's hard to imagine she could do such a horrible thing to Marcus … unless she wasn't herself, of course. Perhaps if she were under the influence of something … something like what the newspaper described."

My tea, I thought. I sank lower and lower in my seat, and Pat's expression grew grimmer and grimmer. I was wrong. It was actually worse than what Pat had said.

"If that's what you think—that Cherry was under the influence of whatever I put in the tea," I said, "why are you here helping me?"

Tilde turned to me, her face puzzled. "Well, clearly you didn't do it. At least not on purpose."

"On purpose?" I nearly yelped. "You think I accidentally tainted her tea with roofies?"

Pat nudged me under the table as Tilde looked startled. "Roofies? Who said anything about roofies? The article talked about you putting some sort of spell on the tea."

"It said no such thing," Pat said.

Tilde waved her hand. "Well, close enough. That's what everyone is going to think."

"And how do you put a spell on something by accident?" Pat continued.

"I haven't a clue, as I haven't cast any spells. But I'm sure it's possible. Right?" Tilde looked at me expectantly.

"How should I know? I don't cast spells, either."

"Well, whatever you did with the tea," Tilde said. "Maybe spell-casting isn't the right word, but you know."

I leaned forward. "I didn't do anything supernatural with Cherry's tea or anyone else's. I'm not a witch."

Tilde patted my hand. "Of course you're not, hon. Whatever you want to call yourself is fine by me."

I opened my mouth to argue with her more, but a slight shake of Pat's hand made me close it. The worry, which had started fading when Tilde appeared, was back in full force. If Tilde, who clearly was on my side, thought I was some sort of witch who had cast a spell on Cherry's tea, what were the others who weren't so strongly in my corner going to think?

"Enough about spells. Let's get back to the roofies. Are you saying there were roofies in the tea, too?" Tilde's eyes were bright behind her huge glasses, and coupled with all her clashing colors, she reminded me of an exotic bird.

Pat gave me an unhappy look, but it was too late. I had let the cat out of the bag. I also figured it probably didn't really matter. If news of whatever was happening to me had spread to the police department, everyone was going to know soon enough about the drugs in the tea. "The police found traces of roofies in the tea Charlie made for Cherry," Pat said.

Tilde's eyes were almost as round as her glasses. "Really? How did that happen?"

"That's the problem ... I have no idea," I said.

Tilde glanced around the kitchen as if looking for a bottle of roofies. "You didn't ... well, you know ... *accidentally* add any to her tea?"

I sighed. "No, I did not. I don't even have any in my house, so that would be impossible."

"Could someone else have added it?"

"That's what we're trying to figure out," Pat said. "But the timing doesn't work."

Tilde cocked her head, looking even more bird-like. "Timing?"

"It was a fresh bag," I explained. "Cherry picked it up that day. So, while it's not impossible that someone could have slipped the drugs into it at some point that day, it would have been tight."

"That is a pickle," Tilde said, a thoughtful expression on her face as she reached for another cookie. "Could a spell have done it?"

"You think Charlie cast a spell to make roofies appear in the tea?" Pat asked.

"Is that even possible?" Tilde asked, but then, she shook her head. "No, no. That's silly. Charlie would never do something so ridiculous."

"I should say not," I chimed in.

"No, I was wondering if the roofies were a byproduct of a spell," Tilde explained. "In other words, maybe what the cops actually found were traces of what appeared to be roofies, but they really weren't. What was really there were just the remnants of the spell." She tapped a finger against her chin. "Or maybe it wasn't *just* remnants of a spell, but actually roofies, as well."

I took a deep, steadying breath. "Tilde, as I said before, I didn't cast a spell on her tea."

"Well, you know, whatever you call it. That part isn't important."

I leaned forward, propping my head up with my hands. "This is a disaster." I had assumed once people learned about the tea being drugged, they would no longer believe I was somehow tapped into the shadow side of Redemption and tainting tea with it, but apparently, there were going to be people who believed I was both some sort of a witch AND someone who drugged teas with roofies.

I had no idea what to do.

"It's certainly quite a puzzle," Tilde agreed. "I wonder how *Matlock* would handle it."

"Well, first off, he wouldn't assume there was any sort of magic or spell-casting involved," Pat said.

"That's only because Matlock doesn't live in Redemption. If he did, it would be a whole different ball game." Tilde's brow furrowed as she played with her wineglass. "He would probably start by asking Cherry's friends."

"Don't you mean Marcus's friends?" Pat asked. "Marcus was the one who was murdered."

Tilde's expression turned to disgust. "I don't know if that boy had any friends. He was a user if I ever saw one. I know it's not nice to speak ill of the dead, but honestly ..." her voice lowered. "If Marcus hadn't been found in poor Cherry's apartment, I doubt much of anyone would be mourning him. Talk about good riddance."

Another memory floated through my head. Sue, at breakfast, saying something similar. I straightened. "You're not the first person I've heard that from."

"I would guess not," Tilde said. "It was well known that Marcus was a cad." She gave a loud sniff. "I don't know what Cherry saw in him."

"If that's the case, maybe we should be talking to Cherry's friends," Pat said, looking at me.

"There's like five or six of them," Tilde said. "They all hang out together. I bet they know more than they're saying. Especially that one with the really long hair. What was her name? Lulu? No, that's not right." She snapped her fingers. "Lola."

"I don't think Lola knows anything," I said carefully. Even though Tilde seemed trustworthy, the fact that Pat didn't want me telling her about the roofies made me hesitant to trust her too much. "What about her other friend, Sage?"

Tilde nodded, a faraway expression on her face. "Oh, Sage. Yes, I remember her. She was in my Sunday School class, as well. Definitely a little squirrely, although not nearly so much as Barbara." She shot Pat an unreadable look.

"Oh, for Pete's sake," Pat groaned. "Don't we have bigger problems to worry about?"

"Yes, yes, of course." Tilde said hastily. "Sage might be a good one to talk to. If I recall, she was one of the girls who didn't have a lot of female friends. If you know what I mean." Her eyebrows wagged up and down.

Was Tilde saying what I thought she was? "But aren't Lola and Cherry her friends?"

Tilde let out a snort. "Cherry is. Cherry is a sweet girl. But Lola?" She shook her head. "What do the kids say? A frenemy? That's what those two are."

"Really." I thought about the five of them sitting around drinking too much after Marcus was killed. Now that I thought about it, Sage and Lola hardly interacted with each other. It might be because Sage and Caleb were going at it, but maybe there was something deeper there. "Why do you think that's the case?"

"Boys. What else would it be?"

I could think of other things, but I figured bringing that up might derail the conversation again. "You mean, that's why Sage didn't have many girlfriends?"

Tilde bobbed her head up and down. "Exactly. Sage was … well, in my day, we called girls like her 'loose.'" Tilde frowned in a disapproving way. "And the worst part is, it didn't seem to matter to her if the boy was with another girl or not."

"Ah," Pat said. "I can see why she had some trouble finding girlfriends."

"Yeah. It's too bad, too, because in other ways, she was a very nice girl. Whip smart, too. She just couldn't keep her hands to herself."

I wasn't sure if I would call anyone who would sleep with other women's boyfriends or husbands very nice, but on the other hand, of all of them, she was the nicest to me, outside of Cherry. "Maybe it would be worth paying her a visit," I said.

As soon as the words were out of my mouth, I regretted them. Tilde immediately brightened. "Absolutely. When should we go? Tonight or tomorrow?"

Chapter 16

It took some doing to convince Tilde that it would be best if she didn't go with us. "But it was my idea," she kept insisting. "And Sage knows me. She'll be more likely to open up with me there."

"You're her former Sunday School teacher," Pat said. "You really think she's going to open up about sexual escapades in front of you?"

It was only after we promised to go by her place and fill her in that she reluctantly agreed to our going without her.

Privately, I wasn't so sure about Pat's presence, either, as I didn't know how to explain both of us showing up. But when I mentioned it to Pat, she said after that newspaper article, my wanting to bring a friend with me would make sense. Plus, Tiki would be there, and she was *always* welcome.

Tiki jumped up and wagged her tail at the sound of her name. She looked at me and tilted her head, and I could sense her letting me know that she would most definitely be a big help with the investigation.

How could I possibly say no to that adorable little face?

Normally, I would have waited to go see Sage—maybe even tried calling her first—but I was feeling too much pressure to get my name cleared sooner rather than later. It was like there was a giant clock hovering right above me, ticking away, each second as loud as a gong. The longer this went on, the harder it would become for people to believe I was innocent. I had to move fast.

So, once we were able to convince Tilde not to come AND politely get her to leave (both activities took far longer than I wanted), Pat, Tiki, and I finally got ourselves loaded up in Pat's car to drive to Sage's. Since I'd already had more than I normally drank, Pat decided to drive.

Luckily, Sage was in the phone book. She was living in a large, well-known apartment complex near downtown Redemption, so she was easy to find. Well, the apartment complex was easy to find. It took a bit to find her specific apartment, as the complex was divided into separate buildings, and there didn't seem to be a directory anywhere. It helped that none of the security doors were working. Two were busted and one was propped open. It all took time, though, so when we finally reached her door, it was getting close to seven.

"Maybe we should have called first," I said, feeling a pang of apprehension as we stood in front of her door. "I didn't realize it was getting so late, especially to just show up like this."

Pat gave me a look. "Well, it's a little late to turn back now. We're here, so we might as well see if she'll talk to us." She loudly knocked on the door.

There was a long silence, which made me wonder if Sage was even there. Pat was just picking up her hand to knock again when the door opened.

Sage, dressed in a pair of soft, comfortable-looking jeans and an old Packers sweatshirt, stood in the doorway. Her hair was pulled back in a messy ponytail, and her makeup was smeared, like she hadn't bothered to touch it up since coming home. She was also wearing pink bunny slippers and holding a glass of red wine, a smudge of lipstick across the rim. I could hear the noise from the television coming from deeper in the apartment, and suddenly, I wished even more that I had called first rather than shown up unannounced. Yes, what I was facing was a really bad situation, but one of Sage's longtime friends was just murdered. I should have shown a little more respect.

Sage, however, simply stood there, looking back and forth between Pat and me. I opened my mouth to apologize for bothering her when she spoke.

"What took you so long?"

I blinked, my apology dying in my throat. "Wait ... you mean you expected me to come by?"

She rolled her eyes as she took a sip of wine. "You think I'm an idiot? Well, don't just stand there ... come on in." She turned and walked away, leaving the door wide open.

Pat and I glanced at each other, then stepped inside. Pat shut the door behind us.

The apartment was larger than I expected. The living room was a good size, with a black leather sectional couch and matching chair in addition to a huge entertainment center, also black. A popular sitcom played on the television, the canned laughter tinny and annoying. A black coffee table was in front of the couch, and on it was a bottle of wine and a pizza box. A plate with a half-eaten piece of pizza sat next to an open wine bottle. The next room seemed to be the kitchen, which was where Sage apparently was, as I could hear her rummaging around. A moment later, she emerged with two more wine glasses, another bottle of wine, and a couple of plates.

"I'm not sure if you two have eaten or not, but there's plenty of pizza," she said, shoving the box aside and carefully setting down everything in her arms. She emptied the first bottle of wine into our glasses and handed us each one, even though the last thing I needed was more wine. Still, I felt obligated to accept it. Then, Sage disappeared into the kitchen to fetch her own glass.

"Sit, sit." She waved at the furniture as she hunted for the remote, which was hidden under a crumpled napkin. I perched on the chair, and Pat sat on the side of the couch. Sage turned off the television before directing her attention to Pat. "You seem familiar."

"I'm Pat Barrone," Pat introduced herself as Tiki poked her head out of the purse. Sage jumped and nearly spilled her wine on her sweatshirt.

"Oh! I wasn't expecting … oh my goodness, is she a cutie."

"Do you want to hold her?" Pat asked as Tiki leaned forward, wagging her tail.

"Um, sure," Sage said, her voice a little uneasy, but Tiki was already scrambling out of the purse and running across the couch to jump on Sage's lap. "Oh my. You're a friendly little one, aren't you?"

I got the impression of watching her that Sage wasn't all that comfortable with dogs, but Tiki refused to be deterred, wagging her little tail and pushing against her. I could see Sage softening as she pet her and oohed and ahhed over her little red sweater and matching ribbons.

"I hope it's okay that we stopped by without calling," I said once Tiki started to settle down.

Sage reached for her wine. "I figured it was just a matter of time before you showed up. Honestly, I thought you'd be here the moment I got home from work."

"It's been a rough day," I admitted. "Otherwise, you're right … I probably would have been here sooner."

Sage's expression softened. "I can imagine. And for the record, I was shocked when I saw that newspaper article. I didn't think Cherry had it in her. Lola, sure. But not Cherry."

For some reason, that made me feel a tiny bit better. Maybe I wasn't the only one who was surprised by Cherry's betrayal. "I was definitely not expecting it."

Sage shook her head as she drank more wine. "If I had to guess, this is all Lola."

"But why would she do such a thing?"

"Because she's a vindictive witch," Sage said, her voice so venomous, it took me by surprise.

I eyed Pat, who shifted uncomfortably. Even Tiki's head jerked up, as if she were startled.

"But I don't even know her," I said. "Why would she target me?"

Sage leaned forward to put her glass down so she could open the new bottle. "It's not you," she said, shifting dishes around to make room in front of her. "But unfortunately for you, she always needs someone to take her frustrations out on, and you're apparently it right now."

I watched her jam the corkscrew into the second wine bottle and contemplated her choice of words. Why would Lola be frustrated rather than grieving? "What does she have to be frustrated about?"

Sage was very focused on the bottle, so for a moment, she didn't respond. I was about to repeat the question when the bottle uncorked with a soft pop. "Aha!" she said triumphantly, putting down the corkscrew and filling her glass. "She's frustrated," she continued, her words coming out slower as she focused on not spilling her pour, "because now, she'll never have Marcus."

"So, she *is* in love with Marcus," I breathed, the image of Lola falling apart on Cherry's bed when she first found out the news replaying in my head. Quickly, I pressed a hand to my lips. "Oh, maybe I shouldn't have said that."

Sage smiled. "Why not? It's true. She was in love with Marcus. Or maybe 'obsessed' is the better word. Either way, it's been that way for years. Since she first met him."

"But she married Flynn," I said.

"Because she knew she could never have Marcus," Sage said. "Lola is one of those girls who can't stand to be alone. And Flynn is perfect, because he works so darn much, he has no idea what she's doing."

All the different pieces that had refused to fall into place started shifting around as I remembered Sue's words about Marcus cheating on Cherry. "Marcus was having an affair with Lola?"

"And others." Sage was staring into her wineglass. "But yes. Marcus and Lola were sleeping together."

"How long?"

Sage picked up a thin hand. "Years. Maybe since they first met."

"But … I don't understand. Why was Marcus with Cherry, if he was sleeping with Lola?"

Sage sighed and tucked her legs up under her, her glass dangling from one hand. "You know who Cherry is, right? Her family?"

"Yes … the Duckworths."

Sage turned to look toward the darkened window. "Marcus was always … ambitious. And pretentious. For as long as I've known him, he's been obsessed with appearances and knowing the right people. Especially those connected politically, which of course the Duckworths are. If you want to run for Wisconsin politics, you better have an in with that family."

"He wanted to be in politics?"

"As does any narcissist." She sipped her wine, her face pensive. "He probably would have been great at it, too. He could be very charming when he wanted to be."

Personally, I thought one less narcissist in politics would be a good thing, although I certainly didn't wish murder on anyone. "So, if I'm understanding you right, he was engaged to Cherry because, with her family connections, she was a better fit for him and his political aspirations."

"That and she would have made a good politician's wife," Sage said. "She's pretty, friendly, oblivious, and doesn't mind being out of the limelight. All good traits for that role."

"Oblivious," I repeated, wondering where that word came from. While all the other descriptions fit, I wasn't so sure about that one. "Because she didn't know Marcus was cheating on her with Lola?"

Sage smiled a self-deprecating smile. "Because she didn't know Marcus was cheating on her with *everyone*. Including me."

I widened my eyes, trying not to let the shock and, dare I say, judgement, show on my face. Cherry was her friend. What was she thinking? "You slept with Marcus too?"

Sage stared into her wineglass. "I'm not proud of it. But yes. I did."

I eyed Pat, noting the same question in her eyes, and decided to ask anyway. "If you weren't proud of it, then why did you do it?" I kept my tone as gentle and neutral as I could.

She kept her eyes trained on her glass. "A lot of reasons, none of them great. He was a good lay," she said pointedly. "And he was close by."

"Close by?"

She nodded. "He and Caleb live here, too. They're in building B. So, it was easy for both of us. And as neither of us were looking for any sort of relationship, it was perfect."

"What about Cherry?"

She paused to take a sip of wine. "I guess I convinced myself she didn't care," she finally said. "I mean, she had to know. Right?" Sage looked at us then, an unreadable expression in her eyes. "How could she not? She was with him for years. He was sleeping with her best friend, who was in love with him. She had to know what was going on."

"You don't sound very sure."

"Probably because I'm not. With the way she's been acting since his death ..." her voice trailed off, and she shrugged. "Although maybe she just has a guilty conscience. I wouldn't blame her if she did snap and kill him."

I truly hoped that wasn't the case, but the more I learned about Marcus, the more concerned I was that that was precisely what happened.

Pat seemed to be on the same page. "What I don't understand is why she still wanted to marry him. He couldn't have been treating her very well."

"You've never seen Marcus in action." Sage turned her head to stare out the window, that faraway expression back on her face. "He was one of those men who would look at you like you are the only woman in the entire world. When he decided to focus on you, look out."

"That's why he would be so good in politics," I said.

"Exactly. Between his charm and that intense focus, he would have gone far."

"So, what about the flip side?" I asked. "If Cherry was so perfect for him in so many ways, why didn't Marcus go ahead and marry her?"

Sage smiled a small, humorless smile. "Ah. The million-dollar question. I don't know for sure, but if I had to guess, I would say as good as Cherry was, Marcus wanted someone a little better."

"Better?" I frowned. "How much better could there be?"

Sage ran a finger around the rim of her glass. "Again, I don't know for sure, but if you know she's a Duckworth, you probably also know she's related to the side of the family that's not so … well-connected, shall we say. They're more the black sheep. And while it's true, a Duckworth is a Duckworth, I would imagine he would be more interested in someone whose immediate family had the wealth and power."

"So you think he was only with her to get access to a different family member to marry?" Despite my best efforts, I couldn't hide the disgust in my voice.

Sage leaned forward to reach for the wine bottle. "I didn't say that. But knowing Marcus, it's certainly possible. I'm sure if a suitable replacement didn't come along, he would eventually have gone through with the wedding."

My worry for Cherry increased a notch. At that point, I suspected people would be hard-pressed to blame her for killing Marcus, if that was what happened.

But then I thought about how upset she was … how she truly seemed to be grieving him. Was it possible, despite all the evidence to the contrary, she did actually love him and didn't kill him?

It was hard to believe, but she certainly wouldn't be the first person to stay in a toxic relationship. Or the last.

"There's another thing I don't understand," Pat said. "Why was Marcus in Redemption? If he was really trying to get in with the Duckworth family, why not live in Riverview? Especially if he wanted to be in politics. Riverview would make far more sense than Redemption."

"For one thing, Cherry was here," Sage said. "They started dating in college, and I think it would have been a bridge too far even for Marcus to break up with her after college and try to start dating another member of her family. Plus, since Redemption is much smaller than Riverview, the opportunities there would be tougher for him to get. You know that he worked in the mayor's office, right? He was a rising star there."

I glanced at Pat and could see her struggling to keep from rolling her eyes. "Why doesn't that surprise me?"

A tiny smile touched Sage's lips. "It made a lot of sense for him to stay here for a while, build his resume, go with Cherry to every family gathering he could get himself invited to, and see what opportunities opened for him."

I closed my eyes and rubbed my forehead, wishing I could erase everything I had heard about Marcus from my memory. No wonder Tilde had called him a "cad." He truly was one. "So, who do you think killed him? Do you think it was Cherry?" I held my breath, waiting for her answer. I didn't want it to be true, for so many reasons, but mostly because I had a feeling Cherry would struggle to live with herself if she had done it. And more and more, it was looking like it might be her—that Marcus had finally pushed her to the brink, either because she found out about the cheating, or he refused to set a date … or maybe both—and she snapped.

Sage's expression was thoughtful. "You know, I don't know. To be honest, I would like to think she did kill him. It would make me respect her more. But frankly, I don't think she has it in her."

I wasn't surprised at her answer, but it did make me sit up a bit. Especially the "make me respect her more" part. "So it wouldn't bother you if you found out Cherry killed him?"

Her eyes quickly shifted to me. "I don't know if 'bother' is the right word. Marcus is dead, and obviously, someone killed him. And the way he led his life, it's not a big shock that it hap-pened."

"Do you know that Cherry thought Marcus was going to set a date that night?"

Her brows went up. "Why would she think that?"

"I guess Marcus had some sort of romantic evening planned. It was supposed to be a surprise. She was in the middle of get-ting ready when she blacked out."

Her forehead wrinkled. "I knew about the second part … that the last thing Cherry remembered was getting ready …

but I didn't know she thought he was going to set a date." She shook her head sadly. "Man, that night was destined to be a train wreck, even if Marcus hadn't been killed."

I cocked my head. "You don't believe he was going to do that?"

"I *know* he wasn't going to do that," she said, her voice definite.

"How could you possibly know that?"

She didn't answer, instead taking a moment to sip her wine. She looked like she was trying to decide how much to say. "Well, screw it," she said, half under her breath. "I guess it doesn't matter now. Marcus had a lead on a new job in the governor's office."

"He was going to leave Redemption?"

She nodded. "It wasn't official yet. And it was with the mayor's blessing. I guess he was the one who pulled a few strings for Marcus."

"Why would the mayor do that?" Pat asked.

"I'm not sure, but if I had to guess, it was probably tied to the mayor's own ambitions, in some way or another. You know he's going to run for something bigger eventually, so his reasons for helping Marcus were undoubtedly self-serving."

"Politicians," Pat said with disgust. "They're all alike."

"That's for sure," Sage agreed.

"But what does Marcus getting a new job have to do with him setting a date?" I asked. "If he was planning to move, wouldn't it make sense to finally marry Cherry?"

Sage looked at me like I had missed the point. "You don't get it. This was Marcus's way of getting a fresh start."

"Did he say that?"

"Not in so many words. But yeah, this was his big opportunity to see if he could find a more suitable bride than Cherry."

"You think he was going to break up with Cherry?" I asked.

Sage let out a long sigh. "Of course not. It's possible he wouldn't find that upgrade, so he certainly wouldn't let Cherry slip through his fingers. This was all about him continuing a long-distance relationship with Cherry while he tested the waters to see what else was out there."

I closed my eyes and rubbed my temples. The deeper I dug, the worse it all looked for Cherry. Although, if Marcus *was* planning to leave town, there could be others who were equally upset. "Who else do you think knew?"

"I would imagine not too many people," Sage said. "Like I said, it wasn't official, so Marcus would keep it close to his vest until it was."

"Why do you think he told you?" I asked.

She shrugged. "I told you, our relationship was simple. It was strictly physical, period. Neither one of us wanted anything more than what we were getting. And because of that, I think Marcus felt like he could open up to me more than he normally would." Her face was pensive as she sipped her wine.

"Do you think this promotion is the only possible reason he was killed?" I asked.

"It wouldn't surprise me in the least," she said. "Politics is a dirty business. And knowing Marcus, he probably stepped on more than a few toes as he climbed the ladder to the mayor's office."

It would certainly make things easier for both Cherry and me if Marcus's death was politically motivated. Unfortunately, when I thought about the method, it didn't quite fit. Would someone who worked with Marcus know that much about Cherry? That she not only drank my tea but was picking up a new order that day? And what about the chocolate-dipped strawberries? Even though I knew Wyle was discounting them, they still niggled at me. "Do you have anyone in mind from the mayor's office?"

"I haven't a clue. I don't work there."

"How about anyone else?"

"Oh man, you want a list?" Sage shook her head. "I mean, just the men whose girlfriends and wives he slept with would be too many to count. And if you add in people from his job or politics in general, who knows how many might want him dead?"

"From what you're telling me, Marcus is no boy scout, and I'm not surprised a lot of people may have wanted him dead," I said. "But I'm still having trouble reconciling an angry husband or a spurned co-worker with how he was killed. If his death was more like a crime of passion or opportunity, like someone ran him over when he was crossing the street, I would agree the suspect pool would be quite large. But this was planned. If it wasn't Cherry, it was someone who took a lot of time and went to a lot of trouble to kill him."

Sage shot me a knowing look. "That's true. Which makes it kind of the perfect crime, does it not?"

Chapter 17

I pulled into a parking spot at the Law Offices of Franklin, Durham, and Jensen, turned the car off, and sat for a moment staring at the stately building. Made of brick and glass, it towered over the nearby structures. *Good for Flynn for landing a job here,* I thought.

The only problem with it was that it was located in Riverview, which meant an hour's commute each way. Maybe a little less, as Flynn's duplex was on the outskirts of town, closer to Riverview. When I thought about it, I wondered if most of the residents living in the up-and-coming homes in that neighborhood were also commuting to Riverview.

I also wondered why Flynn would choose to make that drive instead of relocating to Riverview. Was it because he couldn't leave Redemption? Many of the townspeople believed Redemption decided who stayed and who left. If Redemption wanted you to stay, you were staying. Period. No matter what you did, things wouldn't work out for you to leave. Any job you lined up elsewhere would disappear. Any living arrangements you had worked out would fall through. Conversely, if Redemption didn't want you, nothing you did would get you in.

So, it was certainly possible that Flynn, and any other commuting neighbors, simply couldn't leave Redemption, even though it would be far easier if they could. But in Flynn's case, it was possible he couldn't move, because Lola wanted to be in the same town as her lover. Not only that, but with Flynn's commute, it would be even easier to meet up with him.

I also wondered if Lola had planned it that way. That seemed cold, but after Sage's remarks the night before, I figured anything was possible.

Speaking of Lola, my first thought after talking to Sage was to confront her. The fact that Lola had been sleeping with her best friend's fiancé, and that she since convinced Cherry I was somehow to blame, was irritating me to no end. But Sage changed my mind.

"Who else have you talked to?" she had asked, topping off her wine. I was amazed at how much she had drank without seeming drunk at all.

"Lola and Cherry. And I think it's time for Lola and me to have another chat."

Sage sat back on the couch, tucking her leg underneath again. "Not Flynn?"

"No." I studied her more closely. "Should I?"

She took a sip. "I would."

"Why is that?"

She paused for a moment before speaking, as if arranging her words in her head. "You know how I said I was having difficulty believing that Cherry didn't know about Marcus's infidelities? I also have the same issue with Flynn. How could he not know? Especially since it's been going on for years. Just like with Cherry, I assumed he was fine with it." She shrugged. "Actually, I assumed those two were just in a marriage of convenience. Lola married Flynn because he was going to be a rich lawyer who would be working all the time and not care what she did on the side. Flynn's reason isn't quite so obvious. For a long time, I thought he was gay and was married to Lola just for show, and that still might be what's going on, but ..." she paused and started running her finger over the rim of her glass again, an unreadable expression on her face. "But I suppose it's also possible he didn't know about Lola and Marcus."

"Why do you say that?" I asked.

Again, she hesitated, as if rearranging the words in her head. "Because I'm starting to think Cherry didn't know," she said. "And if Cherry didn't know, then maybe I was wrong about Flynn, as well. I realize Flynn is a lawyer and should be a little savvier about things. Plus, Cherry is a bit of a hopeless romantic, along with being an eternal optimist who always sees the good in people. Flynn isn't quite that bad, but there is a ..."

"Innocence?" Pat asked.

Sage gave her a look. "I was going to say cluelessness. Flynn is one of those book-smart but not street-smart people. He's always been so focused. First in school, then at his job. He's not always all that aware of his surroundings."

"So it's possible he didn't know," I said.

"Yes, it's possible," Sage said. "And if he didn't know and then found out, well, think about it. He just found out his wife and one of his best and longest friends were having an affair right under his nose *for years*. That might cause him to react … badly."

I cocked my head. "So now you're saying you think Flynn might have killed Marcus?"

She held up her hand. "No, I'm not saying that. Like I said before, I suspect a lot of people wanted to see Marcus dead. It's possible Flynn was one of them."

"But the way it was done," I said again. "Look, I agree with you. I think Flynn should be investigated because that would be a massive betrayal. But why would he set up the murder in such a way that would make Cherry look like the prime suspect? Wouldn't he assume Cherry was as much a victim as he was?"

"Not necessarily," Sage said. "He might have thought Cherry knew and was okay with it. Or perhaps he thought with Cherry's family connections, it wouldn't matter anyway, because she wouldn't be convicted. But this way, the cops wouldn't even bother investigating anyone else."

I glanced at Pat and could almost read the same thought I was having in her eyes. *With friends like them, who needs enemies?*

"This would also explain why Lola was so quick to convince Cherry that you're somehow to blame," Sage continued. "I can't really see Lola killing Marcus, although …" she frowned. "It IS true her attachment to him was a little unhealthy. I suppose it's possible she could have snapped and had some sort of *Fatal Attraction* moment, which would also explain her wanting to muddy the waters by throwing you under the bus. But …" she gave her head a quick shake. "Back to Flynn—I would pick him over Lola as the killer. If Lola suspected that Flynn was the one who killed Marcus, she would be looking for a way to help Cherry stay in the clear without turning her husband in."

"But according to you, she loves Marcus," I said. "If Flynn killed him, wouldn't she want Flynn to pay?"

"If Flynn did it, I have no doubt he'll pay," Sage said drily. "But not by going to jail. No, Lola will wield that knowledge over him like a sword for the rest of his life."

"What about Caleb? Should I talk to him, too?"

"You should definitely talk to Caleb. You remember he and Marcus are … I mean *were* roommates. They also worked together."

"In the mayor's office?"

Sage nodded. "It's my understanding that Marcus was the one who got Caleb the job."

"Does Caleb want to be in politics too?"

Sage rolled her eyes. "I don't know what Caleb really wants, and I doubt Caleb knows either, other than to be like Marcus. I've never completely understood why Marcus allowed him to stick around, except Marcus is a narcissist, and narcissists do like having their fans around them. So, to answer your question, I'm not sure if Caleb is actually interested in politics and running himself, or if he's only interested because that was Marcus's dream."

Her tone had the same note of disgust that it did the night of the get-together, except then, she was talking *to* Caleb, not about him. It made me wonder why she continued to hang around that group if she disliked Caleb as much as she seemed to. Was she more like Lola than she wanted to let on, and despite knowing Marcus wasn't faithful to anyone, she still wanted to be close to him? Was it because she had so few female friends, she was willing to put up with Caleb?

Or did Marcus's death push those feelings into the open, whereas before, she had been able to bury them more successfully?

"If that's the case, why do you think I should talk to him?"

She shrugged again. "If anyone would know if something was off with Marcus, it would be Caleb."

What she said made sense, and I decided I would follow the order she suggested—Flynn first and then Caleb. Which was why I was now sitting in the parking lot of a law firm in Riverview.

I opened the car door, which immediately was caught by the wind, and I had to fight with it to make sure it didn't ding the Mercedes Benz next to me. It was another typical cold, gray day, when spring felt like it was still way too far away. I got out of the car, hanging onto my coat and purse as the wind whipped everything around me, and hurried across the parking lot and into the nice warm building.

Once in the lobby, I took a minute to finger-comb my hair and smooth my yellow silk blouse and dark jeans. A man and a woman, both wearing suits, brushed past me to head out into the wind, the woman's heels clicking on the marble floor, and I moved deeper into the lobby. I knew I was taking a chance that Flynn wouldn't see me, but I hadn't wanted to call first, as I didn't want to warn him I was coming. I also didn't want to give him the opportunity to refuse to see me. It was just after 11:00 am, and my hope was that even if he was busy, he would still take a lunch break, and I could finagle some way to see him.

I asked the smartly dressed, very attractive woman at the large desk if I could see Flynn, and she asked if I had an appointment. I told her no, but that it was urgent, and I was hoping he could squeeze me in. She pursed her pale, pink-lipsticked lips as she informed me that Flynn was VERY busy, and I would probably need to make an appointment. Still, she said she would check for me, despite making it seem like she was doing me a huge favor considering how busy she was herself. I simply smiled, nodded, and told her I appreciated it.

However, much to her surprise, Flynn apparently wasn't busy, as he told her to send me right up. I thanked her for her help, ignoring her disapproving stare as she watched me saunter over to the elevator.

Flynn's office was on the fourth floor. Another receptionist met me as the doors opened and led me down a hallway. She opened the door for me, asked if either I or Flynn would like anything, and when we both said no, she gestured me inside and shut the door behind me.

Flynn was sitting behind a large wooden executive desk covered with file folders. He didn't look well. His face was puffy, and his hair was mussed up, as if he had been running his hands through it. He had huge, black circles under his glassy eyes, indicating a likely headache. Or a hangover. Or maybe both.

"So," he said after a moment, gesturing me toward one of the two chairs positioned in front of his desk. "I'm assuming you're here because you need a lawyer."

"Why would I need a lawyer?" I asked as I moved to take a seat.

He gave me an impatient look. "Probably because the police found roofies in the tea that you sold to Cherry."

My jaw dropped open. "How do you know that?"

He smiled grimly. "You don't think we have contacts in the Redemption Police Department? Or that they won't keep us updated on a case that concerns one of their lawyers?"

Of course. I should have realized that myself. But it didn't stop my stomach from sinking into a pit of despair. Even if I found who was responsible for murdering Marcus, would that be enough? Or would I forever be tainted in the townspeople's eyes?

"But," Flynn continued, "unfortunately, I can't help you. Just like I told Cherry the other day, my specialty is contract law, not criminal. But we have an excellent criminal defense department, and I would be happy to introduce you to some of my colleagues." He reached for the phone, presumably to call one of them.

"Actually, I'm not here for an attorney," I said.

Flynn paused, his hand in the air, still holding the receiver. "You're not?"

I smiled at him pleasantly. "No, I'm here to see you."

Flynn became very still, the phone dangling from his finger. "Oh," he said, his voice deliberate as he replaced the receiver. "It's like that."

I cocked my head. "Like what?"

He sat back, folding his hands in front of him. "Don't give me that. You know exactly what I'm talking about. You're trying to shift the blame to someone else."

"I'm not trying to shift anything," I said, crossing my legs. "I want to find the person who is actually responsible for killing Marcus and drugging Cherry's tea, since I can assure you, it wasn't me."

"Well, it wasn't me either," Flynn said. "And besides, you're too late. The police have already questioned me."

I did a double take. "They have?" I wasn't expecting that. I had assumed they were busy looking for ways to frame Cherry or myself, or maybe both of us.

Flynn seemed to realize he had tipped his hand. "Only one did. I'm sure it was standard procedure."

"I'm sure." It had to be Wyle. Bless him. He was still in my corner. "So what did you tell them?"

"Nothing that concerns you," he said. "Other than I didn't do it."

"Well, the police must have some reason why they thought you might have, or I'm sure they wouldn't waste their time driving to Riverview to question you."

"I told you … it was probably standard procedure."

I narrowed my eyes. "*Probably* standard procedure?"

He busied himself straightening the piles of paperwork on his desk. "Again, criminal defense is not my expertise."

"So, there *is* a reason why you might have wanted to kill Marcus."

His head jerked up in surprise. "How dare you. Marcus was one of my best friends."

"That's not what I was asking."

He stared at me, his expression flat and unreadable. "It sounds to me like you have a theory about why I would kill Marcus."

It wasn't a question, which was good, because I still hadn't decided how I was going to bring up Lola's affair. A part of me didn't want to. It was none of my business, after all, and it was still possible Flynn didn't know. And if he didn't know, should I really be the one to tell him? Even though the chances of no one saying anything during a murder investigation were pretty close to zero, it still didn't feel right for me to be the one to tell him.

On the other hand, Lola was actively destroying my life. If her husband found out she was having an affair with the victim because of me, well, maybe she shouldn't have dragged me into it.

"I'm just asking a few questions, that's all," I said.

He leaned forward, resting his elbows on his desk, his gaze intensifying. "You didn't drive here from Redemption because you have a few questions. There's a reason you think I had something to do with Marcus's death, isn't there?"

I held his gaze, refusing to back down. "You tell me."

There was a long pause as we both stared at each other. He broke first. I saw the flicker in his eyes and a muscle jump in his jaw, and I knew the truth.

He must have seen something on my face because he dropped his gaze and started rooting around in his desk. "Who told you?"

"Sage."

He ran a hand roughly through his hair. "Of course she did." He deposited two glasses on his desk along with a bottle filled halfway with an amber liquid. One of the glasses was smudged, and I could see a few drops near the bottom. It suddenly occurred to me that despite the fact it wasn't yet noon, this wouldn't be his first drink of the day. He poured two fingers into the dirty glass and then moved to the clean one.

I held up a hand. "None for me."

His eyes flickered up. "You sure?"

"Positive. I still have a long drive ahead of me." I watched him as he replaced the cap on the bottle and picked up the glass. "You do, too," I reminded him.

He gestured behind me. "That's what that's for." I turned to see a very nice black leather couch against the back wall. There was also a coffee table in front of it that matched the style of the oak executive desk.

In fact, the more I examined the office, the more I realized how nice it was. I didn't think relatively new lawyers had such nice offices.

"That's a sharp-looking couch," I said. "Nicer than mine at home."

I turned to see Flynn staring into his glass. It didn't appear like he had taken a drink yet. "Thanks to Marcus." His tone was full of self-loathing.

"Marcus bought you a leather couch?"

"Marcus got me promoted."

I didn't expect that answer. "How was he able to do that?"

"Our office works with the mayor's office. There aren't a lot of lawyers in Redemption, and since George died, there are even fewer. So, we actually have quite a few Redemption clients. Anyway, there was an opening. Marcus pulled some strings, and voila." He opened his hand like he was doing a magic trick.

That made things a little more complicated with the Lola situation. "That's … awkward."

He shot me a sideways glance. "You could say that."

There was a long silence. He was still staring into his drink as though the solutions to all the worlds' problems were in there somewhere. Finally, I decided to break the silence. "How long did you know?"

It took a minute for him to answer. "Long enough. But not long enough." He tossed half his drink down his throat before setting the glass back on his desk. "And if you're wondering if I knew when Marcus got me the promotion, the answer is yes."

"Did you talk to him about it?"

He folded his arms across his chest. "And say what? 'I know you're sleeping with my wife. Was that why you got me the promotion? As some sort of payment?'" He spat the words.

"Yeah, I see your point." I suspected it probably *was* some sort of payment, although not because he was feeling guilty about sleeping with Lola. He probably wanted to keep Flynn in his good graces in case he ever needed him in the future. "So, what happened? How did you find out?"

He turned his head, studying the wall next to me. "At first, when we were in college, I was completely clueless. I was so focused on school that nothing else really penetrated. Although I think even then, something was bothering me, but it was easy to explain away. I knew Lola and Marcus had dated before we did, so there could of course be a few feelings still there. But Marcus was with Cherry, and I was with Lola, so I figured those feelings weren't much different than a crush you might have on a movie star." He shook his head, picking his glass up. "I was such a fool."

"You're not a fool. You wanted to believe your then girlfriend and now wife. That's a good thing."

He gave me a twisted smile. "Maybe. I still feel like a fool. I'm not sure when it finally dawned on me that they were sleeping together. It was after we were married, and I had suspected something was up for a while, but again, I kept trying to tell myself I was seeing something that wasn't there. There was no way Lola was sleeping with one of my best friends, who was also dating one of her best friends. The Lola I knew, the one I thought I married, wouldn't do such a terrible thing.

"And then, I tried to tell myself it couldn't be happening, because Cherry wouldn't stand for it. She would know if Marcus was cheating on her, right? So, therefore, it must not be happening.

"But eventually, I caught Marcus with another woman ... at a party, believe it or not, that we were all at together. Cherry, Sage, Lola. And Marcus was in the back room with someone else. At the time, I didn't realize he was sleeping with all of them. Actually, that's not quite true. I had no idea about Sage, and I had been busy trying to convince myself he wasn't sleeping with Lola. But that whole episode was what finally got me to admit to myself that he was."

"I'm sorry," I said, even though I knew the words wouldn't help. "That must have been awful."

He nodded, picking up his glass to down the rest of his drink. "It was."

"Does Lola know you know?"

He put the glass back on the table. "If you're asking me if we had a conversation about it, no. I don't think she knows I know, but I can't be sure."

"Is there a reason why you didn't tell her?" The question was none of my business, but it made me wonder. Flynn must have felt a great deal of anger and resentment toward Lola and Marcus and, the longer he tried to force it down and bury it, the more likely it would one day explode out of him. Was it possible when all of that rage started to boil out of him, it resulted in him killing Marcus?

As if reading my mind, he eyed me. "I told you; I didn't kill Marcus." He reached for the bottle and started to twist the cap off. "I loved my wife. I know that sounds stupid and foolish now, but it's the truth. I loved her from the moment I set eyes on her when we were back in college."

"Are you saying you were afraid if you confronted her about her affair, she would leave you?"

His lips twisted as he started to pour his drink. "Not exactly. More like, I didn't think it would last, so it didn't matter."

I cocked my head. "I don't understand."

He picked up his drink but just held it. "Everyone knew Marcus wasn't going to stay in Redemption. He had much bigger plans for his life. Maybe the governorship or becoming a U.S. senator. Maybe even the White House. But whatever it was, he wasn't going to stay in Redemption. It also seemed pretty clear that …" here, he paused to swallow hard, "Marcus wasn't going to be with Lola. So, eventually, Marcus was going to leave her. And I figured by then, I would hopefully have made partner and would be able to spend more time with her. Woo her back." He took a sip of his drink. "I don't doubt it's been rough on her. All the long hours I've put in, first in school and then here. But that's the way it goes when you're just starting out in your career. If you want to get anywhere, it requires putting in 80- or 90-hour weeks. So, I guess … don't get me wrong, I didn't like what Lola was doing, but … a part of me could understand it. At least a little."

"I get it," I said, and I did. In so many ways, Flynn seemed like a good guy. It was too bad he had the misfortune to fall in love with someone who didn't love him back.

Whether or not he was a murderer was still up for debate.

"I was such a fool," he said again, staring back into his drink. His eyes were getting that unfocused look to them that comes with too much booze. I wasn't sure how he was going to get the rest of his work done, but that wasn't my concern. I needed to ensure I got what I needed before he was too far gone.

"What do you think about Cherry?"

His eyes darted toward me. "What about her?" His tone was wary.

"Do you think she could have killed Marcus?"

"Absolutely not." His voice was firm, even more so than when he was talking about himself as the killer. "She doesn't have it in her to kill anyone, much less her fiancé."

"Even if she just found out about the affairs?"

"Even then." Although he didn't sound quite as sure as he did before.

"Do you think she knew about Marcus's infidelities?"

He paused as he thought about it. "I'm not sure," he finally said. "For a long time, I assumed she did, but either it didn't bother her, or she was choosing not to know, like I did. But …" he shook his head. "She's still so close to Sage and Lola. It's hard for me to believe that even if she chose to turn a blind eye to Marcus, she would do the same to either Sage or Lola."

"Why do you think that?"

"Probably because she would expect more from Sage and Lola. Especially if she had decided whatever Marcus was doing was just part of the deal."

That made sense. Cherry probably would hold her friends to a higher standard. "Did you know Cherry thought Marcus was going to set the date the night he was killed?"

That seemed to startle him. He looked at me in genuine surprise. "Really? Why would Cherry think that?"

"I guess Marcus had planned some sort of romantic surprise date, so she thought maybe that was the reason."

"Wow," Flynn breathed, looking back down at his desk. "Poor Cherry."

I studied him, trying to figure out if he was lying. Even though his body language screamed that he wasn't the killer, I still wanted to be sure. The fact that he knew about Marcus and Lola, and Marcus had gotten him a promotion, didn't sit right with me. And I was also having trouble believing that Flynn hadn't said a word to either Marcus or Lola. Could that even be possible? And if it was true, how much resentment was building up inside him?

"So, you didn't know any of this?"

He lifted his head and stared at me. "Of course I didn't. How would I?" He spread his arms out wide. "This is my life. I work all the time. Why would I possibly pay any attention to Cherry and Marcus's dating life?"

He had a point. "Okay, so if you didn't kill Marcus …" I smiled when I said it, but Flynn didn't look amused. "And Cherry didn't kill him, then who do you think did?"

"Where do I even start? Do you want a list?"

He wasn't looking at me. Instead, he was staring at the ceiling, which was a good thing, because I was pretty sure I wouldn't be able to hide how startled I was. Sage had said almost the same thing.

"Did he have a lot of enemies?" I asked.

"Well, yeah. I would say so." He started ticking them off on his fingers. "You can start with the women he slept with.

Chances are he had sex with someone who was a little crazy at some point. And all the husbands and boyfriends. And whoever he backstabbed as he was climbing the ladder at the mayor's office."

He hadn't said anything about Marcus's new job at the governor's office, which of course didn't mean he didn't know. He could just be keeping it under wraps. I decided to keep that detail to myself, as well. "While I agree with you that the more I learn about Marcus, the more I see why it isn't a complete shock that someone finally murdered him. But the problem I'm having is the how. How would a crazy ex-girlfriend know that much about Cherry? Or a husband? Or someone he worked with?"

He gave me a puzzled look. "Why would they have to know so much about Cherry?"

"Well, they knew enough to slip roofies in her tea," I said. "And they also knew Marcus was going over to her place that night, so they were able to plan this."

He pursed his lips. "Yeah, when you say it like that, it probably wasn't an angry husband. However, I wouldn't rule out that it was someone in politics."

"Why do you say that?"

"Because there's a lot of strategy and planning in politics. I could totally see someone who was ambitious coming up with such an elaborate plan. Plus, it also plants the suspicion solely on Cherry. And well … you." He gave me an apologetic look. "If he was killed anywhere else, the cops would probably be looking more closely at his fellow workers. But now …" He shrugged. "It's really the perfect crime, when you think about it."

Again, that was something that Sage had said. Was it just coincidence, or were he and Sage somehow in this together? But why? Sage was also sleeping with Marcus, so why would he and Sage partner to kill him?

"Have you talked to Caleb yet?" Flynn asked.

"I haven't. Should I?"

"Definitely." He picked up his glass and swallowed, his expression resembling someone who had lost an internal battle.

"You know he's Marcus's roommate, right? He would know if someone was hanging around who shouldn't have been. He also worked with Marcus, so he might also know if someone had it in for him there."

"I'll talk to him," I said. "Is there anything else you think I should do?"

He paused, swirling his drink. "I guess I just want to say I'm sorry this is happening to you." He raised his head and looked me directly in the eyes, although his were bleary. "For the record, I don't think you had anything to do with Marcus's death."

The look in his eyes was so intense, I had a feeling what he was really doing was apologizing for his wife dragging me into this mess. "Thank you. I appreciate you saying that." I stood up, brushing my jeans off. "And thank you for seeing me."

"Of course." He stood up as well. I turned to walk to the door when he called out to me. "Oh, Charlie?"

I looked back at him. His expression was unreadable. "I would watch my back if I were you."

Chapter 18

"I'm so sorry ... I've forgotten your name."

Caleb was standing in front of me, wearing a black tracksuit and white tee shirt and holding a glass of red wine. His brown hair was mussed, and his eyes bloodshot. A faint five o'clock shadow darkened his chin.

"It's Charlie Kingsley. We met the other day at Lola and Flynn's house."

It took him a moment to connect all the dots, but when he did, his eyes widened slightly. "Oh yes, that's right. Of course. I recognized you; I just didn't remember your name. Is there something I can help you with?"

"I was wondering if you had time to answer a few questions for me." I gave him my biggest smile. "I promise I won't take long. I'm sure Marcus's death has been really tough for you."

Caleb hesitated, and for a moment, I thought he was going to refuse. But then he seemed to think better of it and held the door of his apartment open wider. "Of course. I was about to make dinner, but that can wait. Can I get you a glass of wine?"

"Oh, I'm fine, but thank you," I said, stepping inside while trying not to wince from the smell of Caleb's breath. There was no way that was his first glass of wine of the day. Was the whole gang a bunch of alcoholics, or had the shock of one of their friends being murdered, possibly by the hand of another in their close-knit circle, pushed them all over the edge?

Caleb and Marcus's apartment—well, just Caleb's apartment, now—appeared to be the exact same floor plan as Sage's. The big difference was the regular thudding overhead that sounded like a herd of elephants learning to tap dance.

"It should stop soon," Caleb said, noticing my expression as he topped off his glass.

"Is it always like that?"

"Not always. Only when the neighbors decide to throw a dance party." His nose crinkled as he glanced up, and I realized he was trying to make a joke. "It never lasts long, though. And it's part of the reason why rent is so cheap. That, and the security doors are constantly broken."

"I noticed," I said. I wanted to ask why he had been rooming with Marcus, if it was so cheap. But I decided that would be just a little too nosy.

Caleb plunked down on the brown plaid couch and gestured for me to sit, as well. I perched on the yellow-orange chair across from him. Nothing in the living room matched, from the black wrought iron coffee table to the wooden entertainment center housing a large television, VCR, and stereo. But it was cleaner than I expected. The only thing on the coffee table was the bottle of wine, a bright, lime-green telephone, and a small pile of unopened mail. The fact that it sounded like he might be cooking something was also unexpected, although it was also possible his cooking entailed nothing more than opening a can of soup.

"How can I help?" He leaned back on the couch, stretching one arm across the back of it, and crossed his ankle over his knee.

I tried to settle in better myself, but the chair was lumpy. "Well, first off, I'm so sorry about Marcus. I'm sure you two must have been close, working and living together, so it must be rough."

A strange expression flitted over his face, but it was gone before I could identify it. "Yeah," he said, scrubbing at his face with his free hand. "Thanks. It has been rough."

"And I am sorry to bother you. I wouldn't, if it wasn't important."

"If this is about the newspaper article, I didn't have anything to do with it," he said. "I'm sorry, but I can't help you."

It was such an unexpected response that for a moment, I could only stare at him. "Well, uh, I didn't think you did."

"Then why are you here?" He fixed his bloodshot eyes on me as he sipped his wine.

"I'm trying to get to the bottom of what happened that night," I said.

"And you think I know?" There was something faintly accusatory in his tone.

"Do you?"

There was a long pause, and he raked his hand through his hair. "Sorry. That was uncalled for. In all honesty, I blame myself." His tone had shifted, sounding more like self-disgust.

I looked at him in surprise. "Why?"

"Because I should have known." He drained his glass, then leaned forward to grab the bottle.

"Why should you have known?"

He didn't immediately answer. Instead, he focused on pouring himself more wine. Mercifully, the pounding overhead had stopped, leaving the room in silence, other than the dripping of an apparently broken faucet that seemed to be coming from the kitchen.

"There were ... things going on that I now wonder whether they might have had something to do with his death."

I sat up straighter. "Things? What things?"

He took a sip of wine. "Just ... things. The kind of stuff that, at the time, you think are a little odd, but then you immediately forget about them. Unless ... something happens. Although usually, it's not as dramatic as murder." His voice kept halting, as if he was taking extra care choosing his words. He also avoided eye contact.

"Did you tell the police?"

He shook his head. "I did, but I don't think they took me seriously."

I gave him a crooked smile. "I know how that feels."

He glanced up at me, a faint smile on his lips. "Yeah. I feel like they've already made up their mind who it is, and they aren't open to anything else."

"You're talking about Cherry. And me, as well."

He stared into his wine. "I kept telling them they needed to take this seriously. Remember, you heard me that night. But instead, they just wanted to bury their heads in the sand. And because of that, who knows what Cherry said to the cops when they were questioning her? Whatever it was, it sure seemed to convince them of her guilt." He sighed, shaking his head again as he raised his glass.

"You don't think Cherry is guilty?"

He shook his head, even though he was in the middle of drinking, and droplets of wine flew everywhere, including onto the plaid couch. "Absolutely not," he said, wiping his chin with the back of his hand. "Cherry couldn't kill anyone. This is all nonsense. Someone obviously set her up."

"Do you have any idea who?"

He paused again. "I have a few ideas," he said, his voice cautious.

I sat up straighter, a thread of excitement starting to burn in my stomach. Maybe I would finally get a solid direction that would lead me to breaking Marcus's case wide open. "Does this have to do with what you saw before Marcus's murder?"

Slowly, he nodded. "That and other things."

I leaned forward, resting my elbows on my knees. "What did you see?"

He hesitated, glancing at me with an almost apologetic expression. "I'm not sure if I should tell you."

"Why not?"

"Because if I'm wrong, I don't want to spread false accusations. The last thing I want is to ruin someone's reputation."

"I completely understand," I said. "My reputation is in the process of being ruined right now, so I can assure you, if what you saw had nothing to do with Marcus's death, no one will ever know."

He eyed me. I could see on his face he was torn. "I don't know …"

"Caleb, please," I said, my voice cracking. "I really need to solve this case. And soon. The longer it goes on, the more likely it is that I'll never be able to repair my reputation. Please help me. And Cherry. You don't want her stuck in the middle of a murder investigation any longer than she has to be, do you?"

His eyes widened, and I could see my words had hit their mark. "Of course I don't. Cherry doesn't deserve any of this. She's the sweetest person in the world. Marcus was lucky to have her." He swallowed hard.

I studied him, wondering if there was something more going on. "Have you known her long?"

"As long as Marcus has. We all met in college. She and I immediately clicked. As friends," he added quickly. "There was never anything more than that. Cherry was always very loyal to Marcus. And from the beginning, it was clear there was a spark between them. It was inevitable that they would be together." He took another long drink of wine, his expression flat.

Even though Caleb said he and Cherry were just friends, and that Cherry had remained faithful, I wondered about their relationship. Was it possible there was something more brewing under the surface, but Cherry wasn't willing to go there? Or was it as innocent as Caleb having a crush on Cherry?

Or were they simply good friends, as Caleb claimed?

I wanted to talk to Cherry and get her take, but I wasn't sure if that would be possible anymore. I made a mental note to see if there was a way I could somehow connect with her without it getting too messy.

Meanwhile, Caleb was fidgeting on the couch, looking like he was fighting with himself about what, if anything, he should say. After a moment, he straightened, his expression resigned. "There are two different … situations, I guess, is the best way to describe them. One is at work. You've probably heard that Marcus and I both worked for the mayor's office?"

I nodded.

"One of our coworkers, Billy Winthrop, is about our age. He's very ambitious. I guess I would call him Marcus's biggest rival. He had been in the mayor's office almost a year longer than Marcus, so when Marcus got the promotion … well, let's just say he didn't take it well."

"He thought he should have gotten it?"

"Most definitely. Needless to say, he's been a thorn in our side for a while, doing whatever he could to sabotage Marcus without it being obvious that he was doing it. Real passive-aggressive stuff. Anyway, about a week before Marcus … died, I walked into the break room and saw Billy. He was standing in front of the fridge with the door open and his back to me. I didn't think anything of it at the time. I figured he was finding his lunch or something, and I headed over to the coffeepot to refill my coffee. And that's when things got strange."

"How so?"

He wasn't looking at me. Staring off at some point in the distance, his forehead was wrinkled in concentration. "I reached for the coffeepot," he held his hand out, as if he was mimicking what he had done, "and the noise it made when I lifted it up made Billy jump. Like I had startled him.

"He looked over at me and said, 'Oh, I didn't see you.' Which I thought was strange, because why should it matter if he saw me or not? I said something like 'Sorry, didn't mean to scare you.' I noticed he was bent over, like he had dropped something. I wasn't paying that close attention, but when he moved to put it back in the fridge, something caught my eye, and I realized it was Marcus's creamer."

"Marcus's … creamer?" I asked. "He has his own creamer?"

"Yes. Marcus liked heavy cream in his coffee. Everyone else uses half and half or skim milk. Or they drink it black."

"So Billy would have no use for heavy cream, I take it."

"Not that I can think of. Billy drinks his coffee black, so why would he be messing around with Marcus's creamer?"

I frowned. "Do you think he did something to it? Or put something in it?" I thought about the roofies in the tea. Was it possible Billy's real target was Marcus and not Cherry? But why would he think Marcus would drink Cherry's tea?

Caleb shook his head. "I'm not sure. It was close to empty, so there wasn't much left, and Marcus brought in a new one the next day."

"Did Billy try it again?"

"Not to my knowledge. At least not with the cream."

"But with something else?"

He was still not looking at me, focused instead on whatever he had seen in his past, but he slowly nodded. "A few days later, Marcus and I were in a meeting, and Marcus realized he had forgotten an important file. He asked me if I wouldn't mind getting it out of his desk. Of course I didn't, so I hurried over to Marcus's office, but when I turned the corner, I saw Billy."

"Billy was in Marcus's office?"

"Not in his office. More like he had been in Marcus's office and was on his way out."

"Did you stop him? Say anything to him?"

"I did. And he claimed he was dropping off a memo. Now, it was true there was a memo on Marcus's desk. But …" he trailed off. "There was just something fishy about the whole thing. Billy was acting really peculiar. And when I went into Marcus's office to find the file, I saw one of his desk drawers partially open. It was where he kept a bottle of whisky."

My eyes widened. "Billy did something to Marcus's whisky?"

Caleb raised his hand helplessly. "I don't know. I can't be sure. At the time, I thought he did, but I figured it was a prank, if anything. Like he had put a laxative or Ipecac syrup in it. You know, like something we would do back in college. Anyway, I wasn't taking any chances, so I poured the whisky down the drain."

"Did you tell Marcus?"

"About the whisky? Yes. I said I'd replace the bottle for him, but he told me not to worry about it."

"What about the cream?"

He made a face as he looked down into his empty wineglass. "No. That one felt too hard to explain. I didn't see Billy do anything, and maybe the cream was sitting toward the front, and he knocked it over when he jumped. But now …" he paused again, his face pensive. "I'm kind of wishing I had. Maybe things would have turned out differently."

"Did Billy do anything else?"

"Not as far as I know. The next day, Marcus put a fresh, unopened bottle of whisky in his drawer, which he never got around to opening. In fact, it's still there." He pointed to a closed box in the corner of the room. "It might never be opened," he said into his empty glass.

"I'm sorry," I offered, even though the words felt empty and meaningless on my tongue. He inclined his head, but didn't lift his eyes.

"So," I said after a moment. Caleb dragged his eyes up to look at me. "While it sounds like Billy had motive—and maybe he was even testing some ideas out at work—what I'm not clear about is how he could have pulled off this particular murder. For one thing, how could he know so much about Cherry?"

"Everyone in the office knows about Cherry," Caleb said. "It's not like Marcus kept her a secret. And she's been to multiple work parties, so everyone has met her, as well. Anything Billy didn't know would be easy for him to figure it out."

That might be true. I made another mental note to put a bug in Wyle's ear about taking Billy more seriously. "You really think Billy is capable of murder?"

Caleb shrugged. "I think we're all far more capable of doing evil than we would like to think. We pretend we're better than that … more 'evolved.' But the reality is, what we call 'society' is a thin veneer that can easily be torn away."

I blinked. I didn't expect Caleb to say that. He must have seen something in my face, because he let out a rusty, self-deprecating chuckle. "Don't mind me. Philosophy minor. A few drinks, and it all comes out."

I gave him a half-smile. "Okay, so thanks for telling me about Billy. You said there was a second situation?"

Caleb stilled. "Yes, but … I don't know if I should say any-thing."

"Why?"

He leaned forward to reach for the bottle of wine. "I just … it doesn't feel right. Marcus was a good guy, for the most part. But he made mistakes, like we all do. And now that he's gone and can't defend himself, is it right to say anything? Especially since it probably was Billy."

I watched him fill his glass, nearly emptying the bottle. "I get your reluctance. He was your friend, so of course you're going to want to protect his reputation, especially now when he can't. Unfortunately, in a murder investigation, things are going to come out, and not all of them are going to paint the murder victim in a good light. But there's no other way to do it if you want to find the killer." I paused as Caleb placed the nearly empty bottle back on the table. "Would it help if I mentioned I already know about some of Marcus's 'mistakes'?"

Caleb's head jerked up, and he stared at me. "What? What do you know?"

I tried to give him a reassuring look, but I suspected it was more sad than reassuring. What Caleb had said about Cherry being loyal still haunted me. "That he wasn't always … faith-ful."

Caleb pressed his mouth into a straight line. "That was vin-tage Marcus. He always felt like no matter what he did, he could somehow talk his way out of it." He swirled the wine in his glass. "And most of the time, he was right."

"I take it something happened around his … extracurricular activities?"

Caleb sighed. "A few days before he was killed, one of his … mistresses, I guess, showed up here, and they got into a huge fight."

"Who was it?"

"I'd rather not say."

I tried to keep from rolling my eyes. This was getting old. It was clear Caleb wanted to tell someone what he knew—the secrets he was carrying were clearly weighing on him. I couldn't figure out if he was still trying to justify telling me, or if he was getting something else out of the game he was playing. I decided it was time to be more direct. "Was it Sage?"

That startled him. He stared at me, his eyes wide. "You know about Sage?"

"I also know about Lola," I said.

His mouth dropped slightly open at the sound of her name, and I knew. "So, it was Lola," I said.

"You have to understand," he said. "They have a really long history. Longer than his and Cherry's."

"Okay," I said, not sure what there was to understand.

"It's complicated with them," he continued. "They have this … connection. It's hard to explain. It's like they were meant to be together or something."

"But they *weren't* together," I said. "Marcus was with Cherry, and Lola is with Flynn."

Caleb hung his head. "I know. That's why it's hard to explain. I know Marcus really cared for Cherry, and in a lot of ways, they were wonderful together. But …" he shook his head. "Lola is the one he should have been with."

While that may have been true, if Sage was to be believed, Lola didn't have the right pedigree for Marcus. Which, in retrospect, considering how it turned out, was probably unfortunate for everyone involved. "What happened with Lola?"

Caleb grimaced. "Like I said, she and Marcus got into a huge fight the day before he was killed."

"You said she came here?"

He nodded as he took another sip. "She was waiting for us in the parking lot when we got home from work. Well, work and a few drinks at The Tipsy Cow. As soon as she saw Marcus get out of the car, she came running over, yelling at him."

"What was she yelling?"

"'How could you? Did you really think I wasn't going to find out?' That sort of stuff."

"Do you know what she was talking about?"

He shook his head. "Marcus took her by the arm and dragged her across the parking lot, all the while telling her to keep her voice down."

"Did you wait for him?"

He shot me a look. "In this weather? Are you kidding? No, I went up to the apartment."

"How long were they out there?"

He shrugged. "Ten, 15 minutes? To be honest, I wasn't looking at a clock."

"Was Lola with him?"

"No. He came up alone."

"Did you ask him about it?"

Another shrug. "Sort of, I guess. I asked him if everything was okay, and he said yes … that everything was fine. It was clear he didn't want to talk about it, so we dropped it."

"Did anything else happen with Lola that night?"

"Not to my knowledge, but I don't know for sure. Marcus wasn't in a great mood, and he didn't stay long. Basically changed his clothes, made a couple of calls, and took off."

"Did he say where he was going?"

"He mentioned the gym. He goes there a lot, at least three or four times a week. And he had his duffle bag with him."

"How long was he there?"

"I have no idea."

"Well, when did he come home?"

Caleb squinted, as if trying hard to remember. "I had the 10:00 news on, so it was after ten. I doubt he was at the gym the whole time, because that would have been like three hours. But who knows, with Marcus."

"So you don't know where he was?"

Caleb looked at me like I was slow. "What, do I look like his mother or something? We were roommates. Plus, we worked together. I didn't need to know his every move."

I stared at him, a little taken aback by the harshness of his tone. While I wouldn't have expected him to grill Marcus on his whereabouts, I also thought it wouldn't be that out of line to ask him what he had done all evening. Not because Caleb was trying to check up on Marcus, but as a topic of conversation. On the other hand, if Marcus was sleeping around as much as Sage made it seem like, maybe it was more like a 'don't ask, don't tell' situation.

Still, Caleb seemed unduly angry at the question and, I wondered why.

One good thing was that it gave me an opening to ask about the roommate situation. "Why were you two roommates, if you don't mind my asking?" I gave him my sweetest smile. "I'm just a little surprised, as you had said this place is cheap. So I'm curious about why you two didn't have your own places."

His lips turned up into that self-deprecating smile again. "Believe it or not, politics doesn't always pay. At least not when you're first starting out. It's a lot of hours and a ton of grunt work with very little money. It does come with some perks, though … like a lot of free pizza."

"Anyway, we both knew the first few years might be a little tough, financially speaking, and rather than stress on our own, it made more sense to keep our expenses as low as possible. That also opened up a lot more options for us, as well … like if we wanted to volunteer for a campaign and cut back work hours. Obviously, once Marcus and I got our promotions, finances became less of an issue. But at that point, it didn't make a lot of sense to mess around moving somewhere else in Redemption when we would both likely have new jobs in a year or so."

He lowered his eyes as he said the last sentence, which made me think that while he may not have exactly been lying, he also wasn't telling the whole truth. Like maybe Marcus really did already have another job with the governor and would be moving soon.

"You got a promotion, as well?"

He nodded. "When Marcus got promoted, so did I. I was part of his team."

"Ah. You two really did work closely together."

"Yeah well, in politics, you quickly learn that most of the time, you're working in a snake pit. People backstab you all the time, so the more you can surround yourself with people you trust, the better."

I wondered if that also meant that Caleb would be going with Marcus to the governor's office. Sage hadn't said anything about Caleb, but she also might not have known.

Caleb sipped his wine, glancing a little pointedly behind him toward the kitchen. I took the hint.

"Well, you were really helpful," I said, getting up. "Thanks for taking the time to talk to me."

He stood as well, moving better than I would have thought after all the alcohol I had just watched him drink. There was only a slight sway as he got to his feet. "I hope I was helpful."

"You were. And if anything else comes to mind, please let me know."

"I will. I just hope … well, I'm sorry you got sucked into all of this." He said it in a rush, the words tumbling over one another.

"I am too," I said. "But you've given me some good leads, especially Billy, so hopefully, we'll get to the bottom of what really happened. And quickly."

Caleb didn't look at all that convinced. "Let's hope," he said.

Chapter 19

Initially, my plan was to call Wyle and find out what, if anything, they were doing in terms of investigating Billy. Even though Caleb didn't feel like the cops had taken him seriously, I wasn't as convinced. I felt like Wyle would at least follow up with Billy, if for no other reason than to ask him a few questions and find out if he had an alibi. If Billy had fallen through the cracks, for some reason, then I planned to push him a bit.

But the more I thought about Lola, the angrier I got. It wasn't about her having an affair with Marcus—I figured something like that was going on as soon as I saw her reaction to Marcus's death. No, it was the hypocrisy of it all. How she was pretending to be Cherry's best friend, when really, she was so involved with Cherry's fiancé that she showed up unexpectedly at his apartment complex, accusing him of hiding something from her. Like Marcus somehow owed her information, even though they were both involved with other people. Not to mention how I was sure she was behind making me the scapegoat of Marcus's murder. If it wasn't her idea, like Sage had seemed to think, then she was at the very least egging Cherry on. Her reaction when I showed up at her house to talk to Cherry made that clear.

Was she just a selfish jerk, like Sage implied? Was she having some sort of mental breakdown at the thought of losing her long-time lover? Or was there something else going on?

And what was she referring to when she was yelling things like "How could you?" and "Did you think I wouldn't find out?" Had she somehow found out about his new job with the governor? I suspected Flynn knew … Flynn seemed to know everything else that was going on in Redemption. And if Flynn knew, then it was very possible he told Lola.

Or maybe Marcus was planning to finally tie the knot with Cherry after all, and Lola somehow found out.

Even though Sage didn't think that was possible, I wasn't so sure. What if Marcus was going to ask her to move with him, even if they didn't get married right away? I couldn't see him leaving Cherry in a completely different town without him. What if she decided she was done with him and broke up with him while he was trying to find his next great relationship? No, until Marcus knew he had a suitable replacement, I didn't see him letting her go. He wouldn't want to start over and find someone new if he didn't have to.

So, if Marcus was planning to move and bring Cherry along, in some fashion, leaving Lola behind, I could see how that would make her angry. Really angry.

Would it be enough to push her to murder?

I thought it was an excellent question to ask. Which was how I found myself pulling into the parking lot at the hospital near the administrative office at nearly ten in the morning. Lola was apparently either an executive assistant or secretary—I wasn't clear on the difference—to one of the vice presidents. I was surprised she still was working full- time, as Flynn looked like he was on the path to making excellent money, but maybe she liked her job.

The wind was brutal, whipping around me. I hurried into the hospital, taking a moment to quickly duck into a bathroom to fix my hair, which had become a tangled mess. Remembering how put-together Lola always was, I thought I should take a little more time with my appearance, so I added some pale-pink lip gloss, as well. I wore a similar outfit to the one I had chosen when I went to Flynn's law office: dark jeans, a cream silk camisole, and an emerald-green blazer with my black wool coat over it. I wasn't crazy about how I looked in black, but it was my best coat, so I dealt with it.

After I had done what I could with my hair, I went in search of an elevator. I knew Lola's office was on the seventh floor— the rest, I'd figure out once I got up there.

It was easier than I thought. I saw her almost as soon as I stepped off the elevator and into the carpeted hallway. She was tucked in a relatively private alcove next to a corner office. She didn't notice me, as she was busy talking on the phone while flipping through a large calendar.

Unlike the rest of the hospital, the floor was mostly quiet and still. The only sound was the clacking of a typewriter from somewhere behind me. The carpet was a dark beige, and the walls were cream-colored underneath watercolor landscapes. It didn't feel like a hospital at all, but more like a high-end executive office.

"Great. I have Mr. Leonard down for 2:00 pm tomorrow. I'll see him then," Lola was saying as I approached. She still didn't look at me, as she was focused on jotting down another note before raising her head, a professional expression on her face. "Can I he …" she started to say, but her voice trailed off as soon as she recognized me. A strange look flitted across her face … was it fear? Within seconds, though, it morphed into something much more sour, as if she had just bit into a lemon.

"You shouldn't be here," she said brusquely.

I smiled pleasantly. "But I'm here to see you."

"I'm working," she said. "If you want to talk to me, you can give me a call when I'm not at work, and maybe we can set something up."

"Of course," I said, busying myself with my purse. "We can talk after I've spoken to the cops, if that's what you'd prefer. I was just extending a courtesy, by giving you the chance to chat with me first. I'll talk to you later." I gave her a little finger wave and turned to head back to the elevator.

"Wait a minute," she said. I slowly turned back to face her, an inquiring expression carefully arranged on my face. "Why would I care if you're talking to the cops? You're the one who drugged Cherry's tea."

"And how would you know about that?"

"Have you forgotten? Cherry and I are friends. Best friends," she said impatiently. "Are you going to answer the question, or are you just here to waste my time?"

"I wouldn't dream of wasting your time," I said. "Nor have I forgotten that you are supposedly Cherry's best friend."

Even with a full face of makeup, she visibly paled. Somehow, she was able to keep up the pretense. "What are you talking about? Of course I am."

I widened my eyes. "Oh. I guess I just assumed that when you're best friends with someone, you don't sleep with her significant other."

She leaped to her feet. "Keep your voice down," she hissed, her eyes darting around frantically. I looked around as well, but didn't see anyone even remotely nearby. She glanced back at me, her lips pressed together. "Fine. Come with me." She stalked off without bothering to check if I was following. I trailed after her.

She led me to the stairwell, holding the door open so I would join her on the gray landing. Her black-heeled pumps clattered on the cement. "Make it quick. You're lucky I haven't taken my morning break yet." Her voice seemed to echo in the cavernous space. I was surprised she chose that area, as it didn't seem particularly private. But on the other hand, it was *her* secret she didn't want exposed, so if she was fine with it, I was fine with it.

"I want to know why you're trying to destroy my reputation," I said.

She stared at me in surprise. "That's what you're going to the cops about? I'm not destroying your reputation. You're doing that yourself. Maybe if you don't want your reputation destroyed, don't add roofies to your customers' teas."

"I did no such thing, and you know it," I said.

"How would I know that? I don't know you at all."

"Because I don't have any reason to," I said. "I didn't even know Marcus. Why would I possibly want him dead? And why would I hurt Cherry? She was a good customer. There was no reason for me to do that."

"You say that, but who knows if it's true or not," Lola said. "You could have done all of that for a reason no one knows about. Or maybe you're just nuts."

I folded my arms across my chest. "Or maybe you're the one with the motive."

Her mouth dropped open. "You're accusing me? I knew Marcus for years. I would never hurt him." Her voice had gone up a notch.

"You showed up at his apartment the day before he was murdered screaming at him," I said.

She turned her head away. "Stupid Caleb," she muttered before turning back to me. "That was private. It didn't have anything to do with his murder."

"So you say," I said. "But as someone who has apparently been sleeping with Marcus since college, you're far more likely to have had a motive than I am. Remember, the two biggest reasons for murder are love and money. All that's tying me to the crime is the fact that someone drugged the tea Cherry drank, which could have been anyone." I shot her a hard look.

"I had nothing to do with drugging your tea," she insisted, her voice raising even more. "How dare you?"

"You seem to be more upset that I'm accusing you of drugging the tea than of killing Marcus," I said.

Her face had turned nearly purple, and her hands were clenched into tight fists. She was so angry, she could barely talk. "How … how … you are *so* out of line!"

I took a step closer to her. "What were you and Marcus arguing about? What was he keeping from you?"

Lola's face was white. "That's none of your business," she stammered.

"I would be more inclined to agree with you if you hadn't dragged me into this sordid affair." I narrowed my eyes. "Are you going to tell me, or would you prefer to deal with the police?"

For a moment, I thought she was going to haul off and punch me. She was still squeezing her hands into tight little fists, and she started to raise her right arm before apparently thinking better of it and dropping it to her side. "You don't understand," she said.

"Then explain it to me."

She was quiet for a moment, her chest rising and falling as if she had run a long race. She was looking down, staring at her designer shoes that went perfectly with the long, black pencil skirt and purple, ruffled silk blouse with a big bow in the front. Her long, thick hair was carefully styled with the front pulled back in a bun while the rest fell in waves halfway down her back. Her perfume was light with floral undertones, and it smelled expensive. Even her nails were perfectly manicured in an understated and elegant French manicure. Looking at her, you would think she had it all together and was living a perfect life. A great job working as an executive assistant for a vice president, a husband who was a lawyer. She had it all.

Which just goes to show how looks can be deceiving.

"I never wanted this," she said, turning her huge golden-brown eyes to me. "You have to believe me."

"I'm not here to judge," I said, softening my voice. "I'm just looking for the truth."

"The truth," she said under her breath. "I'm not even sure I know what that is anymore." She crossed her arms across her midsection, hugging herself tightly. "I've been in love with Marcus forever. Since the moment he sauntered up to me at the dive bar my friends talked me into going to, with that sexy smile of his and oozing charm. Of course I went home with him. I never go home with men like that, but …" she shook her head.

"It didn't last long. A couple of months or so. Basically, until he met Cherry." Her eyes darkened.

"He dumped you for her."

"Not exactly." Lola was silent for a moment. "We were never exclusive, Marcus and me. We had never even gotten to the boyfriend/girlfriend stage. So I knew he was dating other women. I wasn't happy about it, but I also knew that was the price I had to pay to have him. And that was the only thing that mattered … having a place in his life. I thought …" she pressed her lips together. "I really thought that eventually, if I stuck around long enough, he would fall in love with me. Like one of those movies where the girl next door takes off her glasses and shakes her hair out and the hot football star realizes he had actually been in love with her for years without realizing it." She laughed softly to herself.

"Anyway, as you might have guessed, that never happened. Instead, one day I go to a party with a group of friends. Marcus had told me he had to study for a big test and couldn't see me that night. I was a little down about it and thought maybe going to the party would cheer me up.

"Well, imagine my shock when I saw Marcus at the party with his arm around another girl. Worse, I heard him introduce her as his girlfriend!"

"Wow," I said, although I wasn't that surprised after all I had been learning about Marcus. "And he hadn't said anything to you about having a girlfriend?"

"Oh, it's even worse than that." She paused again, her mouth twisted in disgust. "When I was finally able to confront him during the party, he told me yes, Cherry was his girlfriend, but that didn't mean we couldn't still see each other. 'Nothing has to change,' he said."

"And that's exactly what happened," I concluded.

"I was such a fool," she whispered. "Even at the time, I knew it. But I was obsessed with him. I couldn't let him go. I was still convinced that someday, if I just hung on long enough, he would finally realize I was the one he loved, and he would break up with Cherry."

"Yeah, that's the problem with being young and in love. It's easy to become convinced you've found 'the one' when you really haven't."

A tiny smile touched her lips. "That's nice of you to say, but honestly, I don't deserve any kindness." She straightened her shoulders and took a deep breath. "It wasn't enough that I was simply sleeping with Marcus whenever he could get away. I also made a point of befriending Cherry. I was even the one who brought our group together. I didn't do it because I particularly liked Cherry, although it's hard to dislike her. I did it because I thought the more interactions I had with Marcus—especially social interactions at parties and out at dinner—the more opportunities he would have to fall in love with me."

"But you married Flynn," I said.

She nodded. "The night Marcus proposed to Cherry, I think a part of me knew it was over. I set to work convincing Flynn to propose to me. At the time, I had every intention of stopping the affair and moving on with my life. And at first, it worked. Until the night we went out as couples, and after dinner, Marcus and I wanted to go have a nightcap, but Cherry and Flynn wanted to call it a night. Cherry said, 'Oh, it's fine. You two can go catch up, and Flynn will take me home.' Well, you can imagine what happened.

"I told myself it was a onetime thing that would never happen again, but of course, that was a lie, too. We never stopped."

It was a far more sordid story than I had expected. I wondered if I was the first person she ever shared it with. The words were tumbling out of her, almost like she couldn't control them, and she was careful not to meet my eyes. "So, the night before Marcus was murdered. Why were you fighting?"

She took another deep breath, her shoulders trembling slightly. "I guess it doesn't matter if I say it now. I discovered that Marcus had gotten a job with the governor's office. It wasn't official. Nothing was announced."

"How did you find out?"

She shook her head. "It's not important. Redemption is a small town. And my job keeps me well-connected to what's going on." I suppose that made sense, seeing as how she was working for a vice president at the hospital. "Then, Cherry called me all excited about the surprise date she was having with Marcus … she was sure he was going to set a date. That was the tipping point.

"For two days, I tried calling Marcus, but he was never around. I left him messages he didn't return. I was completely irrational. I thought I was losing my mind. And it was so … shocking. My reaction. I didn't expect that. I truly thought I had come to terms with him marrying Cherry. I didn't think it would bother me at all when it finally happened.

"I had been completely fooling myself. If I was being even the slightest bit honest with myself, I would have known better. I would have known that the secret glee I felt every time Cherry came to me wanting a girl's night with lots of wine because Marcus wouldn't set a date meant I was nowhere near coming to terms with Marcus and Cherry actually tying the knot. Or how I was quietly hoping the real reason Marcus hadn't set a date with Cherry was because he was starting to realize he belonged with me, and he was trying to work out the specifics around how we could be together. But no, I hid all of that from myself and was happily living my delusion that everything was fine and dandy. I would be happy for Cherry and Marcus on their wedding day. Just like my delusion that it was somehow okay that I was sleeping with Marcus, even though I was married and Cherry's best friend. I kept telling myself that because Marcus and I had started our affair before either of us was with our significant others, it was somehow okay. Like we were grandfathered in, or something stupid like that.

"Anyway, I had gotten myself so wound up that night, there was no way talking to Marcus on the phone would suffice. I had to see him. So, I told my work I was sick and left early. I waited in the parking lot for Marcus to come home. I sat there for hours in the cold, getting more and more upset. When he finally showed up, I could no longer control myself."

"What was his response?"

She blew the air out of her mouth. "He was angry. He told me I was an idiot. What did I think was going to happen? That he was going to spend the rest of his life in Redemption, and we were going to keep seeing each other on the side? Did I not know him? Was I not listening to him all those years about all the goals and dreams he had? Forget Redemption … if all went according to plan, he would be living in Washington DC. How exactly did I think I would fit in when I would still be living in Redemption with Flynn?"

"Wow. That sounds … harsh," I said.

Her smile was twisted and sad. "That's one way of putting it."

"What did you do?"

She shrugged. "Went home, drank a bottle of wine, ate a pint of chocolate- caramel ice cream, and cried my eyes out. Flynn was working late, which was a good thing, as that would have been impossible to explain to him. By the time he got home, I was already tucked into bed, so he wouldn't see how puffy and red my face was." She paused a moment, and I could see tears in her eyes. "That was the last thing he said to me. I won't even repeat the last thing I said to him, as it … wasn't very nice. I'll regret it until the day I die."

She looked so forlorn, so sick with grief, it was impossible not to feel sorry for her. Even though in so many ways, the whole thing was a situation of her own making. The only way a toxic relationship with a narcissist could end is badly. If she hadn't been so busy lying to herself, she would have probably figured that out years ago and ended it herself. Instead, she doubled down and ended up doing things I suspect she never would have dreamed she would do.

But it wasn't my place to point any of that out. She was going to have to wrestle with her own conscience. What I needed to focus on was making sure the fallout of what she did didn't take either me or Cherry down with it.

"You still showed up at Cherry's apartment the morning after the murder, though," I said.

She nodded. "As you can imagine, I barely slept. I knew in my heart that whatever it was between Marcus and me was over. His cruelty the night before had ensured that. What I needed to do was to decide how to handle it. Was I going to blow up his life, and probably mine right along with it? Or graciously go into that dark night?" She bit her bottom lip, smudging her lipstick. "I guess at this point, it doesn't matter. I've already said more than I've ever told anyone. I'm sure you already think I'm a terrible person."

"I think you made some terrible choices," I said. "And as someone who has made her own terrible choices over the years, I'm not really in a position to judge."

She huffed out something that sounded like a chuckle, but it was too full of self-loathing to have any real humor in it. "Well, I wasn't done making those terrible choices. Even though I had more than 24 hours to stew about it, I hadn't made up my mind when I showed up that morning, coffee and muffins in hand. All I knew was I wanted Marcus to suffer, even if I didn't end up tearing his life apart, and I figured me standing in Cherry's apartment with the two of them, drinking coffee and eating muffins, while all the while he tried to figure out what my plan was, would at least give me some satisfaction." She shook her head, a disgusted expression on her face. "But as it turned out, the joke was on me." She looked up and stared directly into my eyes. "I didn't kill him. Did I do a lot of horrible things? Yes. Did I want revenge? Absolutely. I have a lot of things to atone for, but murder is not one of them. Do you believe me now?"

Even though she sounded sincere, I wasn't sure if I believed her or not. She definitely had motive, and she probably had means and opportunity, as well. What if she had showed up while Cherry was getting ready that evening with some innocent excuse, like she was dropping something off she had borrowed from Cherry? Or maybe with a special treat, like chocolate-covered strawberries? She could have easily slipped roofies into Cherry's tea … maybe she even offered to make Cherry a cup while she finished getting ready. Then, a couple of hours later, when she was sure the drug would have kicked in, she could have returned again with some other excuse and finished the job. Or maybe she never even left, just hid somewhere in that apartment. There weren't a lot of places to hide, but it was possible … and when the time was right, she snuck out and killed him.

It all seemed to fit—except for the killing Marcus with a pillow part. Lola was even more petite than Cherry. There was no way she could have overpowered him. And Marcus likely would have been even more on guard with her after their fight.

"I can see your point of view," I said, which didn't answer her question. "I am curious about what you did the night Marcus was killed, though. Other than try and decide if you were going to ruin his life or not."

"What do you think? More wine and more chocolate-caramel ice cream." She frowned slightly, thinking back. "Not as many tears, though. But I did plan a bunch of different scenarios as to the best way to get my revenge. Oh, and I made lists, too. Pros and cons."

I found it interesting she wrote all of that down. "Did you save those notes?"

"No, I burned them."

Probably for the best. But still, I wondered if any of those plans were about the perfect murder. "What about Flynn? Was he there?"

"Luckily, no. He was working late again."

I tilted my head, studying her. "Does he always work so late?"

"Not always. But often enough. That week in particular, he had a big case, so he worked late all week."

Interesting. Was it possible Flynn wasn't the innocent, injured spouse he portrayed himself to be after all?

At that moment, the stairway door burst open, revealing a woman as impeccably dressed as Lola. "Oh, there you are, Lola. Todd is looking for you." She studied me, one eyebrow raised. "Or are you still on break?" Even though it sounded innocent on the surface, the energy underneath was anything but. She reminded me of a hall monitor who wasn't happy unless she spotted an infraction she could report.

Lola seemed to feel that too, as she quickly straightened up, brushing a hand across her face. "Thank you, Beth. I'll be right there." Her tone was clipped and professional.

Beth stayed where she was, her eyes darting between us, no doubt looking for something she could use against Lola at some point.

"I'd appreciate you letting Todd know I'm on my way," Lola said.

Beth's eyes flickered toward Lola. "Of course," she said smoothly, before stepping back and letting the door close.

Lola ran her hands down the front of her clothes. "I have to go. Even though I know I have no right to ask, I hope you'll keep what I said to yourself." While her voice was still that of the competent executive assistant, there was a pleading underneath I couldn't ignore, even though a part of me wanted nothing more than to ask her what courtesy she showed me when she convinced Cherry to talk to a reporter. But I also now knew how much stress she had been under. The weight of all those bad decisions had obviously taken its toll on her. And if there was one thing I was familiar with, it was how one bad decision could sometimes beget more bad decisions. Sometimes, an avalanche of bad decisions.

"I'll do what I can," I said. "Although I can't make any promises. There is a murder that needs to be solved."

Her eyes darkened. "I understand. And I thank you for your discretion." She stepped around me to head to the stairway door.

"You may want to think about coming clean, no matter what I do or don't do," I said. She hesitated, one hand on the doorknob, but she didn't move it. "Not that you asked for my advice, but I can tell you that you're never going to be able to heal or put this behind you if you don't start owning up and taking responsibly for what you did."

A shiver went through her as she stood frozen in place. After a moment, she pulled open the door and walked through the threshold without another word or glance at me.

I waited a moment, just in case, but I didn't really expect her to come back. I also decided to take the stairs to the lobby. I had no doubt Beth was likely hovering on the other side of the door, just waiting to pounce if she saw me, and I had more important things to deal with than her.

Chapter 20

I found Billy behind City Hall, leaning against the wall. He was smoking a cigarette and brooding. His long, black coat flapped in the wind, and his face seemed to mirror the gray clouds overhead. "Billy Winthrop? I asked.

He jumped at the sound of his name and almost dropped his cigarette. He straightened up, tapped the ash off, and then looked me up and down. "Do I know you?"

"No. I'm Charlie Kingsley." I stuck my hand out.

He stared at it for a moment. He was tall and lanky with a sharp, angular face. He wasn't traditionally handsome, but there was something striking about him, even with the suspicious look that lingered on his face. Then, he quickly smoothed it out and shook my hand. "Hello, Charlie. Nice to meet you. May I ask how you found me out here?"

I waved a hand. "Lucky guess." In truth, after his secretary told me he was "indisposed at the moment," and as his office door was open behind her, I could see she was telling the truth. I then overhead one of the secretaries mention something about Billy being on another smoke break. "I was hoping you could answer a few questions for me about Marcus."

His eyes narrowed, and he looked me up and down again. "You a cop?"

"Not a cop."

"A journalist, then."

"Nope, not that either."

He sucked on his cigarette as he eyed me. "Why do you want to ask me questions about Marcus?"

I stuck my hands in the pockets of my coat. "Do you read the *Redemption Times*?"

He cocked his head. "I thought you said you weren't a journalist."

"I'm not. But there was an article about me in the paper, blaming my tea for Marcus's death."

Understanding flickered behind his eyes. "That's why your name sounded familiar."

"That's why I have questions. I'm trying to find who really killed Marcus."

"Oh, and you think it's me? Oh, no. You aren't going to pin this on me." He blew a mouthful of smoke in the air and moved to stub out his cigarette.

"I'm not trying to pin anything on you. I simply want to get to the bottom of what happened that day."

"How would I know what happened? I wasn't there."

"But you were in Marcus's office, right?"

He stopped putting his cigarette out and slowly turned to me, crossing his arms across his chest. "Who told you that? Was it the police?"

"Does it matter?"

A muscle twitched in his jaw. "I'll tell you what I told the police, which is I'm not in the habit of walking into my colleague's offices when they aren't there, and I certainly didn't touch any whisky bottle."

"*Have* you ever gone into Marcus's office?"

He twisted his mouth, like he had tasted something foul was about to spit it out. "From time to time. If I was dropping something off, like a memo or a file or a note that I didn't want anyone else to see, I'd go in and leave it on his desk. No big deal. We all do it."

"Did you do it these past couple of weeks?"

He stretched his arms to his side. "I have no idea. I can't remember every little thing I do. This is bull." He shook a finger at me. "I will not be the fall guy. Whoever is saying I did it is lying."

"You don't even know who it is or what they're saying about you."

"I know that whoever it is, they're trying to set me up for Marcus's murder. And it's not happening." He dropped his cigarette and started stomping on it.

"Who do you think killed Marcus, if it wasn't you?"

"I have no idea. I told you. I was nowhere near Cherry's apartment that night."

"You know where she lives?"

He glared at me. "Just stop it. No, I don't know where she lives, although I could probably find out if I wanted to. Which is something you would probably discover if you poked around enough. In a place like this," he jerked his head toward the building, "everyone knows everything about everyone. But there's something you ought to know, as well."

"What's that?"

He took a step closer to me. I could smell his aftershave, expensive and subtle. He was much taller than me, and I had to tilt my head to see his face. That gave me a clear view of the stubble on his chin, and I noted how he must be one of those men who needed to shave twice a day. "Everyone also lies."

I met his eyes. "Does that mean you're lying, too?"

His mouth tightened, and I got the distinct feeling he wanted to slap me. "It means you shouldn't believe anyone who works there. Take Marcus, for instance. He was supposed to have some big date with his fiancé the night he died, right?"

"That's right."

"Well, earlier that day, I overheard him in the break room. He was telling one of the new secretaries he'd been trying to bang for weeks that he couldn't meet her that evening because he had some big night out with the boys planned. But according to the paper, he was planning a big surprise date night with the fiancé. So, which was it?"

"Maybe he didn't want the secretary to know he had a fiancé?"

Billy laughed. "Of course she knew. Everyone knew about Cherry. It wasn't a secret. Just like it wasn't a secret that Marcus couldn't keep it in his pants."

"It doesn't matter if she knew or not. If you're trying to se-duce someone, you're not going to throw it in their face that you're already taken."

He cocked his head. "You may be right about that. But here's the thing: there's no question Marcus was a liar and a cheat. There's also no question that at least one person was lying about what happened that night. So the only question is, who was lying?"

* * *

"Lola did it," Tilde said decisively as she reached for another raspberry shortbread thumbprint cookie. Her third. I decided as Valentine's Day was two days away, I needed more cookies. Plus, I still had quite a bit of raspberry jam left, but I didn't feel like messing around with the heart-shaped cutouts, so shortbread thumbprint cookies were the perfect solution. "I always knew there was something off about her. I could feel it."

Pat gave her a bemused look as she fed Tiki a biscuit. We were back in my kitchen, cups of tea and cookies in front of us. I had just finished filling them in on my conversations with Flynn, Caleb, Lola, and Billy. Pat had already told Tilde about our visit to Sage's, as well. "Except Lola wanted Marcus for herself. If she killed him, she'd never have him."

"Yeah, but she knew she was never going to have him," Tilde said. "He made that clear when they argued. And if she couldn't have him, then no one could."

"I don't know," Pat said. "I can't see her suffocating him with a pillow. I don't think she'd have the stomach to go through with it. But Flynn, now that's another story."

"A man wouldn't smother someone with a pillow," Tilde said. "If he was going to kill Marcus, he would do something more manly."

"Manly?" I asked.

"Yes, like stab him or beat him up," Tilde said, gesturing wildly with her hands. "Something like that. Not just hold a pillow over his face." She rolled her eyes dramatically as she said it. She was dressed in an array of bright pinks and purples, which didn't match her hair any better than the last outfit I'd seen her in.

"Plus, it requires more strength than just poisoning someone," Pat agreed. "I don't see how Lola could physically smother Marcus. It wasn't like he was tied up or something."

"But Lola is the only one who makes sense," Tilde said stubbornly. "Why would Flynn kill him? Or, I should say, why would he kill him now? The only thing that had changed was that Marcus was leaving town. So wouldn't Flynn be happy about that?"

"Unless Flynn thought Lola was going to leave him and go with Marcus," Pat said.

Tilde popped a cookie into her mouth as she gave Pat an exasperated look. "Don't you think Lola would have said something to Flynn about leaving him before he ran off and killed Marcus?"

"She might have," Pat said. "But we don't know how the conversation went between the two of them. For that matter, we don't even know if there was a conversation about Marcus. We don't know who told Lola about Marcus leaving. It could have been Flynn, or it could have been someone else."

"No, all we seem to know is that Flynn wasn't home until late the night of the murder and the night before," I said. "If we believe Lola, that is," I added as Tilde rolled her eyes again. "But Tilde brings up a good point. Why kill Marcus now? What changed? Is it because Marcus had a new job in a different city? Who out of the group wouldn't want him to go?"

"Lola," Tilde said triumphantly. It was Pat's turn to roll her eyes.

"Flynn, too, depending on how he thought Lola was going to react," Pat said.

"What about Billy? Maybe he wanted the job in the governor's office," I said.

"You think he killed Marcus to get a job?" Tilde asked.

"I'm just saying it's a possibility. People have killed for less," I said. "If Billy is as ambitious as Caleb said he is, it's certainly possible."

"Plus, we don't know how mentally stable Billy is," Pat added. "Based on what you said, Charlie, he sounded a little paranoid. If that's the case, he absolutely could be the killer."

"He did sound paranoid," I agreed. "Although, what's that old saying? 'Just because you're paranoid doesn't mean they aren't out to get you.' It's possible that Marcus was actively sabotaging him, as well."

"So, maybe he decided it would be a good time to just get rid of the problem," Pat said. "And as an added benefit, he would get the job."

Tilde shook her head furiously, orange-red strands flying around her head. "I don't see it. Whoever did this knows Cherry and Marcus. It has to be someone close to them both."

"Well, if that's the case, what about Sage or Caleb?" I asked. "We didn't talk about them."

"Why would Caleb kill Marcus?" Tilde asked. "Marcus was his meal ticket, right? Marcus gets promoted; Caleb gets promoted, too. Why would he jeopardize that?"

"Maybe because he's sick of living in Marcus's shadow," Pat said.

I thought about Caleb and how his and Marcus's lives were so intertwined. It was possible he was jealous and wanted to be free of him, but something about that didn't seem right. When he talked about Marcus's rising stardom, it was almost in an off-hand tone of voice, like it wasn't a big deal. I was about to say something when the doorbell rang.

Tilde had her mouth open and a fourth cookie on its way in when she paused. "Are you expecting anyone?" Pat looked at me with an inquiring expression, as well.

"No, I'm not," I said, getting up from the table. "Maybe it's a tea customer or a potential customer." Although even as I said it, I could feel my stomach sinking. Since the newspaper article had come out, the only calls I'd received had been from customers wanting an explanation about the article. No one had canceled their orders yet or told me they didn't want to be a customer anymore, but it also seemed like that was only because they were waiting to see what was going to happen. It felt like my entire tea business was collectively holding its breath, just waiting for the outcome.

I couldn't solve this case fast enough.

But it wasn't a current or prospective customer at the door. It was Wyle.

"Do you have a moment?" he asked, his expression flat. My stomach seemed to sink even further. I just knew it wasn't good news.

"What's going on?"

"You might want to sit down," he said.

I found I was having trouble swallowing. "Why don't you come in and join us?" I managed to get out, holding the door open wider.

"Us?" he asked, raising his eyebrow as he stepped inside. "Is Pat here?"

"Yes, and Tilde Tillerson."

Wyle stared at me. "Who?"

"You know. The owner of the Redemption Detective Agency."

"The *what*?"

"What, you mean to tell me you haven't heard of the Redemption Detective Agency?"

Wyle's face went dark. "Charlie, what did you do?"

"I didn't do anything! She came to me."

"Charlie, who was at the door ... oh, hi Wyle," Pat said. "Come on in. There's plenty of tea and cookies. I'll get you a cup. I hope you have an update for us."

Wyle shot me a look. "Charlie, I swear ..." he muttered as he followed me into the kitchen.

Tilde was still sitting at the table with Tiki on her lap as Pat bustled around the kitchen, getting another cup and a plate. "Go on, Wyle. Grab a seat. Make yourself at home."

"I don't think there are enough chairs," Wyle said, glancing around before settling his gaze on Midnight, who was napping in his favorite chair. Midnight, for his part, did not seem inclined to move.

"There's another chair in the family room. I'll grab it," I said. Even though I was dying to know what Wyle had come to tell me, I also welcomed the chance to collect myself. *Deep breaths*, I told myself as I collected the chair and dragged it back to the kitchen.

Pat and Tilde had already rearranged the butcher-block table to make room for Wyle. Tilde was also busy introducing herself and telling Wyle how I was her inspiration and the reason why she had decided to take up sleuthing in her retirement.

"Oh, is she?" Wyle asked, his eyes boring into mine.

"You can never have too many sleuths, especially in Redemption," Tilde said in her cheery voice.

Wyle's eyes bulged in disbelief.

I smiled sweetly and made a point of pulling my chair out, making as much noise as possible before Wyle could start lecturing Tilde on the perils of being an amateur sleuth and getting in the way of professionals. "Wyle has some news he'd like to share. Wyle, do you want to have a seat?"

"Oh, that's wonderful," Pat said. "Hopefully, it's to tell us you've got a different suspect than Cherry."

"It's Lola," Tilde said, patting his hand.

Wyle looked like he might choke. "Lola? Cherry's friend?"

"Oh yes. Trust us. She's the one." Tilde winked at him.

"Wyle, maybe you should start by telling us your news," I said quickly. The last thing I wanted was Wyle distracted and insisting we tell him what we know before sharing his news with us.

Wyle took a deep breath. "Well, yes. We do have another suspect we're investigating." His eyes bored into mine, and I started to get a very bad feeling.

"About time," Pat said. "Who?"

He paused, but I was already bracing myself for what I was sure was going to come out of his mouth.

"You."

Chapter 21

"Charlie?" Pat's voice was incredulous as she stared at Wyle. "Are you serious? I thought we were done with this nonsense."

"I wish we were," Wyle said.

"It's not Charlie," Tilde announced, her voice confident. "Trust me on this."

"What changed?" I asked. I was feeling calmer than I thought I would. Now that I had heard the worst, it was almost a relief.

"We got the toxicology report back on Marcus," Wyle said.

"And?"

Wyle sighed. "He had roofies in his system."

I was floored. "Marcus was drinking my tea?"

"It wasn't your tea," Wyle said. "At least, that's not what it looks like. We found traces of roofies in the bottom of one of the wineglasses."

"But ..." I was having trouble fitting the pieces together. "How am I more of a suspect, then? I didn't give them any wine."

Wyle inclined his head as he reached for a cookie. "And that's why you're not at the police station right now."

"But I don't understand. Why should I be a suspect at all?"

Wyle held the cookie but didn't eat it. "It's highly irregular that both Marcus and Cherry would have been drugged with roofies. Normally, it would be one or the other. So the fact that they were both drugged is puzzling. Was one of them an accident? Like was Cherry the target, but Marcus accidentally drugged himself? Seems unlikely, but stranger things have happened. Maybe he wasn't paying attention and drank out of the wrong glass. But Marcus was the one who was murdered, so that theory doesn't make sense. That leaves Cherry. And we only have Cherry's word that she doesn't remember that night."

"Didn't you test her for roofies?"

He shook his head. "We did, but it was inconclusive. So, we have her statement about not remembering what happened, and we have traces of roofies in the tea you gave her as well as in the wine glass. Did she drug Marcus and then the tea, so she could pretend they were both drugged that night? It's possible, and that's one very strong theory going around the station."

I closed my eyes briefly. "Poor Cherry."

"A third possibility is that someone else drugged both of them," Wyle continued. "That would explain the roofies being in the tea and in the wine. Plus, it's the perfect crime, in a lot of ways. Cherry doesn't remember, so she can't be a good witness, and Marcus would be incapacitated, making it easy to smother him. It's perfect. And because they found roofies in the tea you made, you become the obvious suspect."

"But … why would I do such a thing?" I asked. "I didn't even know Marcus."

Wyle looked truly unhappy. "It's true that no one has figured out a motive, which is another reason you're sitting here and not in the station. But I did hear a few whispers that it might be because you're really some sort of dark witch, channeling the shadow side of Redemption … and you killed Marcus as a sacrifice."

"*What*?" I yelped.

"I told you," Pat said, shaking her head. "All that talk about the tea being cursed was not going to end well."

"This is ridiculous," I said.

"It IS ridiculous," Wyle agreed. "And if it was anyone else besides you, I don't think anyone in the department would be floating such an absurd theory."

"So it's personal," I said.

"I knew it," Pat interjected again, eying me as she reached for a cookie. "You've made some powerful enemies."

"Well, yeah," Wyle said. "But we knew this."

Tilde was watching all of us intently. "I don't understand. How did you make powerful enemies?"

"Because she keeps investigating crimes instead of leaving it to the professionals," Wyle said, giving Tilde a hard look.

Tilde looked confused. "Is that bad?"

Wyle stared at the ceiling. "Yes, it's bad. The professionals have been trained. Civilians like you and Charlie haven't. Not only is it possible you could mess something up, but it's dangerous."

Tilde still looked confused. "But there are so many unsolved crimes in Redemption. No offense, but it seems to me that the police need all the help they can get."

I looked down to hide my grin.

"That may be true," Wyle said with less heat. "But that doesn't stop people from being embarrassed."

"Ohhh," Tilde breathed.

"So, what are we going to do?" I asked. "How can we stop this?"

Wyle sighed and ran a hand through his hair. "Well, I think we need to figure out who killed Marcus as quickly as possible …" he paused and gave me a look. "And it could very well have been Cherry."

I bit my lip and looked down again.

"But we don't have to go there yet. Let's talk about what you've uncovered these past couple of days and why …" here, he gave Tilde a hard look, "you think Lola is the killer."

"Well, because she's guilty, that's why," Tilde said, as if it should be obvious.

I held out a hand. "Hold on. Let me tell you what's been going on. I've got a lot to share." I filled him in as succinctly as I could, even with Tilde, and then Pat, throwing in their two cents. Wyle, for his part, quietly listened as he took notes, ate a couple of cookies, and drank a little tea.

"Now do you see why we think it's Lola?" Tilde asked when I was more or less finished.

"Flynn is a possibility, as well," Pat added. "Although now that I know Marcus was also drugged, it seems more probable that he could have been killed by a woman."

"What about Billy?" I asked Wyle. "Did you look into him?"

"It wasn't Billy," Wyle said. "He has an alibi for that night. I suppose it's not out of the range of possibilities that he paid someone to do it, but this feels more … personal, to me. It doesn't feel like a crime committed by an angry boyfriend or a jealous political rival. Whoever did it knew both Cherry and Marcus intimately. They knew that Cherry didn't drink a commercial-brand tea from the grocery store, but that she ordered a special blend from Charlie, which meant they could throw suspicion on Charlie. That wouldn't have worked with a store-bought brand. They also knew about the surprise date and where Cherry lived, and presumably, how to get into Cherry's apartment without it looking like a break-in. None of that points to someone who was just after Marcus."

"That fits Lola to a T," Tilde insisted.

"Yes, it does, but not just her," I said. "There's also Sage, Caleb, and Flynn."

Tilde made a face. "Those three didn't fight with Lola a day before the murder."

"That you know of," Pat said. "The only reason we know about Lola's fight is because she had an audience. The other three could have been more discreet."

"Maybe they weren't as upset with Marcus as Lola was," Tilde said.

"Actually, Tilde has a point," I said. I had been sitting there mulling about all the pieces that didn't quite fit together, but when Tilde said that, it was like a lightbulb went off. "This really does seem like the definition of a crime of passion." I started ticking things off with my fingers. "It took place a couple of weeks before Valentine's Day; it happened on what was supposed to be a super- romantic surprise date night; the living room was trashed, indicating a huge fight took place in it; the drug that was found in Marcus's and Cherry's system is called 'the date-rape drug,' and all the suspects loved someone who didn't love them back. Plus, let's not forget about the elusive chocolate-dipped strawberries and rose."

"There's no evidence the strawberries or rose even existed," Wyle said.

"There's also no evidence that roofies cause hallucinations like Cherry described," I said. "Typically, when someone has been roofied, they don't have any memories at all. But Cherry has a distinct, specific memory of receiving that package before she blacked out. I suppose it's possible she had something other than roofies in her system, which might cause something like that to happen, but if she were hallucinating, it feels like she would have hallucinated a lot more than receiving a package."

Wyle shifted to sit back in his chair. "So, you think whoever left that package took those items away with them?"

"I think it's the only thing that makes sense," I said. "So, imagine the killer knows that Cherry loves chocolate-covered strawberries. It's her favorite dessert, so they're pretty confident she'll indulge and have one or two immediately. And they also know that romantic surprises of that nature are right up Marcus's alley, so Cherry wouldn't have any issue believing they were from Marcus. The drugs were actually put in the strawberries, not my tea. And later that night, along with cleaning up any traces of the package, they also added the drug to my tea, so the cops would assume I was the one who roofied her."

"Hmm, that could work," Wyle said. "It would also explain why the vase was in the wrong cupboard, as well."

"Exactly. They knew Cherry kept it in the kitchen, but not where."

"But how does Marcus fit in?" Pat asked.

"Well, again, if it was someone close to both of them, maybe they timed their arrival with Marcus's," I said. "They knew that Cherry would be acting drunk with the drugs in her system, so maybe they made up a story that Cherry called them to come over. Marcus would surely be disappointed, as whatever he had planned would have been a bust. So maybe the killer offered to have a drink with him at Cherry's apartment as a sort of consolation. In that case, you can probably guess the rest."

Wyle was nodding. "It's a decent theory."

"Hold on," Pat said. "I want to go back to what you said about all of them being in love with someone who doesn't love them back. Lola was, obviously. And so was Flynn. He loved his wife, who didn't love him back. But what about Caleb?"

I thought back to Caleb's face when he talked about Cherry. "I think Caleb is in love with Cherry. If he's not, he certainly cares for her deeply. A little too deeply, in my opinion, for friendship."

"If that's the case, maybe it *was* Caleb," Pat said, reaching for a biscuit to feed Tiki. "Maybe he thought if he got Marcus out of the way, Cherry would fall in love with him."

Tilde gave Pat an exasperated expression. "But why would he kill Marcus at Cherry's apartment? He would be effectively framing the woman he loves for a murder she didn't do."

"Maybe he wanted to punish her for not seeing Marcus for who he really was," Pat said.

"That's quite a punishment," Wyle said.

"Or maybe something went wrong," Pat reconsidered. "Maybe Marcus was never supposed to show up at Cherry's apartment, and Caleb drugging Cherry was meant to protect her. But wires got crossed, and Marcus arrived at the wrong time, so Caleb had to improvise."

"It's possible," Wyle said.

"So the only one left is Sage," Tilde said. "And she doesn't seem to be in love with anyone."

I thought back to Sage in her lonely apartment with her takeout pizza and wine. "Actually, I would argue that Sage was also in love with Marcus."

"Why would you say that?" Pat asked. "She seems to be the only one who gets that the only person Marcus loved was himself."

"Yet she continued to sleep with him," I said. "Was the sex really that good? Or was it because she was also secretly in love with him?"

"That's a good question," Pat said thoughtfully. "She also rented an apartment in the same complex he lived in."

"Exactly. From the outside, it sure seems like she built her life around her relationship with Marcus. Including not getting involved with anyone else."

"Unlike Lola," Pat said. "But why would she kill Marcus? The same reason as Lola? If she couldn't have him, no one could?"

"If Marcus left Redemption, she would really have no one," I said. "Her only friends are Cherry, Lola, Flynn, and Marcus. If Marcus moved, and let's say he was planning on asking Cherry to go with him, and it seemed Caleb would likely follow him, where would that leave Sage? Flynn works all the time, so it's not like she's going to hang out with him, which would only leave Lola. And I don't get the feeling that Sage and Lola are exactly bosom buddies. Cherry seems to be the glue in that threesome, so if she left, it would likely all fall apart."

"So, she really could have felt like Marcus owed her," Pat said.

"Plus, we don't know where Marcus was the night before he was killed," I said. "After he fought with Lola, it's possible he went to Sage's. Maybe he wanted to complain about Lola to someone, and he knew Sage would be an understanding audience. But maybe that time, she wasn't so understanding."

"Yes, because it finally sunk in that Marcus was never going to marry her, either," Pat concluded.

"Right. She could have decided that enough was enough, and Marcus needed to pay," I said.

Wyle tapped his notebook with his pen. "The problem with this whole case is that it's all circumstantial. Without a confession, I don't see how we're going to figure out which one of them is behind it."

"Well, I have an idea about how we can get a confession," I said. "But first, there's someone I need to talk to."

Chapter 22

It was already starting to get dark when Cherry emerged from the travel agency. Her head was down, so she didn't see me right away, and the wind blew her reddish-golden curls that seemed duller than normal around her head.

As she came closer, I was shocked by the change I saw in her. She had definitely lost weight. Even though I would never have called her "fat," she had been on the curvy side. But now, her curves were gone, and her clothes hung awkwardly on her. Under her makeup, which looked like it had been carelessly applied, her skin was as gray as the weather.

She had almost reached her car when she finally noticed me. Her eyes went round, and she stumbled. "You shouldn't be here," she said, her eyes darting around the half-empty parking lot. "My lawyer said I shouldn't talk to you."

I bit back a retort against her lawyer. "You know I didn't do this," I said instead.

"But you did," she threw back. "You put roofies in the tea you made me. The police found it."

"Just because they found it doesn't mean I put it there."

Her look was skeptical. "Then who did?"

"That's what we have to figure out," I said. "I know I didn't do it. I know you didn't do it. That's why we need to come together … to figure out who did."

Cherry hadn't moved, but a strange expression drifted over her face, and for a moment, I thought she might cry. "You don't know that."

"Of course I know that," I said. "And you must know it, too. We're both being framed."

She shook her head violently, her hair whipping around her face. "No. That's not true."

"What isn't true?"

She didn't answer, just kept staring at me with that squished-up face that looked like she was holding back tears. "I don't know it." Her voice was a whisper.

I wanted to throttle her lawyer. Or Lola. Or both of them. They really did a number on her about me. "Cherry, you *know* me," I said urgently. "I've been making you tea for months now. Why would I suddenly put roofies in it? And for what reason? I didn't even know Marcus. I had never met him before. Why would I do such a thing?"

She kept shaking her head. "I … I … I can't."

Something clicked inside me, and I took a step closer to her. "Cherry … are you saying you think you were the one who killed Marcus?"

At that, a couple of drops spilled out of her eyes, her tears finally overflowing inside her. "I don't remember. Don't you see? Maybe the roofies caused me to … go crazy, or something. And maybe I did kill him."

I took another step toward her. "Cherry, you did not do this." My voice was confident.

She blinked her eyes quickly, her mascara running down her face. "How can you possibly know that? You weren't there, and I can't remember. How can anyone know?" She flapped her arms helplessly.

"I know because I also know I was not the one who put the roofies in your tea," I said. "Which means someone else was in your apartment and drugged it to make it look like I did it. Unless you did it yourself?"

She gave me a confused look. "No, of course not. I don't even know where to get roofies."

"Well, I don't either. So, if you didn't do it, and I didn't do it, someone else did, which means someone else killed Marcus, too. We need to put our heads together to figure out who it was before one or both of us ends up in jail… or worse."

Cherry bit her lip, thinking about what I said. "But I just don't understand. Who would want Marcus dead?"

I stamped my feet on the concrete. I had been standing outside for a while at that point, and the cold was starting to seep into my clothes and shoes. "Can we sit in your car and talk about it? It's kind of freezing out here. Not to mention it's getting dark."

She hesitated, her eyes darting around the parking lot one more time, though it seemed to finally sink in how dark and cold it actually was. "Okay. For a few minutes."

"Great," I sighed and hurried around to the passenger side of her car as she unlocked the doors.

It wasn't much warmer in her car, but at least we were out of the wind, and that helped. Cherry put the key in the ignition but didn't turn the car on. "Who would want Marcus dead?" she asked again. "Everyone loved him."

I took a deep breath. "Cherry, you have to know that isn't true."

Her face jerked toward me. Even though it was dark in the car, my eyes had adjusted, and since we were in closer proximity, I could see how bad her makeup was. Along with the mascara trailing down her cheeks like some sort of sad clown, her eyeshadow had creased in the folds, and her lipstick was mostly gone. "What are you talking about? How dare you say such a thing. Marcus is dead! You shouldn't speak ill of the dead."

"Cherry," I said as gently as I could. "Believe me, I'm very sorry about Marcus. And I'm sorry you have to go through this. But you must know that there were … things happening that aren't being talked about."

"That's a lie," Cherry said, but her voice was almost a whisper. Her hands, which were in her lap, were clenched into tight fists. "No one is hiding anything from me. They're my friends. They wouldn't do that to me."

"I'm so sorry," I said sadly.

She turned her head and stared down at her clenched fists. Her knuckles had turned white. "I don't believe it. I can't believe it. If you didn't do it, and you're saying I didn't, then it must have been a stranger. Someone broke into the apartment that night. Marcus and I just had the bad luck to be there when it happened. That's all this was. Horrible, rotten luck."

I didn't say anything. Cherry kept staring at her fists as she rocked slightly back and forth, her lips moving, but no sound escaping them.

Finally, I put a hand on her knee. "I've got an idea. What if we created a test to see if your friends are being as honest with you as you are with them?"

She didn't look at me, but she stopped rocking. "How can we do that?"

"You're back in your apartment, right?"

She nodded.

"Okay, so this is what we'll do …"

Chapter 23

I stood in Cherry's tiny kitchen, putting the finishing touches on an appetizer platter filled with a variety of cheeses, sausage, olives, grapes, and crackers. Another plate was filled with my raspberry thumbprint cookies. Bottles of red wine lined the counter like little soldiers. A red tablecloth lay on the table along with heart-shaped plates and napkins. Six chairs were crammed around the table.

"I don't know about this," Cherry said, wringing her hands and pacing, which was basically what she had been doing since I had arrived an hour before. I was the one to set everything up and decorated as she muttered to herself and circled her apartment. "What if it doesn't work?"

"Then I'll admit to you that you were right, and I was wrong," I said.

She stopped in her tracks. "But what about my relationships? They're going to know that not only did I not trust them, but I thought they might be capable of killing Marcus!" She wrung her hands more fiercely than before. Her manicure, which had been so perfect the day of her romantic date, was chipped and peeling. Her makeup was also not as perfect as it had been that fateful day, but it was better than it was when I met her in the parking lot a couple of days ago. She was still too thin, but at least she had taken a shower and was dressed in a clean pair of jeans and red sweater.

I stepped toward her and took one of her hands in mine. It was ice cold, and I could feel her trembling. "Look, if anyone is angry with you about this, you can blame it all on me, okay? You can tell them I took advantage of you. Or, if you really want, you can tell them I drugged you again."

She stopped fussing and stared at me, her mouth dropping open slightly. "You'd let them think that? For me?"

I nodded gravely. "Cherry, I'm not here to hurt you. I want to help you, and yes, help myself. But if this ends up backfiring,

I'll do whatever I have to in order to take the brunt of it instead of you."

The tension in her shoulders started to relax, and her expression began to soften. She took a deep, shuddering breath.

The doorbell rang, causing her to jump. I gave her hand another squeeze. "You got this. I know you do."

She bit her lip as her eyes gazed into mine. She must have seen something there that bolstered her, because she straightened up, took another deep breath, and turned to answer the door.

I went back to the kitchen to lean against the stove and listened as Cherry greeted her guests and invited them to the kitchen. "I brought wine," Lola said, her voice floating in from the living room. "You know, you really didn't need to do this at your apartment. I would have been happy to host at my place."

"No, it's better I do it here," Cherry said. "I need to lay some ghosts to rest."

Lola appeared first. "Wow, this is lovely, Cherry. You didn't need to do all of this." She turned toward the row of wine bottles, saw me, and froze.

Sage, who was right behind her, almost crashed into her. "Lola, what gives?" she asked crossly before seeing the reason Lola had stopped. One eyebrow went up as she first regarded me, then Cherry.

"You both remember Charlie, right?" Cherry asked.

All the blood instantly drained from Lola's face. "What is she doing here?"

I smiled pleasantly. "Hi Lola, Sage. It's nice to see you both. And Happy Valentine's Day."

The doorbell rang, and Cherry disappeared to answer it. Lola still hadn't moved, but her eyes narrowed. "What game are you playing?"

I shrugged. "Why would I be playing a game? It's Valentine's Day, and Cherry needs some closure, which I'm sure you can understand."

"Where's the wine?" Flynn asked, strolling into the kitchen. As soon as he saw us, a hesitant look appeared on his face. "Uh …"

"We're leaving," Lola said decisively, spinning around on her heel and beginning to march out of the kitchen.

"Lola, no," Cherry said, her face ashen.

"Are you walking?" Sage asked, picking up one of the bottles and the opener. "Because I have the keys."

Lola spun back around, glaring at everyone. "Well, come on."

Sage shook her head and started to uncork the bottle. "I'd like to hear what Charlie has to say. After all, we made her life a living hell. The least we can do is hear her out."

"What?" Lola practically screeched. "We didn't do anything. She's the one who put roofies in Cherry's tea."

Sage uncorked the bottle with a pop and started pouring. "Sure. Because it makes such good business sense to roofie your customers."

Lola whirled back around and confronted Flynn. "Flynn. Let's go."

"But I just got here," he said. "I took off early because Cherry said it was important."

"It IS important," Cherry said. "And I'd very much like you to stay."

Lola moved toward Cherry. "Cherry, she's filled your mind with poison," she hissed. "She's a witch. We've talked about this."

Cherry glanced at me, then away. I could see her chest heaving, and for a moment, I thought she was going to buckle and ask me to leave. Instead, she raised her head and met Lola's eyes. "The thing is, I have some of the same questions Charlie has. I think it would be good for us, for all of us, to sit down and talk. We owe it to Marcus."

Lola's mouth dropped open in shock. After a moment, she tried to speak, but no sound came out.

"Lola, why are you making such a big deal out of this?" Flynn asked, accepting the glass of wine that Sage handed him. "You have nothing to hide, right?" His tone was mild, but was it my imagination, or was there an edge to it?

Lola turned her head to stare at him, a haunted expression on her face. She looked like a predator that had just been backed into a corner and was coming to the realization that the only way out was to fight. Maybe to the death.

The doorbell rang again, and Cherry trotted off to answer. Wordlessly, Sage handed Lola a glass of wine.

"Oh, I guess I'm the last one," Caleb said as he stepped into the kitchen. He cocked his head, a puzzled expression on his face as he stared at everyone before his gaze finally fell on me. "Oh," was all he said.

Sage handed him a glass of wine.

"You shouldn't drink it," Lola advised as everyone turned to her. She pointed at me. "She probably drugged it." I tried hard not to roll my eyes.

"You saw me open the bottle, Lola," Sage said.

"She still might have," Lola insisted.

"I was right here the entire time. She didn't do anything," Cherry said.

"Oh please," Sage said as she tipped the glass back into her mouth. She swallowed and looked at Lola. "Happy? I'll be the test case. You can all see if I keel over or something."

"Fine, your funeral," Lola muttered as Flynn also took a drink. Lola shot him an icy look.

"Shall we sit?" Cherry asked, gesturing toward the table. Everyone made their way over, including me, with the two platters of food to place in the middle of the table. Sage grabbed a couple more bottles of wine.

"Thanks for coming," Cherry said once everyone had been seated and was eyeing each other awkwardly. "So, I'm sure you already saw the paper and have some idea as to why Charlie is here."

"Actually, I'd like to better understand that. Why *is* she here?" Lola asked. "She drugged you, Cherry. Why would you possibly allow her into your home? Not to mention to prepare food for us." She waved a hand toward the platters.

"Oh for Pete's sake," Sage muttered as she took another sip of wine.

Cherry visibly tensed and opened her mouth to speak, but I raised a hand to stop her.

"That's a great question, and I'm sure Lola isn't the only one thinking it." I smiled pleasantly as I looked around the table. "You see, there's been some interesting developments over the past few days, and I thought … well, Cherry and I thought, that you all might be able to shed some light on them."

"Us?" Lola looked at me like I had grown two heads. "How would we be able to shed any light on what happened? None of us were there."

"I can understand your confusion," I said. "Especially since I also wasn't there, and Cherry was unconscious. That's why we were hoping we could do some group brainstorming about what you all think might have happened. After all, the five of you not only knew Marcus the best but also Cherry, so if anyone might have ideas, it would be all of you."

"Makes sense to me," Sage said before Lola could answer. "I'd like to hear about the new developments."

"So would I," Flynn said as Caleb nodded. Lola had a grouchy look on her face, but I could see even she was leaning in.

"Great," I said. "So, you probably all saw that roofies were found in the tea I made for Cherry." I looked around the table as everyone nodded. "What you might not have heard is that Cherry did not test positive for roofies; her test was inconclusive. Of course, her symptoms seem to indicate she actually *was* drugged, even if the test didn't prove it."

"So what?" Lola said. "I was told that it's not that unusual to have an inconclusive test."

"That's true," I said. "But what IS unusual is that Marcus also tested positive for roofies."

There was silence as everyone processed that information. "Are you saying that Marcus drank your tea, as well?" Flynn asked.

"No. Well, he might have," I corrected myself. "Again, I wasn't there, so I don't know. But the police found traces of roofies in a wine glass, too. So, it would appear that it was the glass of wine that did it."

Another silence, this one longer. "So, you're saying both Marcus and Cherry were drugged with roofies that night?" Sage asked.

"That's exactly what I'm saying. And it actually makes sense, considering how Marcus was killed. He was smothered with a pillow, which would have been very difficult to do if he wasn't significantly impaired." I looked at Lola as I said it, and she blanched.

"What are you implying?" she snapped.

I held up my hands. "I'm not implying anything. Other than it would be far easier to smother someone who was as fit as Marcus if he was drugged. I suspect even a woman could have done it."

Lola slammed a hand against the table. "Are you accusing me?"

I held up my hands. "I'm just stating the facts, is all."

Lola's eyes glittered. "It sounds like you're insinuating a lot more."

"Lola, that's enough," Flynn said. Lola's head jerked up, and she glowered at him.

Sage seemed to be thinking through what I said. "So, if both Marcus and Cherry were roofied that night … I don't understand. How does that happen? And who killed Marcus?"

"Excellent questions," I said. "Because you're right … why would anyone roofie themselves? It's called the 'date rape drug' for a reason. So, let's just say that Cherry had a cup of tea before Marcus got here, which she remembers doing, right?" Cherry nodded. "And let's say, for argument's sake, that my tea was laced with roofies. The drug would have been in her system by the time Marcus arrived. This much is consistent with Cherry's story, because she doesn't remember Marcus arriving. So, if this was the case, when Marcus showed up, she would have appeared to be completely inebriated … drunk out of her mind. Which begs the question, how did Marcus get roofied? Did he pour himself a glass of wine and drink it while Cherry stumbled around him? And who would want to roofie them?"

"It must have been you," Lola accused, her voice cracking slightly. "You roofied the tea, so you must have roofied the wine, too." Her tone sounded a lot less sure than her words. I also noticed she must have gotten over her fear of my messing with her wine, as she was drinking it.

"So, let's talk about that," I said. "But first, let's talk about the timing, because I think that's important. Cherry called me the morning of her big date. I didn't even know about the date until she showed up to pick up the tea, but let's put that aside for a moment. She called me that morning in a panic because she realized the night before that she was almost out of tea. She apologized for the late notice and asked if I wouldn't mind whipping her up a batch that she would pick up that afternoon. Right, Cherry?" I turned to her.

"Right," Cherry said. "In fact, it was a little weird, because I was sure I had a lot more tea left than what was there, and I couldn't figure out where it had gone. I thought maybe I had spilled the bag without realizing it."

"So, I went to work making her a batch," I continued, "and according to the cops, I decided to add some roofie to this batch, even though I had never done anything like that before nor could the cops find any of that drug in my house. But we can set all of that aside for now, too. So, Cherry picks up her tea and tells me about her big date, and that's when I make the decision to somehow slip into Cherry's apartment and add roofies to a bottle of wine, too, that Marcus would decide to drink, by himself, in his fiancé's apartment while his fiancé is basically incapacitated. And then, once he was also adequately drugged, I could smother him."

The story was ridiculous, and I knew even Lola couldn't deny it.

"Okay, so what do you think happened then?" Flynn asked. "Obviously, someone must have slipped the roofies into both the tea and the wine. And it seems like a huge stretch for it to have been two different people. But who would have done that?"

"That's the question of the hour," I said. "But before we go there, there's one other detail I think you should all know." I leaned forward slightly. "My tea wasn't the only thing Cherry consumed that night before Marcus showed up."

I paused and looked around the table. The others were also leaning forward intently. I noticed they seemed to have all forgotten about their wine in front of them.

"About an hour or so before Marcus was supposed to arrive, a package was delivered. It was just left on the doorstep, but Cherry assumed it was from Marcus."

"What was in it?" Sage asked.

"A single red rose and a box of chocolate-dipped strawberries," I answered.

"Wow," Sage said. "That was very romantic."

"It was. And that's what Cherry thought, too. Which is why she had one."

"Actually, I had more than one," Cherry clarified. "I had either two or three; I can't remember. But it was definitely more than one."

Sage was looking between us, a confused expression on her face. "I don't understand. What happened to the chocolate-dipped strawberries? I haven't heard that mentioned anywhere."

"That's because the police didn't find them," I said. "There was no trace of any chocolate-dipped strawberries anywhere in the apartment."

"Or the rose, either," Cherry said.

Sage looked even more confused. "Then why are we talking about chocolate-dipped strawberries?"

"Ah … because as it turns out, there WAS a chocolate-dipped strawberry still in the apartment."

"It was in the bedroom," Cherry said, her voice apologetic. "All of you know how much of a slob I am. So, I ate a couple. I'm pretty sure I ate two in the kitchen and then took a third with me to the bedroom, so I could finish getting ready. But it's also possible that I took the second one into the bedroom."

Lola put her hands against her temple and shook her head. "Oh, for goodness' sake. What does it matter if you had two or three? Or if you took one into the bedroom with you or not?"

"Because she didn't finish it," I said.

Cherry nodded. "Yeah, they found it under the dresser. Half of one strawberry. I must have passed out and dropped it."

Silence again, as the pieces began falling into place.

"And wouldn't you know it?" I smiled sweetly. "There was enough strawberry left for them to test. And it tested positive for roofies."

This time, the silence was like a taut wire stretched nearly to the breaking point. "So, what are you saying?" Flynn finally asked. "That the person who sent the chocolate-dipped strawberries is the one who killed Marcus?"

"I'm saying that someone delivered Cherry chocolate-dipped strawberries that were tainted with roofies, knowing she would eat at least one before Marcus showed up. Then, once they knew the drug was taking effect, they either let themselves into the apartment to be there when Marcus arrived—in which case, I'm guessing they pretended Cherry called them to come over— or they simply met Marcus outside, using the same excuse. Either way, once Cherry was taken care of, maybe tucked safely into bed, that same person offered to have a drink with Marcus. Like a small consolation, as he was supposed to have this hot date with Cherry that obviously couldn't happen. Marcus accepted, and that person then had the opportunity to slip some roofie into his wine, as well. You can guess the rest."

The others had started edging away from the table, almost like they were unconsciously trying to distance themselves from the rest. "If that's what happened, then that would mean one of us killed Marcus," Flynn said slowly.

"Precisely," I nodded. "That's exactly my thought. It would have to be someone who knew how much Cherry loved chocolate-dipped strawberries and who Marcus would feel comfortable enough to have a glass of wine with in Cherry's apartment … someone who Marcus wouldn't be surprised Cherry might have called."

"But why would any of us do that?" Sage asked.

"The why is trickier, I agree," I said. "Especially now, as all of you have been friends for a long time. So what recently changed? Only one thing that I know of … Marcus got a job with the governor's office and was going to be moving soon."

"But," Sage still looked bewildered, "why would one of us kill Marcus because he was moving away?"

"I suspect because that move would cause a relationship to change dramatically," I said. "Each of you had a … special relationship with Marcus. And some of you might not have wanted to see that relationship end."

"What are you talking about?" Lola asked, clearly frustrated. "We were friends. All of us. And we would still be friends even if he lived in a different city or even a different state."

I cocked my head as I studied her. "Would you still be … friends? Or would the relationship … end?"

Lola opened her mouth then shut it. Even Sage looked a little shook up.

"Lola, how would you characterize your relationship with my fiancé?" Cherry asked, her voice direct and uncharacteristically bitter. "How about you, Sage?" She looked between the two women as they both seemed to shrink in their seats. "You think I didn't see it all of these years? The looks? The flirtations? The little touches? I just assumed it was all innocent. Sure, you found my fiancé attractive. Who wouldn't? He was a very attractive man. And maybe you had a little crush on him. But it was more than that, wasn't it? Wasn't it?" At this, she pounded both hands on the table, making everything jump.

"Cherry, it wasn't like that," Lola started to say.

Cherry whirled toward her. "Oh, then how was it? Why don't you explain how it was then? I think we would all be interested to hear it … especially Flynn. Wouldn't you, Flynn?" Flynn was staring into his wineglass and didn't answer.

Lola licked her lips, a trapped expression in her eyes. "Cherry, this isn't the time or the place. Let's talk about it later."

Cherry gave her a disdainful look. "No. We don't have to talk about it later. I'm a big girl. I can figure it out."

"Cherry," Lola's voice was pleading, but Cherry deliberately looked away. Sage hadn't said a word. She kept her head down, avoiding eye contact.

"Both of you," Cherry spat. "I thought you were my friends. My *best* friends. I can't believe you would do this to me!" Here, I saw the tears well up in her eyes. "Did you kill Marcus, too? Because he was finally going to set a date?"

"He wasn't going to set a date," Sage said softly, her voice tired. "Don't you get it? He was never going to set a date."

Cherry looked stunned. "Oh … so you think he was going to marry you instead?"

Sage gave her a small smile full of self-loathing. "No. He had no intention of marrying any of us." She shot a hard look at Lola. "*None* of us," she repeated.

Lola blinked, as if it suddenly occurred to her what was going on. "Wait," she said, pointing at Sage. "You were sleeping with Marcus …?" I got the impression she almost said "too" but just barely caught herself.

"I am deeply ashamed," Sage said. "I have no excuse."

"But not ashamed enough to have stopped," Cherry snapped. "You could have stopped!"

Sage inclined her head. "You're absolutely right."

"I can't believe it," Lola said, glaring at Sage. "I can't believe it."

"Oh, give it up, Lola," Sage countered. "You must have known."

Lola was shaking her head violently. "No! I didn't think …" she caught the looks of Flynn and Cherry and shut her mouth firmly.

Cherry was still staring at her. "Did *you* do this, Lola? Did you kill Marcus?"

"No!" The sound was a yelp. "I could never kill him. I could never kill anyone. I can't believe you would ask me that."

"I can't believe you would sleep with my fiancé, either," Cherry threw back.

No one spoke. Cherry finally naming the betrayals seemed to have drained all the energy out of the room.

Caleb cleared his throat. "So, to be clear, you're assuming one of us killed Marcus because he was taking another job and leaving Redemption."

"I'm saying that something changed, and that's why one of you killed him," I said.

"But we've been friends with Marcus forever," Caleb said. "You really think one of us is capable of first drugging choco-late-dipped strawberries in order to get Cherry out of the pic-ture, then drugging Marcus, killing him, and then having the presence of mind to remove the strawberries and the note and drug your tea in order to frame you?"

I cocked my head and studied Caleb. "I never said anything about a note."

Caleb sat very still. Everyone else at the table slowly turned their heads to look at him. "You must have," he sputtered.

I shook my head very slowly. "No, I didn't. Did I?" I turned to Cherry for confirmation.

Cherry's face had gone very white. "Caleb?" Her voice was small.

"You must have told me about it," he said, his voice plead-ing as he stared at Cherry. "You must have."

"No, I didn't tell anyone about the note. Officer Wyle asked me not to."

"But … you must have," Caleb said, pushing his chair away from the table. Unfortunately for him, he was in the corner, so he would basically have to climb over us to get out. Or try and escape through the busted fire escape door. "Otherwise, how would I know?"

"That's a good question," I said as the reality of his mistake sunk in around the room. "And the answer is because this was all you, wasn't it?"

"What are you talking about?" Caleb's eyes were desperately searching the room for a way out.

"There was no date that night, was there?" The final pieces were finally clicking into place, and it was all coming clear. "Billy mentioned that he had overhead Marcus say he was going out with the boys. Cherry, how did Marcus tell you about the date?"

She was still staring at Caleb, and she looked just like she did when she found Marcus dead in her kitchen—like she was about to faint. "He … he … he left me a beautiful handwritten note in my mailbox. He told me it was a secret and not to ask him about it, as it would spoil the surprise. I was to be ready by 7:00 sharp for the night of my life."

I couldn't help but think that it had turned out to be the night of her life, but not in the way she had hoped.

"So, what did you tell Marcus?" I asked Caleb. "That you were taking him out for a night on the town?"

Caleb licked his lips. "I don't know what you're talking about."

"Marcus would have been easy for you to drug. You could have slipped the roofies into any one of his drinks, at any time. Maybe even into the bottle of whisky in his drawer. Is that what you said? 'Let's have a quick one here before going out?' And then, you replaced that bottle with a fresh one, and made up that silly story about Billy being in his office, so no one would find it strange that he had a new, unopened bottle there? Once he was drugged, it was just a matter of helping him into your car, and then leaving the package on Cherry's doorstep. Once she took the bait, all you had to do was wait for the drugs to work. Then, you would have all the time you needed to set the stage. You would have all the time in the world to add roofies to my tea, the wine, trash the living room and, of course, kill Marcus."

"Caleb," Cherry said. She sounded like her heart was breaking. "Was it really you? Did you really do it?"

"I don't have to listen to this," Caleb snarled, jumping to his feet.

"That's fine," Wyle said, sauntering in from the living room. "We can talk about it at the station."

Caleb froze, his mouth falling open. "Where did you come from?"

"I've been here the entire time," he said, glancing at me. "And yes, I heard it all."

Caleb took a step back, his eyes frantic as he looked for an escape.

"Come on, you don't want to do this," Wyle said. "I've already called for backup. You're not going to be able to get away. We will bring you in, and all that's going to happen is that I'm going to charge you with more crimes."

"What does it matter?" Caleb demanded as Flynn got to his feet and moved to block off the other side of the table. "Who cares if I'm also charged with evading arrest, if I'm going to be charged with murder?"

"You may not like your plea deal options if you're charged with more crimes," Wyle said. "But if you cooperate, we'll definitely put in a good word for you."

Caleb swore under his breath as he took another step backward.

"Caleb, come on," Flynn said, taking a step toward him. "You don't want to do this."

Caleb whirled on him. "What do you know about what I want to do or don't want to do? You married a woman who has never been faithful to you." Flynn winced, and Lola dropped her head, but otherwise, neither of them moved. "Why should I possibly want to take any advice from you?"

"What about me?" Cherry was on her feet, though I hadn't even noticed her getting up. Her face was very pale, and she was swaying slightly, but there was something else in her expression I hadn't seen since her middle-of-the-night phone call. Determination. "How could you do this to me?"

The air seemed to go out of Caleb, and he stared at her, his mouth opening and closing like a fish gasping for air. "I … I … I didn't mean …"

"You *killed* Marcus," she said. "Which is bad enough. He was supposed to be your best friend. But you also drugged me! Why would you do that to me? Why would you make me think I … I killed Marcus?" Her voice choked on the words. "You made everyone think I killed Marcus. Why would you do that?"

"Cherry, that was never the plan." Caleb's tone was pleading.

Cherry's eyes were huge in her face. "But you killed him *in my apartment.*"

"I know, I know," Caleb said, wringing his hands. "That's why you were supposed to call me, not Charlie."

"What?" Cherry looked completely bewildered. "Why would I call you?"

"Because that's what I do," Caleb said. "I clean things up. You were supposed to call me, and I was going to come over. I would have been here when the cops arrived. I would have made sure they never would have charged you. You're a Duckworth, after all … it wouldn't have been hard. And Billy was the perfect fall guy."

"Billy had an alibi," Wyle said.

Caleb waved his hand. "It didn't matter. I had … well, it doesn't matter now. Even though he was never charged, I could have muddied your case enough that no one would ever have been charged. I have friends, you know. Powerful friends. Plus, it's not like the Redemption Police Department has that stellar of a record when it comes to solving crimes."

Wyle opened his mouth, then shut it. He didn't look at me, but I could feel what he was thinking. Caleb wasn't completely wrong.

"But why would you put me through all of that?" Cherry asked. "I don't understand."

Caleb's eyes went wide. "You don't understand? How could you not understand?" His voice grew louder. "You were supposed to be with me! Not Marcus. I was the one who loved you. Me! You were supposed to call me that night. I was supposed to save you, and then you would finally realize you loved me. That you had always loved me. None of this was supposed to happen. But you had to go and call Charlie. Why would you call your tea lady, anyway?"

Cherry looked puzzled. "Why wouldn't I call her? She's not just a tea lady. She also solves cases."

Wyle shot me a sideways look. I could almost feel his exasperation. *This is what happens when amateurs mess around with things they have no experience in or training to deal with.*

"You were supposed to call me," Caleb practically howled. "You've called me before when things went wrong with Marcus. Why didn't you call me that night?"

Cherry looked confused. "I only called you when I was trying to find Marcus. You were his roommate and best friend. Plus, you worked with him. You're the natural person to call to track him down when he's been in a mood and not talking to me. That's a lot different than calling you in the middle of the night because Marcus was dead."

Caleb's eyes were wild, and he raked his hands through his hair. "But you love me! I know you do, deep down inside. You just didn't want to admit it because you were engaged to Marcus and, unlike Marcus, and everyone else here ..." His eyes swept across the table. "You actually ARE faithful."

Cherry was shaking her head. "Caleb, I'm so sorry, but no. I don't love you. I *like* you. I consider you a good friend. But, no, I don't want to be with you in any way other than as a friend."

"No, you don't know what you're saying ..." Caleb pleaded.

"But I do," Cherry said gently. "I don't love you. I never will love you. And it never even occurred to me to call you when I found Marcus dead."

Caleb's face had gone slack. In fact, his entire body deflated, like a balloon, as the fight had drained out of him. He let Wyle approach him, handcuff him, read him his rights, and lead him away. His head lolled on his neck, like he no longer had the strength to hold it up.

It was only after the front door clicked that the spell was finally broken. A shell-shocked Cherry fell into her seat, almost like her legs had given out. Lola tried to say something to her, but Cherry shot her a quick, hard glare and held up a hand to stop her. Lola fell silent. Flynn also resumed his seat as Sage began to refill the wineglasses.

"Caleb," Sage mused, shaking her head. "I never would have guessed that of all of us, Caleb would snap first."

Chapter 24

"So it was Caleb after all," Pat said, slipping Tiki a piece of cookie despite the plate of homemade dog biscuits sitting right next to the leftover Valentine's Day cookies. All of us were in my kitchen, including Tilde, who insisted on hearing all the details, so she could learn my "secrets."

"And only Caleb," I said, pushing the dog biscuits a little closer to Pat, hoping she would get the hint.

Once Wyle had brought him in, Caleb ended up confessing everything. It seemed Cherry's reaction had broken him, and he no longer cared what happened to him anymore.

"I still think Lola was involved somehow," Tilde said. "Maybe she was the one who gave Caleb a key to Cherry's apartment."

"Actually, Caleb was using Marcus's key," I said. "Cherry and Marcus had exchanged keys for emergency purposes only, and it doesn't sound like Marcus ever used Cherry's key, so it was basically Caleb's key."

"And he was using it a lot?" Pat asked.

"Apparently. He's been watching Cherry for a long time now, so he knew her habits fairly well. It was how he knew about her nightly tea-drinking ritual, and he figured if he dumped out most of the last batch of tea I had made her, she would very likely call me for a new batch the next day. He knew if he roofied a batch she had already been drinking, no one would believe I had anything to do with it, so he had to get her to buy a fresh bag."

Pat shivered. "That's so creepy."

"But what about the note?" Tilde asked. "Cherry thought Marcus wrote it, right? But he didn't. It was Caleb. Right?"

I nodded as I picked up my mug. "Caleb had gotten pretty good at mimicking Marcus's handwriting. Apparently, Marcus was better at the networking and politicking, and not as good at all the other parts of being in politics, so Caleb did a lot of the grunt work. It sounded like it started back in college."

"Caleb was doing Marcus's homework?" Pat asked.

"Sounds like it," I said.

"Man, no wonder why he wanted to kill him," Pat said, breaking off another bit of cookie for Tiki. I tried not to sigh.

"But what I don't understand is why now?" Tilde asked. "If Marcus was leaving Redemption for another job, wouldn't that be Caleb's chance?"

"Except Caleb was going with him," I said. "And Marcus wasn't going to break up with Cherry. So, he and Cherry would be in a long-distance relationship, and Caleb wouldn't have the chance to try and woo Cherry when Marcus wasn't around."

"So why leave?" Pat asked. "Why not tell Marcus he wasn't going with him and stay here?"

I reached for a cookie. "Because this was about him replacing Marcus. Or maybe, more accurately, becoming Marcus. You have to understand, Caleb thought he was getting away with it, so I think he assumed he would still be off to the governor's office, and I think he also might have assumed that, with Marcus gone, he would get Marcus's job. And, of course, he believed that Cherry would realize she loved him, and when that happened, he would have successfully stepped into Marcus's life. He would have Marcus's job and Marcus's fiancé. In essence, he would be Marcus."

"Sounds a bit delusional," Tilde murmured.

"Well, yeah. That level of planning someone's murder does require a certain amount of delusion," I said.

***

I was cleaning up the kitchen after Tilde and Pat left when the doorbell rang again. I went to answer it, assuming one of them had come back to retrieve something they'd forgotten.

But I was wrong. It was Wyle.

"This is a surprise," I said, holding the door open wider. "Do you want to come in?"

"I can't stay long," he said.

"Well, I'd rather not stand here with the door open, heating the outside, either," I said, taking a step back.

He half-smiled as he stepped inside. "This is for you," he said, handing me a huge heart-shaped box of chocolates that he had been holding behind his back. "Happy belated Valentine's Day."

"Thank you, but you didn't have to," I said, taking the box. A tingly warmth was forming in the pit of my stomach, and I suddenly didn't know what to do with my arms or where to look.

"I wanted to," he said, his voice deepening. "You made me cookies. This was the least I could do."

"Well, yeah, but … that's what I do. Bake cookies," I said, my voice sounding awkward.

"Yeah, and what I do is buy things," Wyle replied, a smile in his voice. He paused and cleared his throat. "You saw the article, right?"

I nodded. "Thank you." Along with a full-page article about Caleb and how he was behind Marcus's murder, the *Redemption Times* had printed a retraction regarding their report on my tea and involvement. I suspected that was because Wyle had threatened a lawsuit if they didn't print it. My nemesis, Tad Clark, had written the original, but I wasn't sure who was responsible for the retraction, as it didn't have a byline.

"Did it help?"

"I think so," I said. While it didn't appear like I had lost any tea customers over the first article, I had noticed a palpable sense of relief around my tea business.

He nodded. "Good." He hesitated again. "I also wanted you to know I would have liked nothing better than to ask you out for Valentine's Day."

The tingles in my stomach grew stronger, and I was finding it hard to breathe. "But we were busy catching a bad guy," I said, trying to lighten the energy that was suddenly feeling very dangerous. *I can't be dating a cop,* I reminded myself. *I can't be dating anyone, but especially not a cop.*

He gave me a slanted smile. "I meant after that. But I wanted you to know. I wish I could, but the more I dig into whatever is going on at the Redemption Police station ..." he hesitated. "The less I say, the better. At least for now. Just like how, at least for now, it's better for us to keep our relationship strictly business."

"I get it," I said, feeling a strange mixture of relief, disappointment, and the same warm tingles.

He nodded and took a step backward so he could put a hand on the door. "It's not going to last forever," he said. "I will get to the bottom of whatever is going on." He flashed me one of his charming smiles that took my breath away. "I'm giving you plenty of notice, so you can get over whatever reluctance you have about dating me."

My mouth dropped open. I had no idea how to respond to that.

His smile widened. "Have a good night, Charlie. And enjoy the candy."

A Word From Michele

Can't get enough of Charlie? I've got you covered. Keep going with book 7, *A Cornucopia of Murder,* now available on preorder.

When Charlie accepts an invitation for a pot luck Thanksgiving feast, she immediately decides to bring dessert. Homemade pies, of course.

And they look so delicious that two of the guests decide to sneak a few bites before the meal.

Which wouldn't be an issue except they both end up dead!

Obviously, Charlie didn't poison the pies, but that's not what it looks like. Can she solve the case in time to save the day?

Grab your copy right here:

www.MPWNovels.com/r/w-rhm

* * *

You can also check out exclusive bonus content for *Red Hot Murder,* along with the other Charlie Kingsley books. If you ever wanted to learn more about Officer Brandon Wyle and how he first came to Redemption, well, here's your chance.

The bonus content reveals hints, clues, and sneak peeks you won't get just by reading the books, so you'll definitely want to check it out. You're going to discover a side of Redemption that is only available here:

MPWNovels.com/r/q/rhm-bonus

* * *

If you enjoyed *Red Hot Murder*, it would be wonderful if you would take a few minutes to leave a review and rating on Goodreads:

www.goodreads.com/book/show/122936316-red-hot-murder

or Bookbub:
www.bookbub.com/books/red-hot-murder-charlie-kingsley-mysteries-book-6-by-michele-pariza-wacek

(Feel free to follow me on any of those platforms as well.) I thank you and other readers will thank you (as your reviews will help other readers find my books.)

The *Charlie Kingsley Mysteries* series is a spin-off from my award-winning *Secrets of Redemption* series. *Secrets of Redemption* is a little different from the *Charlie Kingsley Mysteries*, as it's more psychological suspense, but it's still clean like a cozy.

You can learn more about both series, including how they fit together, at MPWNovels.com, along with lots of other fun things such as short stories, deleted scenes, giveaways, recipes, puzzles and more.

I've also included a sneak peek of the first book in the Secrets of Redemption series, *It Began With a Lie*, just turn the page to get started.

It Began With a Lie - Chapter 1

"You're right. It's perfect for us. I'm so glad we're here," I said, lying through my carefully pasted-on smile.

I tried to make my voice bright and cheery, but it sounded brittle and forced, even to me. I sucked in my breath and widened my smile, though my teeth were so clenched, my jaw hurt.

Stefan smiled back—actually, his mouth smiled but his dark-brown eyes, framed with those long, thick lashes any woman would envy, looked flat … distracted. He hugged me with one arm. "I told you everything would be okay," he whispered into my hair. His scent was even more musky than usual, probably from two straight days of driving and lack of shower.

I hugged him back, reminding myself to relax. *Yes, everything is going to be okay. Remember, this move represents a fresh start for us—time for us to reconnect and get our marriage back on track. It's not going to happen overnight.*

His iPhone buzzed. He didn't look at me as he dropped his arm and pulled it out of his pocket, his attention already elsewhere. "Sorry babe, gotta take this." He turned his back to me as he answered the call, walking away quickly. His dark hair, streaked with silver that added a quiet, distinguished air to his All-American good looks was longer than normal, curling around his collar. He definitely needed a haircut, but of course, we couldn't afford his normal stylist, and not just anyone was qualified to touch his hair.

I wrapped my arms around myself, goosebumps forming on my skin as a sudden breeze, especially cool for mid-May, brushed past me—the cold all the more shocking in the absence of Stefan's warm body.

He has to work, I reminded myself. *Remember why we're here.*

I remembered, all right. How could I forget?

I rubbed my hands up and down my arms as I took a deep breath, and finally focused on the house.

It was just as I remembered from my childhood—white with black shutters, outlined by bushy green shrubs, framed by tall, gently-swaying pine trees and the red porch with the swinging chair. It sat all by its lonesome in the middle of a never-developed cul-de-sac, the only "neighbors" being an overgrown forest on one side, and a marshy field on the other.

Okay, maybe it wasn't *exactly* the way I remembered it. The bushes actually looked pretty straggly. The lawn was overgrown, full of dandelions going to seed, and the porch could definitely use a new paint job.

I sighed. If the outside looked like this, what on earth waited for me on the inside?

Inside.

I swallowed back the bile that rose in the back of my throat. It slid to my stomach, turning into a cold, slimy lump.

The house of my childhood.

The house of my nightmares.

Oh God, I so didn't want to be here.

Stefan was still on the phone, facing away from me. I stared longingly at his back. *Turn around*, I silently begged. T*urn around and smile at me. A real smile. Like how you used to before we were married. Tell me it's going to be okay. You don't have to leave tonight like you thought. You realize how cruel it would be to leave me alone in this house the first night we're here, and you don't want to do that to me. Please, tell me. Or, better yet, tell me we're packing up and going back to New York. Say this was all a mistake; the firm is doing fine. Or, if you can't say that, say we'll figure it out. We'll make it work. We don't need to live here after all. Please, Stefan. Please don't leave me alone here.*

He half-turned, caught my eye, and made a gesture that indicated he was going to be awhile.

And I should start unpacking.

I closed my eyes. Depression settled around me like an old, familiar shawl. I could feel the beginning of a headache stab my temples.

Great. Just what I needed to complete this nightmare—a monster headache.

I turned to the car and saw Chrissy still in the backseat—headset on, bobbing to music only she could hear. Her long, dark hair—so dark it often looked black—spread out like a shiny cloak, the ends on one side dyed an electric blue.

Oh, yeah. That's right. I wouldn't be alone in the house after all.

Chrissy closed her eyes and turned her head away from me.

It just kept getting better and better.

I knocked on the window. She ignored me. I knocked again. She continued to ignore me.

For a moment, I imagined yanking the door open, snatching the headset off and telling her to—no, *insisting* that—she get her butt out of the car and help me unpack. I pictured her dark brown eyes, so much like Stefan's, widening, her pink lip-glossed mouth forming a perfect O, so shocked that she doesn't talk back, but instead meekly does what she's told.

More pain stabbed my temples. I closed my eyes and kept knocking on the window.

It's not her fault, I told myself for maybe the 200th time. *How would you act if you were sixteen years old and your mother abandoned you, dumped you at your father's, so she'd be free to travel across Europe with her boy toy?*

I squelched the little voice that reminded me I wasn't a whole heck of a lot older than said boy toy, and started pounding on the window. Stefan kept telling me she was warming up to me—I personally hadn't seen much evidence of that.

Chrissy finally turned her head and looked at me. "What?" she mouthed, disgust radiating off her, her eyes narrowing like an angry cat.

I motioned to the trunk. "I need your help."

Her lip curled as her head fell back on to the seat. She closed her eyes.

I had just been dismissed.

Great. Just great.

I looked around for Stefan—if he were standing with me, she would be out of the car and helping—a fake, sweet smile on her face, but he had moved to the corner of the street, still on the phone. I popped the trunk and headed over to him. Maybe I could finally get him to see reason—that it really was a dreadful idea to leave the two of us alone in Redemption, Wisconsin, while he commuted back and forth to New York to rescue his failing law firm. "See," I could say, "She doesn't listen to me. She doesn't respect me. She needs her father. I need you, too. She's going to run wild with you gone and I won't be able to deal with her."

Stefan hung up as I approached. "The movers should be here soon. You probably should start unpacking." Although his tone was mild, I could still hear the underlying faint chords of reproach—*what's going on with you? Why haven't you started yet? Do I need to do everything around here?*

"Yes, I was going to," I said, hating my defensive tone, but unable to stop it. "But there's a problem I think you need to deal with."

His eyes narrowed—clearly, he was losing his patience with me. "What?"

I opened my mouth to tell him about Chrissy, just as her voice floated toward us, "Can I get some help over here?"

I slowly turned around, gritting my teeth, trying not to show it. Chrissy stood by the trunk, arms loaded with boxes, an expectant look on her face. The pain darting through my head intensified.

"Rebecca, are you coming?" Stefan asked as he headed over to his charming daughter, waiting for him with a smug expression on her face, like a cat who ate the canary. I took a deep breath and trudged over, the sick knot in the pit of my stomach growing and tightening.

What on earth was I going to do with her while Stefan was gone?

Chrissy threw me a triumphant smile as she followed her father to the house. I resisted the urge to stick my tongue out at her, as I heaved a couple of boxes out of the trunk.

Really, all the crap with Chrissy was the least of my worries. It was more of a distraction, than anything.

The real problem was the house.

The house.

Oh God.

I turned to stare at it. It didn't look menacing or evil. It looked like a normal, everyday house.

Well, a normal, everyday house with peeling paint, a broken gutter and a few missing roof shingles.

Great. That probably meant we needed a new roof. New roofs were expensive. People who had to rescue failing law firms tended to not have money for things like new roofs. Even new roofs for houses that were going to be fixed up and eventually sold, ideally for a big, fat profit.

Would there be *any* good news today?

Again, I realized I was distracting myself. New roofs and paint jobs—those were trivial.

The real problem was *inside* the house.

Where all my nightmares took place.

Where my breakdown happened.

Where I almost died.

I swallowed hard. The sun went behind a cloud and, all of a sudden, the house was plunged into darkness. It loomed in front me, huge and monstrous, the windows dark, bottomless eyes staring at me … the door a mouth with sharp teeth …

"Rebecca! Are you coming?"

Stefan broke the spell. I blinked my eyes and tried to get myself together.

I was being silly. It was just a house, not a monster. How could a house even BE a monster? Only people could be monsters, which would mean my aunt, who had owned the house, was the monster.

And my aunt was dead now. Ding, dong, the witch is dead. Or, in this case, the monster.

Which meant there was nothing to fear in the house anymore. Which was exactly what Stefan kept telling me back in New York, over and over.

"Don't you think it's time you put all this childhood nonsense behind you?" he asked. "Look, I get it. Your aunt must have done something so dreadful that you've blocked it out, but she's dead. She can't hurt you anymore. And it couldn't have worked out any more perfectly for us—we have both a place to live rent-free right now, while I get things turned around. And, once we sell it, we can use the money to move back here and get a fresh start."

He was right, of course. But, still, I couldn't drop it.

"Why did she even will the house to me in the first place?" I persisted. "Why didn't she will it to CB? He was there a lot more than I was."

Stefan shrugged. "Maybe it was her way of apologizing to you all these years later. She was trying to make it up to you. Or maybe she changed—people said she was sick at the end. But, why does it matter why she willed it to you? The point is she did, and we really need it. Not to mention this could be a great way for you to finally get over whatever happened to you years ago."

Maybe. Back in New York, it had seemed so reasonable. So logical. Maybe the move wouldn't be a problem after all.

But, standing in the front yard with my arms filled with boxes, every cell in my body screamed that it was a really awful idea.

"Hey," Stefan whispered in my ear, his five o'clock shadow scratching my cheek. I jumped, so transfixed by the house that I hadn't even realized he had returned to me. "Look, I'm sorry. I should have known this would be rough for you. Come on, I'll walk in with you."

He rubbed my arm and smiled at me—a real smile. I could feel my insides start to thaw as all those old, exciting, passionate feelings reminiscent of when we first started dating swarmed over me. I remembered how he would shower me with red roses and whisk me off to romantic dinners that led to steaming, hot sex. He made me feel like a princess in a fairy tale. I still couldn't fathom how he ended up with me.

I met his eyes, and for the first time in what seemed like a long time, I felt the beginnings of a real smile on my lips. *See, he does care, even if he doesn't always show it. This is why the move was the perfect thing for our marriage; all we needed was to get away from the stress of New York, so we could rekindle things.* I nodded and started walking with him toward the house. Over her shoulder, Chrissy shot me a dirty look.

The closer we got to the house, the more I focused on my breathing. *It's going to be okay, I repeated to myself. It's just a house. A house can't hurt anyone. It's all going to be okay.*

An owl hooted, and I jumped. Why was an owl hooting in the daytime? Didn't that mean someone was going to die? Isn't that what the old stories and folklore taught? My entire body stiffened—all I wanted to do was run the other way. Stefan hugged me closer, gently massaging my arm, and urged me forward.

"It's going to be okay," he murmured into my hair. I closed my eyes for a moment, willing myself to believe it.

We stepped onto the porch, Chrissy impatiently waiting for Stefan to unlock the door. He put the boxes on the ground to fumble for his keys as I tried hard not to hyperventilate.

It's just a house. A house can't hurt anyone.

After an eternity that simultaneously wasn't nearly long enough, he located the keys and wrenched the door open, swearing under his breath.

His words barely registered. I found myself compelled forward, drawn in like those pathetic moths to the killing flame.

I could almost hear my aunt excitedly calling, "Becca? Is that you? Wait until you see this," as I stepped across the threshold into the house.

It was exactly like I remembered.

Well, maybe not exactly—it was filthy and dusty, full of cobwebs and brittle, dead bugs lying upside down on the floor with their legs sticking up. But I remembered it all—from the overstuffed floral sofa where I spent hours reading, to the end table covered with knick-knacks and frilly doilies, to the paintings lining the walls. I found myself wanting to hurry into the kitchen, where surely Aunt Charlie would have a cup of tea waiting for me. It didn't feel scary at all. It felt warm and comforting.

Like coming home.

How could this be?

Stefan was still muttering under his breath. "I can't believe all this crap. We're going to have put our stuff in storage for months while we go through it all. Christ, like we need another bill to worry about." He sighed, pulled his cell phone out, and started punching numbers.

"Dad, what do you mean our stuff is going into storage?" Chrissy said, clearly alarmed.

Stefan waved his arms. "Honey, look around you. Where are we going to put it? We have to put our things into storage until we get all this out of here."

"But Dad," Chrissy protested. I stopped listening. I walked slowly around, watching my aunt dashing down the stairs, her smock stained, arms filled with herbs and flowers, some even sticking out of her frizzy brown hair, muttering about the latest concoction she was crafting for one of the neighbors whose back was acting up again ...

"Earth to Rebecca. Rebecca. Are you okay?" I suddenly realized Stefan was talking to me, and I pulled myself out of my memories.

"Sorry, it just ..." my voice trailed off.

He came closer. "Are you okay? Are you remembering?"

There she was again, the ghost of Aunt Charlie, explaining yet again to the odd, overly-made-up, hair-over-teased, forty-something woman from the next town that no, she didn't do love potions. It was dangerous magic to mess around with either love or money, but if she wanted help with her thyroid that was clearly not working the way it should be, that was definitely in my aunt's wheelhouse.

I shook my head. "No, not really. It's just ... weird."

I wanted him to dig deeper, ask me questions, invite me to talk about the memories flooding through me. I wanted him to look at me while I spoke, *really* look at me, the way he did before we were married.

Where had it all gone wrong? And how could he leave me alone in a lonely, isolated and desolate house a thousand miles away from New York? Sure, Chrissy would be there, but the jury was still out as to whether she made it better or worse. The memories pushed up against me, smothering me. I *needed* to talk about them, before they completely overwhelmed and suffocated me. And he knew it—he knew how much I needed to talk things through to keep the anxiety and panic at bay. He wouldn't let me down, not now, when I really needed him.

Would he?

It Began With a Lie - Chapter 2

The empty coffee pot mocked me.

It sat on the table, all smug and shiny, its cord wrapped tightly around it.

I had been so excited after unearthing it that morning—yes! Coffee! God knew I needed it.

The night before had been horrible, starting with the fights. I ended up in the living room, where I spent the night on the couch, a cold washcloth draped over my face in a feeble attempt to relieve the mother of all headaches.

Several times, I'd have just dozed off when the sound of Chrissy's footsteps would jerk me awake, as she paced up and down the upstairs hallway. I couldn't fathom what was keeping her up, so finally, after the fourth or fifth time of being woken up, I went upstairs to check on her. She must have heard me on the stairs, because all I saw was of the trail of her white nightgown as she disappeared into her room. I stood there for a moment, wondering if I should go talk to her, but the stabbing pain in my head drove me back downstairs to the safety of the couch and washcloth. I just couldn't face another argument then, in the middle of the night.

She must have decided to stay in her room after that, because I finally drifted off, only waking when the sun shone through the dirty living room window, illuminating all the dust motes floating in the air.

Coffee was exactly what I needed. Except … I had no beans to put in the coffeemaker. Not that it mattered, I realized after digging through the third box in frustration. I didn't have any cream or sugar either.

Well, at least my headache was gone, although what was left was a weird, hollow, slightly-drugged feeling. Still, I'd take that over the headache any day.

I sighed and rubbed my face. The whole move wasn't starting off very well. In fact, everything seemed to be going from
bad to worse, including the fight with Stefan.

"Do you really need to leave?" I asked him again as I followed him to the door. He had just said goodbye to Chrissy, who
had immediately disappeared upstairs, leaving us alone. I could
see the taxi he had called sitting in the driveway and my heart
sank. A part of me had hoped to talk him out of going, but with
the taxi already there the possibility seemed even more remote.

He sighed. I could tell he was losing patience. "We've been
through this. You know I have to."

"But you just got here! Surely you can take a few days—a
week maybe—off to help us unpack and get settled."

He picked up his briefcase. "You know I can't. Not now."

"But when? You promised you would set it up so that you
could work from here most of the time. Why can't you start
that now?" I could tell his patience was just about gone, but I
couldn't stop myself.

He opened the door. A fresh, cool breeze rushed in, a sharp
contrast to the musty, stale house. "And I will. But it's too soon.
There are still a few things I need to get cleaned up before I can
do that. You know that. We talked about this."

He stepped outside and went to kiss me, but I turned my
face away. "Are you going to see *her*?"

That stopped him. I could see his eyes narrow and his mouth
tighten. I hadn't meant to say it; it just slipped out.

He paused and took a breath. "I know this whole situation
has been tough on you, so I'm going to forget you said that. I'll
call you."

Except he didn't. Not a single peep in the more than twelve
hours since he had walked out the door. And every time I
thought of it, I felt sick with shame.

I didn't *really* think he was cheating on me. I mean, there
was something about Sabrina and her brittle, cool, blonde, perfect elegance that I didn't trust, but that wasn't on Stefan. I
had no reason not to trust him. Just because my first husband

cheated on me didn't mean Stefan would. And just because Sabrina looked at Stefan like he was a steak dinner, and she was starving, didn't mean it was reciprocated.

Worse, I knew I was making a bigger mess out of it every time I brought it up. The more I accused him, the more likely he would finally say, "Screw it, if I'm constantly accused of being a cheater, I might as well at least get something out of it." Even knowing all of that, I somehow couldn't stop myself.

Deep down, I knew I was driving him away. And I hated that part of myself. But still nothing changed.

To make matters worse, it didn't take long after Stefan left before things blew up with Chrissy. I asked her to help me start organizing the kitchen, and she responded with an outburst about how much she hated the move. She hated me, too—her life was ruined, and it was all my fault. She stormed off, slammed the door to her room, and that's how I ended up on the couch, my head pounding, wishing I was just about anywhere else.

Standing in the kitchen with the weak sunlight peeking through the dirty windows, the empty coffee maker taunting me, I gave in to my feelings of overwhelm. How on earth was I ever going to get the house organized? And the yard? And my aunt's massive garden? All the while researching what it would take to sell the house for top dollar, and dealing with Chrissy? My heart sank at that thought, although I wasn't completely sure which thought triggered it. Maybe it was all of them.

And if that wasn't difficult enough, I also had to deal with being in my aunt's home. Her presence *was everywhere*. I felt like an intruder. How could I do all of this, feeling her around me? How could I be in her home, when she wasn't? It wasn't my house. It was Aunt Charlie's. And I wasn't even sure I WANT-ED it to feel like my home.

Because if it did, then I would probably remember every-thing.

Including what happened that night.

The night I almost died.

God, I felt sick.

I needed coffee. And food.

Maybe I should take Chrissy out for breakfast as a peace of-fering. We could get out of the house, which would be good for me at least, and then go grocery shopping before coming home to tackle the cleaning and organizing.

I wanted to start in the kitchen. It was Aunt Charlie's favorite room in the house, and I knew it would have broken her heart to see how neglected and dingy it had become. When my aunt was alive, it was the center of the home—a light, cheery place with a bright-red tea kettle constantly simmering away on low heat on the stove. Oh, how Aunt Charlie loved her tea—that's why the kettle always had hot water in it—she'd say you just never knew when a cup would be needed. She was a strong believer that tea cured just about everything, just so long as you had the right blend. And, surprise, surprise, you could pretty much always find the right blend outside in her massive garden, which I had no doubt was completely overgrown now. I didn't have the heart to go look.

I could almost see her, standing in that very kitchen, prepar-ing me a cup. "Headache again, Becca?" she would murmur as she measured and poured and steeped. The warm fragrance would fill the homey kitchen as she pushed the hot cup in front of me, the taste strong, flavorful, and sweet, with just a hint of bitterness. And, lo and behold, not too long after drinking it, I would find my headache draining away.

I wondered if I would still find her tea blends in the kitchen. Maybe I could find that headache tea. And maybe, if I was even luckier, I would find a blend that would cure everything that ailed me that morning.

With some surprise, I realized just how much love encom-passed that memory. Nothing scary. Nothing that could possibly foretell the horror of what happened that dreadful night.

Could my aunt actually be the monster?

My mother certainly thought so. She forbade any contact, any mentioning of my aunt even, refusing to allow her to see me once I woke up in intensive care following the stomach pump.

She refused her again when I was transferred to a psych unit, after becoming hysterical when I was asked what had happened that night.

My mother blamed my aunt.

And, I, in my weakened, anxious, panicked state, was relieved to follow her lead. Actually, I was more than relieved; I was happy, too.

But sitting in that kitchen right then, I felt only love and comfort, and I began to question my choices.

My mother had been completely against us moving back here, even temporarily. At the time, listening to her arguments, I had chalked it up to her being overly protective. Now, I wondered. Was that it? Or was something deeper going on?

Chrissy chose that moment to stroll into the kitchen, her hair sticking up on one side. She was wearing her blue and red plaid sleep shorts and red tee shirt—the blue plaid almost an exact match to the blue highlight in her hair. Staring at her, something stirred deep inside me—a distinct feeling of wrongness … of something being off—but when I reached for it, I came up empty.

She leaned against the counter and started checking her iPhone. "How sweet, you're being domestic."

I shook my head—that off feeling still nagged at me, but I just couldn't place it. I really needed coffee. Coffee would make everything better.

She tapped at her iPhone, not looking up. "Anything to eat in this God-awful place?"

I sighed. Maybe I should be looking for a tea that would cure Chrissy.

Want to keep reading? Grab your copy of **It Began With a Lie** here:

MPWNovels.com/r/rhm-ibl

More *Charlie Kingsley Mysteries:*
A Grave Error (a free prequel novel)
The Murder Before Christmas (Book 1)
Ice Cold Murder (Book 2)
Murder Next Door (Book 3)
The Murder of Sleepy Hollow (Book 5)
Red Hot Murder (Book 6)
A Cornucopia of Murder (Book 7)
A Wedding to Murder For (novella)
Loch Ness Murder (novella)

Secrets of Redemption *series:*
It Began With a Lie (Book 1)
This Happened to Jessica (Book 2)
The Evil That Was Done (Book 3)
The Summoning (Book 4)
The Reckoning (Book 5)
The Girl Who Wasn't There (Book 6)
The Room at the Top of the Stairs (Book 7)
The Search (Book 8)
The Secret Diary of Helen Blackstone (free novella)

Standalone books:
Today I'll See Her (free novella or purchase with bonus content)
The Taking
The Third Nanny
Mirror Image
The Stolen Twin

Access your free exclusive bonus scenes from *Red Hot Murder* right here:
MPWNovels.com/r/q/rhm-bonus

Acknowledgements

It's a team effort to birth a book, and I'd like to take a moment to thank everyone who helped.

My writer friends, Hilary Dartt and Stacy Gold, for reading early versions and providing me with invaluable feedback. My wonderful editor, Megan Yakovich, who is always so patient with me. My designer, Erin Ferree Stratton, who has helped bring my books to life with her cover designs.

And, of course, a story wouldn't be a story without research, and I'm so grateful to my friends who have so generously provided me with their expertise over the years: Dr. Mark Moss, Andrea J. Lee, and Steve Eck. Any mistakes are mine and mine alone.

Last but certainly not least, to my husband Paul, for his love and support during this sometimes-painful birthing process.

About Michele

A USA Today Bestselling, award-winning author, Michele taught herself to read at 3 years old because she wanted to write stories so badly. It took some time (and some detours) but she does spend much of her time writing stories now. Mystery stories, to be exact. They're clean and twisty, and range from psychological thrillers to cozies, with a dash of romance and supernatural thrown into the mix. If that wasn't enough, she posts lots of fun things on her blog, including short stories, puzzles, recipes and more, at MPWNovels.com.

Michele grew up in Wisconsin, (hence why all her books take place there), and still visits regularly, but she herself escaped the cold and now lives in the mountains of Prescott, Arizona with her husband and southern squirrel hunter Cassie.

When she's not writing, she's usually reading, hanging out with her dog, or watching the Food Network and imagining she's an awesome cook. (Spoiler alert, she's not. Luckily for the whole family, Mr. PW is in charge of the cooking.)